THE ARRIVAL OF MR. HANDS

Within the pit of the sculpture, something began to form around the carved figure of Mr. Hands. A soupy, shapeless pool at first with no discernable hint of structure—bits of dead leaves, pieces of tree bark, pebbles and exposed bones of dead birds and squirrels mixing with the mud and water—but there was life there, pulsating like a spurting heart suddenly torn from a chest, and it continued to grow as the ground drank in the essence of Sarah, hidden in her blood, which still clung to Mr. Hands's body, as he slowly came into awareness.

And Mr. Hands felt his limbs growing, unfurling into life, and Mr. Hands took in his first sentient breath, sucking in the pain and anger and grief like a vacuum taking in dust; moving, yes, he was moving now, growing....

MORE PRAISE FOR
GARY A. BRAUNBECK!

IN SILENT GRAVES

"A genuinely disturbing book. Braunbeck taps into a power cable."

—*The New York Review of Science Fiction*

"An indelible experience."

—*DarkEcho*

"This is an incredibly ambitious novel, and it is an absolute wonder."

—Mehitobel Wilson, Gothic.net

"Good Lord, what a novel! I'm still reeling! A splendidly disturbing gem!"

—Elizabeth Massie, author of *Sineater*

"Braunbeck is one of the brightest talents working in the field."
—Thomas Monteleone, author of *The Blood of the Lamb*

"A phenomenally talented writer who never seems to make a misstep."

—*Shocklines*

"Gary A. Braunbeck is simply one of the finest writers to come along in years."

—Ray Garton, author of *Night Life*

GARY A. BRAUNBECK

MR. HANDS

LEISURE BOOKS NEW YORK CITY

A LEISURE BOOK®

August 2007

Published by

Dorchester Publishing Co., Inc.
200 Madison Avenue
New York, NY 10016

ISBN-10: 0-8439-5610-0
ISBN-13: 978-0-8439-5610-8

This one is for 2 people:

For Alan Clark, who once showed me a painting of the damndest monster I've ever seen, and then said to me: "I know there's a story behind this. Would you tell it to me?"

and

For J.N. Williamson (1932 – 2005), my second father who could weave a damned good story himself; I miss you, and hope you approve of what I've done here. I wanted to write the kind of novel you yourself might have penned.

AUTHOR'S NOTE

The author would like you to know that 10% of all royalties from the sales of this book will be donated to Protect.org, an organization dedicated to helping children who are in danger; but don't let that prevent you from logging on to their Web site and making a donation of your own.

"When the gods wish to punish us, they answer our prayers."

—Oscar Wilde

PROLOGUE
Intersections

1

—*Shall there be mercy, then?*
—*Not for monsters like them, no.*
—*Under no circumstances?*
—*Anyone who would do such a thing doesn't de-serve it.*
—So, then . . . under no circumstances?
—*Goddamn right, under no circumstances.*
—*So be it.*

2

The next cliff on the mountain was not as steep as he had first thought, but there was no doubt in his mind that it would probably get steeper before he reached the top. He came to the bulge, went over, placed his foot firmly on the edge, and found a solid hold with his left hand on what felt like a root. Pulling upward, kneeing and toeing into the gold-colored stone, kicking steps into the shale-like rock wherever he could, he positioned both hands and one foot before moving into a new, higher position.

He thought of his family—all of them now gone back to earth, dirt, rock, soil, and dust, the forgotten rot of molding ages—and had to steady himself against tears.

It wasn't my fault, really, it wasn't, I didn't mean for any of it to happen. Oh God, please, please, can all of you forgive me . . . ?

The mountain was starting to shudder in his face and against his chest. His own breath was whistling and humming crazily against the stone. The rocks were steepening and he backbreakingly labored for every inch. His shoulders were tiring and his calves ached and the muscles in his arms felt like iron. Panic was courting him, and it was only the thought of what he might find somewhere above that kept him going.

Proof-positive that what had happened years ago had indeed been real.

That he had not imagined it, as the doctors insisted.

Somewhere above, he would find the remains of the giant, the Terrible Miracle, the Demon, the Thing beyond all Things called Mr. Hands.

He thought of those years when he'd been a child, afraid of the dark, afraid of the shadows cast by the tree branches and leaves against his window at night, terrified of the scratching noise those branches had made when the wind came up ever so softly and pressed them against the glass, causing them to move back and forth, back and forth, back and forth, *let me in, let me in, I'm coming for you, always here, I'm coming for you scritchscritchscritch* . . .

Always he'd cry out for Mommy or Daddy, and always one—or more often than not *both*—of them would come running into his room, holding him, soothing him, stroking his hair and gently rocking him back and forth, whispering *there, there, shhh, c'mon, hon, it's all right, there's no such thing as monsters, it's all right, there, there. . . .*

God, how wrong they had been. So much love in their hearts, such good intentions, but so fucking *wrong. . . .*

It occurred to him—not for the first time since he'd began this journey, this climb—that maybe he was doing this as much for his long gone family as he was for himself.

He concentrated everything he had to become ultra-sensitive to the mountain, feeling it more gently than before, though he was shaking badly. He kept inching upward. With each shift to a newer, higher position, he felt a deeper tenderness toward the mountain. He caught part of a rock with his left hand and started to pull, but could not rise. He let go with his right hand and grabbed onto the wrist of his left, the fingers of his left hand shuddering and popping with the weight.

"You won't stop me," he hissed upward, knowing the creature could hear him.

He got one toe into the cliff but that was all he could do. He looked up and held on. The mountain was giving him nothing. It no longer sent back any pressure against his body, no longer returned his tender embraces. Something he had come to rely on had been taken away from him by the thing that waited somewhere above.

So much of life had been denied him because of what it had done.

"I won't stop. I won't. Hear me? I don't . . . care if it . . . kills me. . . ."

He was just barely hanging on.

He concentrated all of his strength into the fingers of his left hand, but they were dying on him.

He didn't know how much longer he could hold on.

3

She came awake around five thirty in the morning, when her bladder announced to her in no uncertain terms that she'd had too much Pepsi with the pizza they made for dinner. She pulled herself up—careful not to jostle the child beside her—and sat on the edge of the sofa. Her side hurt like hell from where the gun and holster had been pressing into it while she slept, and her head was screaming for codeine.

She slowly rose and shuffled toward the bathroom, leaving the door open so she could lean back from the sink to see the child; then she took a Dixie cup from the dispenser on the wall beside the sink, pulled a bottle of water from one of the bags, and found the codeine tablets. Part of her wondered if taking them would be a good idea—they tended to make her feel woozy and shiny—but then realized that if the thing chasing after them *did* manage to find them, she'd be no good to the child if she were half-blinded with the agony of a migraine.

Six of one, a half-dozen of the other . . . damned if you do, damned if you don't . . .

Having exhausted her repertoire of early morning clichés, she thought, *To hell with it,* and took two of the tablets.

Gripping the edge of the sink, she leaned forward, eyes closed, and pressed her forehead against the mirror, taking several deep breaths until her heart rate steadied and her arms and legs stopped trembling. When she was certain she had herself under control, she released a slow, even breath, and opened her eyes to see herself staring back at her.

Jesus. You look like hell.

She splashed some cold water on her face, dried off with a towel, and then turned off the bathroom light.

She checked on the child—sleeping peacefully. God, did you ever sleep as soundly as you did before you turned thirteen? If a time machine were ever invented, she'd use it not only to go back and repair the wrongs of the past, but to be thirteen again so she could get a good night's sleep.

She wandered over to the front window and stood there, staring out into the night. The moon was full and made the snow shimmer. Light moved like glissandos over the treetops in the distance as the wind caused them to sway side to side, sometimes forward, then backward, just once, and—

And then she saw him. *It.*

He was so still among the towering trees and swirling snow that he'd looked like part of the scenery.

Mr. Hands just stood there, gigantic, cold, motionless, merciless, staring with his black pit eyes.

She moved quickly and quietly, grabbing up the Mossberg, a knife, three road flares, and her coat, disabling the alarm, and marching out onto the porch, pumping a round into the shotgun's chamber.

Mr. Hands did not move, only continued staring dispassionately, an entomologist observing the behavior of an insect under glass.

She looked back into the cabin only once—*I won't let him harm you*—then stepped off the porch, down the steps, and crossed the distance between herself and the thing that had been pursuing them for what seemed years.

She raised the shotgun and thought about firing, but that would wake the child and the last thing she wanted right now was for the child to awaken and be alone in the dark in a strange place.

Still, she kept her finger near the trigger.

"Leave us alone," she said.

Mr. Hands still did not move or give any indication that he'd heard . . . or cared.

The wind came up again, blowing snow against her face. She blinked, stopped moving, and brushed her eyes clear.

Mr. Hands began to bend down toward her. For a crazy second, she thought he was falling, the movement was that stiff; but then she didn't think about it any longer because she knew what it meant when he started to bend down toward a person (sixty seconds left to live—less if you were lucky). She had no choice, so she pumped off three shots from the Mossberg in rapid succession, straight into his gut, and that must have done something because he seemed to explode from the center as he closed the distance between them, falling toward her, and—

4

The place is called Hangman's Tavern, one of the most legendary watering holes in the self-proclaimed "Land of Legend." It's located halfway between Cedar Hill and Buckeye Lake, but if you look for a clearly marked sign to guide you there, you'll never find it; instead, you need to watch for the crossroad two miles after you get off the I-70 exit toward Buckeye

Lake. Can't miss it. If the weather's bad and visibility is low, then keep an eye peeled for the eight-foot 'T' post on the left, the one with the noose sculpted in iron dangling from it. The Ku Klux Klan used to bring their victims out there and hang them, then go down the road for a few drinks. That's how the business came by its name.

Grant McCullers, owner/bartender/sometimes short-order cook (who can play a mean harmonica despite a severely arthritic hand), is the latest—but hopefully not the *last*—of the men in his family to own the place; although Grant's great-grandfather was Klan and built the tavern, the rest of Great-Grandpa's male descendants decided not to pursue membership in that particular boys' club. Not that it helps erase the shame of the family's history, or make it any easier to forget that somewhere on the acreage surrounding the tavern there are still dozens—if not hundreds—of undiscovered bodies buried by the Klan during the heyday of their necktie parties.

While the Hangman's history will never be fully forgotten (as well it shouldn't be), Grant, like his father before him, has managed to remove much of the taint from the tavern's reputation. The Hangman, you see, is *the* place to go if you're looking for good company, decent food, homemade brew, and, most of all, stories. All the regulars who patronize the Hangman have one—consider it the unofficial cover charge. Some of these stories will break your heart; some will have you doubled over with laughter; some will leave you shaking your head in wonder; and some—a very exceptional few—will leave you feeling a bit more wary about what lies hidden in the night outside.

The interior is long and narrow, with the bar on the right, small round tables on the left, a comfortably scuffed polished-wood dance floor in between, a stage set against the far wall, and an ancient but superbly functioning jukebox off to the side (the selections lean heavily toward old blues standards). Gleaming brass horse rails run along the opposite wall and the bottom of the bar itself, while electric lanterns resting on thick wooden shelves just barely wide enough to hold them keep an air of perpetual twilight inside, regardless of the time of day. The place smells of cigarettes, pipe to-bacco, beer, hamburgers, and popcorn, all of the scents mixing with the lemon oil Grant uses to polish the bar. It smells somehow safe and welcoming, a perfect place to tell stories.

Except this had not been a good night for stories; in fact, it hadn't been a good night at all, in Grant's opinion. Oh, business was fine, the drinks were flowing and the kitchen was busy and it was all Grant could do to keep the popcorn machine filled, but everyone was tight-lipped and perfunctory with him, sometimes bordering on outright rude. Around nine p.m. Grant quietly decided, *To hell with it,* and stopped trying to make small talk with the customers. Even the regulars seemed out of sorts tonight, and it wasn't hard to figure out why: the guy at the end of the bar.

He'd come in around seven thirty looking and smelling like he'd just crawled out of a grave. At first Grant assumed he was homeless, but after the guy downed two drinks in quick succession, placed a large dinner order, and paid for it up front with a fifty (one of *many* fifties the guy had in his pocket), that conclusion almost went right out the window. Almost. There was something undeniably disturbing about him, and Grant was glad he'd made the call to the sheriff shortly after the man arrived.

While waiting for his meal to come out of the kitchen, the guy picked up his backpack and went into the men's room. No sooner did the door to the restroom close behind him than two more Hangman regulars entered: Sheriff Ted Jackson, perhaps Grant's best friend in the world, and a man both Jackson and Grant knew only as the Reverend, who ran the open shelter in downtown Cedar Hill. The Reverend attracted more than a few uneasy glances himself whenever he entered a place; dressed in a traditional black clergy shirt and white collar, his long dark hair and sharply trimmed beard—both peppered with a not-unbecoming amount of gray— gave him an eerie resemblance to a post-lithium Grigori Efimovich Rasputin . . . an eeriness that the Reverend was not above exploiting to the hilt when it came time to ask the city council for additional funding for the shelter every year.

"So where is he?" said Jackson, scanning the bar.

"Went into the men's room just before you came in." Grant poured the two men their usuals—a Bailey's Irish Cream on the rocks for the Reverend, a Pepsi with a wedge of lime for Jackson—and gestured for them to sit down a couple of seats away from the end of the bar.

"I'm sorry that I had to bother you, Ted," said Grant, casting a quick glance toward the restroom doors, "but there's something about this guy that . . . well, he doesn't exactly give me the willies—or, hell, maybe he *does,* I don't know—but there's this . . . this *air* about him that's been making everyone a little uncomfortable."

"Hence the traditional bellow of conversation from the room," said the Reverend. "That was intended as irony, by the way."

"Sarcasm," said Grant. "It wasn't quite witty or observant enough to qualify as irony."

"I beg to differ; in the dictionary sense of the word, irony is defined as 'a type of humor based on using words to suggest the opposite of their literal meaning.' I think credit should be given where credit is due. I was being ironic."

"You really think so?"

The Reverend nodded. " 'Further, deponent sayeth not'—or to put it in the vernacular, 'That's my story and I'm sticking to it.' "

Jackson took a sip of his Pepsi and reached for a bowl of popcorn. "Think this guy might be trouble?"

"I don't know. I'm tempted to say no, but . . ." Grant parted his hands before him and shrugged.

"Gotcha," replied Jackson.

"So why am *I* here?" asked the Reverend.

Both Grant and Jackson looked at him.

"I think that would be obvious," said Grant.

"I'm not entirely dim, Grant. I've already figured out that part of your anxiety is born from concern—and despite the rumors, that will *not* be the cause of your downfall someday—so I'm guessing that it's fairly obvious he has no place to go."

Grant nodded. "He's got a lot of cash on him, but the more I think about it, something tells me he's . . . well, *lost,* I guess. I'd bet the farm on it, if I owned one."

"You *know* there's always room at the shelter, and I never turn anyone away, so what—"

"His eyes," said Grant. "There's something about his eyes."

The Reverend nodded. "Something *in* his eyes, or something that's missing?"

"Catches on fast, doesn't he?" said Jackson, smiling at both men.

"Something missing," replied Grant. "There's this awful *emptiness* in his gaze—not like he's crazy or anything like that, but you can take one look at this guy and know he's seen or been through something that just . . . tore the center right out of him."

"A 'thousand-yard stare'?" asked Jackson.

"Something like that, yes."

Grant saw Jackson's hand go to his holster and unsnap the cover.

The Reverend, who'd seen this, as well, cleared his throat and said, "Either of you guys ever heard of a writer named Gerald Kersh?"

"*Night and the City*?" asked Jackson. "*That* Gerald Kersh?"

"I never read that one," said Grant. "But I've got a copy of a story collection called *Men Without Bones* that I've read about a dozen times."

The Reverend grinned. "A regular Algonquin Roundtable are we three. Why doesn't it surprise me that both of you have—oh, never mind. The point is there is a line from Kersh—I'm not sure from which novel or story—that goes: 'There are men whom one hates until a certain moment when one sees, through a chink in their armor, the writhing of something nailed down and in torment.'"

"That about covers it," said Grant. "There's something about this guy that's seriously hurting, and it's kind of scary."

Jackson signaled for a refill. "Only *kind of*? You called us both up here and away from our jam-packed social calendars for *kind of* scary? Sorry, Grant—*no one* pulls me away from an all-night *Gilligan's Island* marathon for 'kind of' scary."

The Reverend turned toward Jackson. "That may be the saddest thing I've ever heard come out of your mouth."

"Oh, bite my bag, Reverend. You forget I've seen those boxed sets of *Green Acres* DVDs you have stashed back in your room. You got no room to pass judgment on taste."

"That's true," said the Reverend. "After all, I chose the two of you for friends, didn't I?"

Grant laughed as he slapped a five-dollar bill onto the bar. "First zinger of the evening, Ted. Pony-up time."

Jackson slipped his wallet from his back pocket and pulled out a five. "I suppose that whole 'bite my bag' thing doesn't count?"

"No," said the Reverend, holding out his hand. "Though it was a refreshing change from your standard 'Lick my left one,' so heartiest congratulations on further expanding your repertoire. And in my defense, I'd like to add that Arnold the Pig remains one of the wisest and most articulate characters in the history of American television." He snapped his fingers. "Grace the palm; grace it now."

Grant and Jackson handed him their money; as they did so, the door to the men's room opened and the guy from earlier emerged, washed and shaved, wearing a fresh shirt, and smelling of Old Spice. Grant went over to the pass-through window, retrieved the guy's dinner, and set everything down in front of him.

The guy looked from Grant to Jackson (his gaze dwelling for a few moments on the gun dangling from the sheriff's hip), and then to the Reverend. He nodded a wordless hello at them, and then turned his attention toward the food.

He ate his meal in silence, his eyes never coming up to meet anyone else's gaze, and then ordered some cheesecake for dessert. After that came his third drink of the night; he was now two away from the Hangman's limit.

Holding up the empty plastic bowl near his corner of the bar, the guy cleared his throat and said, slurring a few words here and there, "Could I get some more popcorn, please?"

"Sure thing." Grant took the bowl, filled it with a fresh batch from the machine, and set it down just as the guy asked for another gin and tonic.

"This'll be your fourth drink, friend," said Grant. "I realize I'm probably way the hell too late in asking this, but are your driving?"

The guy shook his head and then stuck out his thumb. "Hitching. I caught a ride with a trucker in New Jersey and got out at the truck stop at Buckeye Lake."

Jackson leaned forward. "You *walked* here from the truck stop? That's got to be at least, what? Eight miles?"

The guy shrugged. "It's a nice evening."

"You could've eaten there," said Grant. "The food's pretty damn good—hell, they've even got pay showers you could've used instead of having to wash up in the sink."

The guy smiled, but there wasn't a lot of joy in it. "I heard the food's better here." He took a few sips from his fresh drink, set the glass down on the bar, and then removed a prescription bottle from his pocket, popped one of the tablets into his mouth, and chased it with another sip.

"Is that a good idea?" asked Jackson. "I'm not an expert, but it seems to me taking any kind of medicine with alcohol isn't high up on anyone's 'Smart Things To Do' list."

"I never claimed to be smart, Sheriff, but I also don't believe I'm breaking any laws, so if you don't mind . . ." The guy reached for his drink again but Grant was faster, pulling it from the bar and setting it on the sink.

"Look," said Grant, "I don't have many rules here, but there are a couple that I won't compromise for anybody. The first one is, no one gets more than five drinks over the course of the evening. And the second one is, I reserve the right to lower that number if I've got a good reason."

The guy shook his bottle of pills. "And these would be your 'good reason'?"

Grant nodded. "Afraid so. You walk out of here with your pills and my liquor in your system and anything bad happens, it's *my* ass that can legally be held responsible. This might not be the fanciest place of its kind, but it's been in my family for four generations and I won't risk that for anyone." He pointed at the pills. "Especially someone who mixes prescription meds with booze. You wanna play Russian roulette with liquor and pills, do it somewhere else."

The guy stared at him for a moment, and then gave a slow, sad nod. "I'm not trying to hurt myself. Really, I'm not."

"Then why mix your meds with booze?" asked the Reverend.

"Because every once in a while, neither one works well enough on its own." He reached into his back-pack once more and removed a small object that he looked at for maybe two seconds before closing his hand around it.

"Did ya ever wonder," he said to Grant, his slur worsening, "why it is that all the bad stuff that happens to us we equate with the hand?"

Grant shook his head. "I'm not sure I follow you, friend."

"Every time something goes wrong, every time there's a natural disaster or a bunch of people get killed when a balcony or bridge or something like that collapses, you always hear folks talk about things like 'the hand of fate,' or 'the hand of destiny.' When someone dies they say, 'the hands of time stopped running for them.' Stuff like that."

"Sure, I've heard those phrases."

"D'ya know why they *use* those phrases?"

"No idea."

With the index finger of his right hand he traced the ball of his left thumb. "This area of the hand, it's what's called the Mount of Venus. The first phalange symbolizes willpower, the second, logic." He then touched the base of his index finger. "This is the the Mount of Jupiter, and it symbolizes . . . what? Ah, hell, you'd think I could remember what . . ."

"Arrogance, haughtiness, and pride," said the Reverend.

Jackson shook his head. "Figures you'd know that."

The guy was only half listening to them as he pointed toward other areas of his hand, talking aloud, seemingly, to reassure himself he remembered everything. "The Mount of Saturn, the *digitus infamis* of the Romans . . . fate and destiny, that one. The Mount of Apollo at the base of the third finger stands for music and imagination and art—see how weak mine is? Bull*shit* I imagined all of it. But I've got a pretty strong Mount of Mercury; that's for learning, so maybe there's some untapped potential there."

He continued tracing patterns across the Mount of the Moon and the Mount of Mars, both at the heel of the hand. "These symbolize violence and lightheartedness, respectively." He pointed this out to Jackson, in particular. "They're both equally as strong in me. You think maybe that's something we need to worry about?"

Jackson made no reply, only exchanged a quick, worried glance with Grant.

"If you look at the line on the heel of my hand," the guy continued, "you'll see it joins the line of life and runs parallel to the line of the heart. The line of fate runs up the center of the palm, and parallel to that on the heel-side of the hand is the line of fortune. Mine don't intersect very well, do they? That's the odd thing about the lines in the hand—sometimes lines that *should* intersect come nowhere near one another, while other lines that *shouldn't* intersect run straight into each other. See, if you look closer, you can see that fortune crosses over into violence, and fate meets with lightheartedness. Those lines don't usually intersect."

"And this means what?" asked the Reverend. "That your destiny is to become a rich middleweight boxer who can tell a good joke and play a mean *Moonlight Sonata*? How fickle is the universe . . ."

For the first time, the guy genuinely laughed, and then moved his fingertip along the curved line that ran from below his little finger to the base of the first. "This one's called the Girdle of Venus."

"In my case," said Jackson, "it'd probably be more of a truss—but why get picky this late in life?"

"Where did you learn all of this?" asked Grant. "I mean, I don't know that I've ever had someone come in here who knows this much about palmistry."

"A woman I once knew. She had the most exquisite hands. Long, delicate fingers, smooth fingertips, and her skin, especially on her palms, was so thin and soft it felt like tissue paper. She used to tell me that a person's hands were the sexiest part of their body. And she was right." He leaned in, lowering the volume of his voice. "I know it sounds weird, like maybe there was some kind of fetish thing going on, but her fascination with hands, with their power and their complexity, their dexterity and grace, it gave me a . . . a *mystery,* I'd guess you'd call it, to carry with me for the rest of my life. A person needs one unsolvable mystery to carry with them to keep life interesting, don't you think? Consider the hand. It can touch, it can grasp, it can add dimension, it can kill with tenderness, it can save or end a life, and it's usually the first thing that comes into direct physical contact with another human being. I'm sorry, it's just that I—and please don't laugh at this or—"

"I won't laugh," said Grant. "I promise."

"None of us will," added the Reverend, whose presence—as Grant had been hoping—seemed to be having a calming effect on the guy.

"It's just that . . . I used to love the hand. Even the *idea* of the hand excited me. Look at it. The miracle of the whole thing. Your whole life is mapped out in the lines and curves and ridges and whorls, all the answers are *right there*—even those hidden within the lines that shouldn't intersect—but you'll never have the time to find all of them. So many sentient sensations enter the body through the hands, ya know? A baby grasping your finger, that crackle of electricity when you first touch someone you hope will become important in your life, cupping them together to splash cold water over your face when you come inside on a hot day. . . ." He shook his head. "But that's all ruined now. I look at this thing at the end of my arm and all I feel is . . . scared."

Jackson moved even closer to the guy. "Why's that?"

The guy leaned back, almost whispering. "Because of Mr. Hands."

Jackson's hand began to slide down toward either his holster or handcuffs; the Reverend caught sight of this and quickly—but subtly—gripped the sheriff's wrist, shaking his head.

Grant gave a slight nod of thanks to the Reverend and then turned back to the guy at the bar. "Okay . . ."

"I'm serious."

"About some guy named Mr. Hands?"

He stared at Grant for a moment before answering. "Uh-uh. Not a guy. A thing. A monster. A demon." He placed the object in his hand on the bar.

For a moment, Grant thought it was some kind of plastic toy that fast food places put in their kids' meals, a promotional tie-in for an animated movie, because the thing on the bar was so silly-looking it *had* to be from some kind of movie or cartoon; but as he leaned over to get a closer look he realized two things: it was not made of plastic, but hand-carved from a piece of wood; and once you got a good look at it, it definitely *wasn't* silly.

"Makes an impression, doesn't it?" asked the guy. Grant could only nod, unable for the moment to find his voice.

It stood about four inches tall, a gourd-shaped figure that had only stumps for legs, long arms, and almost ridiculously large hands with lengthy, skeletal-thin fingers. Its head was semirounded, with two deep chasms where eyes should have been, no nose, and the too-wide rictus grin of a mummified corpse. The detail was all the more remarkable because it was so hideous, and Grant couldn't help but wonder what sort of a mind came up with such a thing.

"Did you make that?" he finally managed to ask.

The guy at the bar shook his head. "No. It was a gift."

Grant reached out and touched the top of the thing's head; why, he wasn't sure. Maybe to make certain it was just a lifeless figure.

As soon as his finger touched the top of the thing's head, it moved.

Startled, Grant pulled his hand away and took a stumbling step backward. The guy at the bar waved an apology, then also touched the figure's head. It moved again.

"It's got something to do with the kind of wood that was used to carve it," he said. "This thing probably doesn't weigh three ounces. It's really delicate." He turned toward Jackson and the Reverend. "See how it's standing just on its fingertips? Yet it somehow manages to stay perfectly balanced." He touched it once more, and once more it moved—*glided*, to be exact. "I guess it's because of the pressure, y'know? You touch its head, and that creates a small amount of pressure all the way down to the fingertips, and when you pull your hand away and the pressure's relieved, the fingertips kind of act like a spring."

Jackson shook his head. "Sorry, friend, but I was watching. You hardly touched it. *Grant* hardly touched it."

"Like I said, it doesn't take much. It's real delicate."

Grant quickly scanned the customers to make sure none of them had seen him jump away from the figure like a spooked little kid. Satisfied that no one had noticed, he moved toward the corner of the bar once more. "So what's it supposed to be, anyway?"

"Mr. Hands."

"Really?" asked the Reverend. "This is your monster, your demon? The one that's responsible for 'the hands of fate' and all the rest of it?"

The guy shrugged. "I don't know if it's responsible for everything bad, but it's done some serious damage. I know. I've seen it."

Despite his rising anxiety, Grant smiled. He'd been hoping the guy was leading up to an interesting story. He turned away to pour himself a cup of coffee before getting comfortable, but the guy must have thought he was turning away in disgust or pity because his hand shot over the bar and grabbed Grant's arm. "No! You gotta listen to this! I have . . . have to tell someone. Please? I . . . have to."

Jackson was on his feet at once, gripping the guy's shoulder. "Take it easy, there, buddy, hear me?"

The guy nodded his head, took a couple of deep breaths, and tried to compose himself. "I know how it sounds, I *do*. Even if you don't believe it, just . . . just listen, okay? I've been trying to get someone to listen for most of my life, but the doctors and everyone else tell me I must have imagined it, or that my mind turned it into something else. . . . They tell me what I've got is . . . oh, what's it called?"

"Post-traumatic stress disorder," said the Reverend. It was not a question.

The guy nodded. "Yeah, but . . . but they're *wrong*, you understand? I mean, okay, yeah, maybe that's part of it, PTSD or whatever in the hell it's called— that's what I have to take all the fucking pills for, but they don't always work on their own, you understand?" He faced each man in turn. "So please, *please*, even if you think I'm full of shit, even if you think I'm nuts, would you just please *listen*?"

Grant covered the guy's hand with his own and gently pulled it from his arm. "Settle down, friend. I was just going to pour myself a cup of coffee and pull up a chair. Would you like to have some coffee with me? It'll be on the house."

The guy stared into Grant's eyes for a few seconds. "You really *want* to hear it?"

"Sure do. Whole thing, beginning to end. And I don't think you're crazy—no more so than half the people who come through that door with a story they want to get off their chests."

The guy looked unconvinced. "But I said it's a de-mon; a monster."

"I heard you the first time." Grant poured two cups of coffee, set one down in front of the guy, and then pulled up the chair he kept behind the bar. "I make a good pot of java, if I do say so myself. And before you start quizzing me again about everything you've said up to this point, you need to understand that I've seen some seriously weird shit in my day."

"That's putting it mildly," said Jackson.

The Reverend only nodded, and for a moment the three of them looked up toward the shelf that ran above the length of the bar, a shelf with an odd but eye-catching assortment of items, knickknacks, and bric-a-brac, among which could be seen a handmade model of a lighthouse with a clipper ship crashed upon the shore, an old harmonica, and the highly polished broken neck of an acoustic guitar. Each of these items held a special meaning for the three men, each had its own story, and every story, as Grant had told the guy at the bar, contained its own element of "seriously weird shit."

"So," said Grant to the guy, "if someone walks in here and wants to tell me a story about a demon or a monster, I don't shake my head or pass judgment or jump to the worst possible conclusion. Now, why don't you drink some of my unjustifiably unfamous coffee and get on with it?"

The guy took a couple of sips. "I, uh . . . Sorry, no one's ever *asked* me to tell the whole thing before. At best I get about halfway through before someone whips out a prescription pad and starts scribbling."

Grant said nothing. This was a guy who desperately needed to talk to someone. If Grant waited in silence long enough, the guy would get the idea that he wasn't going anywhere and begin wherever he needed to begin.

"You're right," the guy said. "This is really good coffee." He took another sip, set down the cup, and pulled in a deep breath as he steadied himself and his hands. "Wow. Somehow I thought it'd be easy to start this, y'know?"

"It's *your* story," said the Reverend. "Start it wherever you wish."

"That's just it," said the guy. "It's not *just* my story."

The Reverend nodded. "Most stories usually aren't."

The guy rubbed his eyes. "Anyone got a smoke? I mean, is it okay to smoke in here?"

Jackson laughed. "Can't you smell it in the wood?" He fished a pack of smokes from his shirt pocket. "This is one of the few businesses left in the state where you can still smoke."

"When did you start again?" asked the Reverend, gesturing toward the cigarettes.

"I didn't," said Jackson. "But you'd be surprised how many confessions I've gotten from people after they've had a chance to relax with a smoke." He looked at the guy at the end of the bar. "Not that this is an interrogation or anything."

"No," replied the guy. "But I suppose it's a confession, nonetheless." He took the cigarette, fired it up, and pulled in an almost desperate drag of smoke; if you listened closely enough, you might have heard the cancer cells cheering. "Oh, *man,* that tastes good." Another sip of coffee, another deep drag on the smoke. "Have any of you ever heard the name Ronald Williamson?"

None of them had.

"I'm guessing at least one of you know him by his other name," said the guy. "Uncle Ronnie."

"Holy shit," whispered Jackson.

The Reverend stared at him for a moment. *"Well . . . ?"*

"Uncle Ronnie was the name of a serial killer from a ways back—at least fifteen, twenty years ago," said Jackson. "He targeted children in Kentucky, Indiana, and Ohio. He always left a note of apology on the victim's body, and always signed it, 'I'm Sorry. With Love, Uncle Ronnie.' The killings stopped around nineteen eighty-three. He was never caught." Jackson's gaze was now intensely focused on the guy at the end of the bar. "How old are you, friend—and while we're on the subject, what the hell is your name, anyway?"

"I just turned twenty-eight. I was three when the Uncle Ronnie killings stopped, so I think that qualifies as an alibi."

Jackson continued staring at him. "And your name?"

The guy cupped the mug of coffee in his hands, staring down into the dark liquid. "What's it matter?"

Before Jackson could answer, the Reverend said, "I think we should call him Henry—after William Sydney Porter, better known, of course—"

"As O. Henry," said Jackson. "I thought we'd already established that we're an incongruously literate bunch." He regarded the guy at the bar for a moment. "All right, for the sake of getting on with things, I'll go along with calling you Henry—*for now.*"

"Thank you," said Henry.

Grant refilled both his and Henry's coffee mugs. "So, what about Uncle Ronnie?"

Henry took another drag from his cigarette, picked up the figure of Mr. Hands, and said, "Well, for one thing, his full name was Ronald James Williamson, and he killed his first child when he was still a child himself. . . ."

PART ONE

THE MOUNT OF SATURN

"Procul omen abesto!"
Far be that fate from us!

—Ovid
Amores, I.xiv.41

"Where're she lie,
Locked up from mortal eye,
In shady leaves of destiny."

—Richard Crashaw (1612(?)–1649)

CHAPTER ONE

His full name was Ronald James Williamson, and he killed his first child when he was still a child himself—not that killing had been his intention; it never was the *intention*. It was often his only choice (hence the notes of sincere apology he began leaving on the bodies of his victims); he simply wanted to find a way to make the hurting stop.

Ronnie (as everyone called him, though he would have preferred R.J.—R.J. sounded like someone cool, someone strong, someone others looked up to; Ronnie, on the other hand, was the name of a sometimes-friend you called whenever your A-number-one friends were busy and there was no one else to call, but we're getting off the point) couldn't remember a time when he hadn't been the odd one, the strange one, the one the other kids always whispered about and from whom they stayed far away unless it was absolutely necessary they interact with him, like for a school project or if the others in their clique felt like terrorizing or beating up on him.

Had any of them known about Ronnie's special talent, his unspoken facility, his—and let's call it what it was—his particular power, they might have been much nicer to him.

Try as he did, Ronnie could never figure out why he was able to do the things he could do. He didn't ask for it, this . . . *ability* he was born with. Most of the time he didn't even *understand* it, not really, because every time he felt as if he were getting a grasp on what exactly this ability, this facility, this *power* could and couldn't do, it would reveal a new facet to him, and leave him twice as confused as before.

Ronnie was never one hundred percent certain how he came to posses this power, but one night he heard his mother talking on the phone to one of her friends—this was on a night that Daddy was out at the bars with his friends from work—and Mommy mentioned something about how Daddy had hit her "as usual" while she was pregnant with Ronnie and she'd fallen down the short flight of stairs that led from the back porch to the patio in the backyard. "I thought for sure I was going to lose the baby," she said to her friend. "I landed right on my stomach. The other kids came running to help me, and all of them were so *scared*. . . ."

Ronnie was the youngest of five children, the one who had to make do with hand-me-down clothes and toys, but he didn't mind, not really. The only thing that he minded, the only thing that bored him to tears, were the trips he and Mommy had to make to the doctor four times a year. The doctor would make Ronnie take all these tests (match the wooden shapes to the proper holes; what does this blotch on the paper look like?; name the animal; can you recognize this word?) and then ask him all sorts of questions about school and what he watched on television and could he add two and two and what about subtraction. . . . Geez, it was dumb; but Mommy seemed to feel better after these boring visits—well, if not *better,* exactly, then no worse, and that made Ronnie happy because he loved his mommy.

Daddy . . . not so much. Daddy was stingy with his affection but generous with his fists, at least as far as Ronnie was concerned. The other kids, well, Daddy was real nice to them; but Ronnie, Ronnie he didn't like, and after a few drinks never hesitated to tell him. "Never wanted you," he'd say; "You were a fuckin' mistake," he'd say. "Damn, you little half *ree*-tard, I wish you'd never been born," he'd say. Ronnie learned to ignore it—especially after he discovered his special power.

It happened the day he heard Mommy talking on the phone with her friend about how Daddy had knocked her down the back porch stairs. Mommy had started to cry, and Ronnie came into the kitchen so quietly that she didn't hear him, and he touched her hand. That was all. But it was enough, because in an instant he *knew* everything, he *knew* all about the *hurting.*

Mommy was supposed to be using something called a diafram but she'd forgotten to put it in so she and Daddy had made Ronnie one night (he wasn't sure what "doggy-style" meant, but that's how he'd been made) and when Mommy found out, she waited eight weeks before she told Daddy, and Daddy had been mad and hit Mommy real hard and then dragged her out the back door and hit her again so she'd fall down the porch steps and land real hard, land facedown on the concrete patio, and Daddy shouted "That ought to do it!" and then went back inside to open a fresh beer because it helped him to not worry about the layoffs at the plant that everybody knew were coming while the other kids came running to help Mommy, and one of the neighbors, Mr. Wade, he'd insisted on driving Mommy to the hospital where she sat in the emergency room for four hours before a doctor saw her, and that's when she'd found out that Ronnie was okay but something had been damaged in her you-ter-us so she'd have to make weekly visits to her obeey-gee-why-en to make sure nothing went wrong, but when it came time for Ronnie to be born something did go wrong, Mommy lost a lot of blood and the doctors had to perform a sissy-air-eyan to get Ronnie out and then do something called a history-ect-omy on Mommy so she couldn't have any more babies (that part made Ronnie very sad because he thought it would be neat to have a baby brother or sister someday) and ever since then Daddy and Mommy hadn't had any secks or even kissed and Mommy was so lonely. . . .

Ronnie smiled at her and left the kitchen after that because it was too sad and confusing. He was almost six years old that night, and if he understood nothing else, he understood that the boring visits to the doctor made Mommy . . . if not *happy*, then at least not any more sad, so he decided that he wouldn't whine and complain about going to the doctor or riding on the short bus to school or getting upset when the kids called him a "ree-tard" or a "sped."

He wondered, though, if there were anything he could do to make Mommy's hurting stop, but he couldn't think of anything.

Then one day he was out in the backyard playing by himself (he was the Green Hornet spying on a bad guy) when he spotted a small bird lying on its side, twitching. He crawled over on his hands and knees (didn't want the bad guy to spot him; the Green Hornet was a phantom, he was invisible) and saw that the bird was bleeding.

Ronnie stared at the bird for a few seconds before reaching out to touch it, and as soon as he did, he knew what had happened: there was a neighborhood cat whose owners didn't feed it very often, and they were mean to it most of the time even when it rubbed up against them and purred in hopes they'd pet it, and this cat (Reuben, that was its name, but how Ronnie knew that he didn't understand) would run outside any chance it got to get away from its mean owners, and sometimes this cat felt mean itself, and it had been feeling mean earlier today when it hopped the fence into Ronnie's backyard, and it was feeling meaner when it saw this little bird on the ground poking around for worms, and it felt the meanest of all when it pounced on the little bird and tore into its neck and clawed one of its wings until the thing almost came all the way off, but then the Rueben heard one of its owners calling for it, and they'd sounded worried, like maybe they'd be nice this time, and Reuben had run off, leaving this bird lying here.

And the bird was *hurting*.

Ronnie was very careful, very gentle, as he cupped his hands and slid them underneath the bird and lifted it close to his face, and no sooner had he looked into the bird's eyes than he *knew*: that the bird was in agony and was going to die a slow, terrible death; that the bird was a mommy-bird; that she'd been gathering up worms to feed to her children in their nest; and—worst of all, most terrible of all—that the baby-birds were going to die from starvation because Mommy was never going to return. (For an instant Ronnie flashed to the mommy-bird's view from her nest, and he thought he recognized the street she saw, the one with the tree where her starving babies waited for her to come back.)

But first thing, he had to make the hurting stop; so he did the only thing he could think of—he grasped the mommy-bird by her neck and quickly snapped it to the side, hearing a little *crunch* at the same moment the bird's eyes glazed over and her body went limp and lifeless in his hands.

He sat there and cried for almost half an hour before finding a spot to bury her, and then—not telling Mommy where he was going—set off to see if he could find the street with the tree where the bird's babies were waiting for her, so hungry.

He walked all over the neighborhood, and even went beyond, looking for the tree, but he never found it. He cried himself to sleep for almost a week because he *knew* that the baby-birds were all dead, having starved because Mommy didn't come home and he hadn't been able to find them. He cried so much that Daddy stopped hitting him (for a little while, anyway) and Mommy called the doctor to see if she and Ronnie could get in to see him a week early.

The visit went as most of them did; the tests, the pictures, the questions—only this time the doctor kept asking Ronnie if anything was bothering him, if he felt sadder than usual. Ronnie knew it wasn't right to lie to someone, but he couldn't figure out a way to make the doctor understand what had happened without sounding like a "ree-tard" or a "sped" . . . so he said everything was okay, he was just having bad dreams. The doctor nodded his head and made the *hmmmm* sound that he made a lot whenever he saw Ronnie, and then took out his square gray pad and began writing on it. Ronnie knew what that meant: more pills. That seemed to be the doctor's solution to everything: the gray pad and pills.

The doctor asked Ronnie to go out to the waiting room and oh, by the way, would he please ask his mommy to come back here for a few minutes? Ronnie did as he was asked.

Mommy was back there an awful long time and Ronnie quickly became bored with the toys and back issues of *Highlights for Children*, so he looked around the waiting room to make sure no one was watching him (no one was), slipped out of his chair, and made his way outside like a phantom, like he was invisible, like he was the Green Hornet.

The doctor's office was in a strip of doctor's offices located across the parking lot from the hospital, so there were always lots of cars and people coming and going. Ronnie liked to watch the people as they came and went, so he found a bench and sat down and for a little while had a grand old time just watching the people. Then he became aware of the sound of someone crying nearby.

He looked around and saw her, sitting two benches away from him. She was a lot older than he was— maybe even in her twenties—and she was kinda fat (not *really* fat, just a little, all of it in one spot where her tummy was) and she was holding a bunch of square gray pieces of paper (pills, pills, pills) and she seemed so sad.

Ronnie stared at her for a minute, looked around

again, then jumped down off the bench and walked over to her.

"How come you're so sad?" he asked her.

The woman looked up at him and wiped her eyes, then tried to smile. "Oh, hon, I'm . . . I'm okay, really." Then she looked around. "Where's your mommy?"

"She's inside talkin' to the doctor. He's tellin' her that I ain't ever gonna be real smart like the other kids." And this was true. Ronnie had overhead the doctor and Mommy talking once; the doctor had said something like "He'll never be older than ten or eleven, mentally and emotionally. . . ." Ronnie didn't understand what the doctor meant by that, and as the days went on, he didn't really care.

The crying lady stared at him for a moment, then blew her nose into a tissue she was holding. "Don't you say that, hon. You're going to turn out to be just fine."

"Promise?"

Now her smile seemed less sad. "Promise." She stood up, gathering her purse and square gray slips of paper, and offered her hand. "Show me which doctor's office you came from, okay? Let's get you back so your mom doesn't worry."

" 'Kay," said Ronnie, and then noticed how her belly bulged, like she wasn't fat at all. "Hey—you gonna have a baby?"

She looked shocked for a moment, but then the smile came back. "Yes, yes, I am."

"Can I . . . can I touch it?" asked Ronnie. He'd seen a lot of people do this before, that is, ask if they could touch the woman's belly to feel the baby before it came out.

"Why . . . oh, what the heck? *Of course* you can, hon. Go right ahead."

Ronnie wiped his hands on his jacket to make sure they were clean, and then placed both of them on the woman's protruding belly.

And he knew. And it scared him. And it hurt him. And it made him sad. And sick. And he made a wish. He wished away the hurt of her unborn baby and, he hoped, the nice lady herself.

He looked up at her, nearly in tears, and said: *"Mirror, mirror, tell me true / Am I pretty or am I plain?"*

She stared at him for a moment, looking as if she hadn't understood what he'd said, and then asked: "What did you s-say, hon?"

Ronnie could tell that he'd scared her, maybe even made her think he was weird, a ree-tard, a sped, and he didn't want that, she seemed so nice, so he just shrugged and said, "Nothing."

She took him back to the doctor's office, and met his mother, and they were nice to one another, and before she left, the woman knelt down and gave Ronnie a hug and said, "My name's Lucy, hon, and I hope my baby grows up to be just as sweet and considerate as you." She rose to her feet, wished Ronnie's mom a nice day, and walked outside.

Ronnie was too confused to speak for several minutes after this encounter, because the ability, the facility, the power had just revealed a new and frightening facet to him.

We need to leave him right here for the moment; a confused, lonely, damaged little boy watching a young woman named Lucy walk away from him. Oh, they'll meet again—in fact, they'll meet two times more before our story is done, though only one of them will remember the other.

But for the moment, we need to leave Ronald

James Williamson standing here, in the waiting room of his doctor's office, clutching his mommy's hand, watching a pregnant woman named Lucy walk away.

The thing to remember, though, is this: at this precise moment, both of them are feeling confused and helpless. It unites them, binds them together; a nearly invisible silver thread running through time and space, alive and vibrating, feeling their every breath, their every heartbeat, their every thought and want and pain and need. It knows them as well as they know themselves, perhaps even *better* than they know themselves, and it will never allow them to separate.

Never, ever; now and forever.

CHAPTER TWO

The expectant mother who met Ronald James Williamson that afternoon was named Lucy Thompson (one day to be Lucy Holcomb, at least for a while), and when Ronnie laid hands upon her, this is what he knew, completely and utterly:

She had been forced to leave state college one semester into her second year because her father had gotten laid off from the plant and her parents needed her help. Though the letter her mother sent wasn't obvious in its manipulations, it nonetheless managed to push all the right guilt buttons. Two days after receiving it, Lucy withdrew from school and used her last forty-five dollars to buy a bus ticket back to Cedar Hill. It was during the three-hour bus ride that she began to wonder about the price a person paid for so-called "selfless" acts. From the moment she'd stepped into the iron belly of the road lizard her throat had been expanding, then contracting at an alarming rate, finally forcing her to open the window next to her seat so she could breathe more easily. Her chest was clogged with anger, sorrow, confusion, and, worst of all, pity. Everyone knew the plant was on its last leg, that the company had been looking for an excuse to pull up stakes ever since that labor riot a few years back, and when it happened, when the plant went down, so would the seven hundred jobs that formed the core of the town's financial stability.

More than anything, Lucy didn't, dear God, didn't want to end up like every other girl in town; under- to uneducated, with no dreams left, working nine hours a day in some bakery or laundry or grocery store, then coming home to a husband who didn't much like her and children who didn't much respect her, wearing a scarf around her head all the time to cover the premature gray hair, watching prime-time soap operas and getting twelve pounds heavier with each passing year.

As she stepped off the bus she promised herself that, regardless of what eventually happened with the plant, she wouldn't betray herself for anyone or anything. That alone was her hope.

"I thank God for a daughter like you," said her father, embracing her as she stepped through the door. "Come on in and sit down and let your mother fix you something to eat. It's good to see you, hon. Here, I saved the want ads from the last couple days. Maybe you'll find something. . . ."

She wound up taking a cashier job at the town's only all-night grocery store. Lucy smiled at her late-night customers, and spoke with them, and tried to be cheery because there was nothing more depressing than to find yourself in a grocery store buying a loaf of bread at three thirty in the morning in a town that was dying because the plant was going under and no one wanted to admit it.

Still, Lucy smiled at them with a warmth that she hoped would help, from a heart that was, if it could be said of anyone's, truly good and sympathetic.

The customers took no notice.

For eleven months she lived in a semi-somnambu-listic daze, going to work, coming home, eating something, handing her paycheck over to her parents once a week, then shuffling off to bed where she read until sleep claimed her.

Outside her bedroom window, the soot from the plant's chimneys became less and less thick but still managed to cover the town in ashes and grayness.

She read books on sociology, countless romance novels and mysteries, biographies of writers and film stars, years-old science magazines, and developed an understanding and love of poetry that had eluded her in high school. Of course she went for a lot of the Romantics, Byron and Keats and Shelley, as well as a few modernists—T. S. Eliot and James Dickey, Rainer Maria Rilke and the lyrical, gloomy Dylan Thomas. Cumulatively, they gave eloquent voice to her silent aches and hidden despairs.

Crime began to spread through the town: holdups, street fights, petty thefts, and acts of vandalism.

And in the center of it all stood the plant, a hulking, roaring dinosaur, fighting desperately against its own extinction as it sank into the tar of progress.

Lucy discovered *Jane Eyre* in the library one day. Over the next month she read it three times; and the dinosaur howled in the night; and her mother, at day's end every day, sat alone staring at the television or listening to her scratchy old records; and her father's eyes filled with more fear and shame as he came to realize he was never going to be called back to work; and somewhere inside Lucy a feeling awakened. She did what she could to squash it, but it never really went away. So sometimes, very late at night when shameful fantasies are indulged, she took a certain private pleasure as she lay in her bed, and usually felt like hell afterward, remembering the words to a nursery rhyme her mother used to read to her when she was a child:

Mirror, mirror, tell me true
Am I pretty or am I plain?
Or am I downright ugly?
And ugly to remain?

No man would ever want her in that special, heated, passionate way. She was too plain, and the plain did not inspire great passion.

Then Larry Parre, one of the stockroom workers, asked her if she wanted to go to a party on Wednesday evening, her only night off.

She smiled, stunned (no one had ever asked her out on a real date before), then decided that she deserved to enjoy herself a little.

She said yes, and Larry smiled, really smiled, and she felt wonderful, as if she were Miss Eyre meeting Rochester for the first time.

She had managed to save a little over four hundred dollars from her twice-monthly twenty-dollar allowance, and spent nearly a third of it on a new outfit to wear to the party that Wednesday. The thought of having a date and meeting some new people, making some friends, having someone else besides her parents to talk to . . . well, for the first time since coming home she felt there was something to look forward to.

She even sprang for some new makeup and perfume at the local K-Mart.

Might as well do it up right.

The party had been nice enough, and Larry had complimented her on how she looked, and for a while Lucy had been able to forget about the desperate faces of her parents and the feeling that she was dying inside.

After the party, when they climbed into his pickup truck, Larry leaned over and kissed her. It was so sudden, so abrupt and unexpected, that Lucy froze. Larry pulled back and blushed. "Sorry. I didn't mean to just, y'know, surprise you like that."

"Oh, it's . . . it's okay," said Lucy. "I mean, I just didn't expect it." She laughed softly, shaking her head.

"What is it?" asked Larry.

"I'm just . . . sometimes I think maybe I'm really out of it. I mean, I didn't think you even knew I existed."

"I noticed you."

"I noticed you, too."

"A lot of the girls who work in the store, they got this superiority problem. They think that just because they get to wear uniforms and deal with customers that they're, I don't know, better than us guys who work the stockroom, that because we don't come to work in nice shirts and wearing ties that we're low-class hicks. I don't think it's right, judging someone on account of how they dress or what kind of work they do. Do you?"

"No," she whispered, unable to meet his gaze. "Not at all."

Larry looked at his watch and smiled. "Wanna go on a picnic?"

"Yeah, that might be nice. Maybe next week on my day off we could—"

"I mean now," he said, reaching behind the seat and pulling out a wicker picnic basket.

Lucy stared at the basket. "You're kidding?"

"Uh-uh. Hasn't anyone ever taken you on a picnic at night before? It's pretty cool, out there on a blanket at night, chowing down under the stars. It's only ten thirty. C'mon, what do you say?"

"Did you plan to do this all along?"

"Yeah. I would've brought you flowers but someone said you were allergic."

"I am." She felt as if she'd awakened in some old Russian fairy story to discover that she was a princess.

How could she have said no?

They wound up on Horn's Hill (a popular make-out spot in Cedar Hill), overlooking the abandoned rock quarry just beyond the county line. Another couple, Jim and Wanda, who hadn't been at the party, were already waiting for them, a red-and-white checkered tablecloth spread on the ground and paper plates and plastic forks all set. They'd even brought along a portable cassette player to provide music. Gordon Lightfoot. Larry introduced Jim and Wanda, and they seemed nice enough.

They had brought wine and cheese and some sandwiches to go with the cold fried chicken in Larry's basket. They'd also brought along some grass. Despite her more sensible instincts, Lucy drank a little

too much wine and took a few too many tokes off one
of the joints and, after a while, began feeling light-
headed and lighthearted, the most relaxed and happy
she'd been since coming home. After a few more
swigs of wine she realized that Larry's hand was resting on the inside of her thigh. She gently pushed his
hand away and smiled at him. Then, after another hit
of the joint, she began thinking maybe she liked having his hand there, and he asked her if he could put
his arm around her and Lucy said "Yes, that would be
fine if you want to" and Larry said that he wanted to
because she was a "nice-looking chick" and that made
her laugh because wasn't a chick a little thing you saw
running around a barnyard, and Larry laughed at
that and told her once again how he'd been watching
her for quite some time and she told him "I've noticed you, too, from time to time," and that made Jim
and Wanda laugh, and Larry laughed, then Lucy
started laughing and took another swig and another
toke and was feeling really good now, really fine, fine
like a princess in an old Russian fairy story, and Larry
started a fresh joint and offered it to her and she
asked him "Isn't this expensive?" and he said "Yes,
baby, it is but you're worth it," then ran his hand up
under her dress and she giggled because, for some
reason, she liked the feel of his hand on her body.
Then Jim asked if everybody was ready to "get serious
and party down hearty" and took off his pants and
Wanda took off her blouse and bra as Larry reached
over and squeezed one of Lucy's breasts and Lucy said
"Pleeeeze don't do that it hurts when you squeeze like
that," but Larry kept at it and soon had her dress unzipped in the back and she was feeling truly fine now

and helped him to undress her and soon all of them were naked and rolling around on the blanket and smoking more grass and smiling as Wanda kept screaming "fuckmefuckme*FUCKME*" in Jim's ear and Lucy giggled and Larry asked what was so funny as he parted her legs and Lucy, thinking of her mother, said "This is better than television because you can touch," then Larry touched her and climbed on top and slid inside of her, hard and firm as they pushed together, and there was a moment of blinding pain as Lucy felt something tear and leak between her legs, up and down, up and down, he felt *good* there, deep inside of her, and she pushed up and kissed him through the sweet pain as his hands squeezed and tickled her all over, and she said, "That feels so good am I doing all right I've never done this before," and Larry rammed in deeper and said she was "doing just fine, fine baby, I'm gonna come, baby, hold on," and Lucy did, held on tight as she felt his hardness swell inside her and then she pushed up and felt the spurts as he came and came and came. . . .

By the time Larry dropped her off in front of her house she was starting to feel nauseated, but he didn't seem to care because he just said something about how he didn't know if he should apologize or not because he didn't mean for it to happen like that. Sure, he wanted to kiss her and stuff, and it was really great but "Ah, hell, I don't know what to say, maybe you should've said no and not let me" and then he drove away, leaving her by the curb, and she almost made it onto the porch before she vomited on the steps. Then Mom was there, holding her up and asking what was the matter and all Lucy could say was, "Aren't you going to miss something on the television that you like to watch?" Then the world started spinning like a top and she felt dizzy as Mom put her into bed and she wondered if maybe she'd been a bad girl, and after her father had thanked God for a daughter like her.

Five weeks later she discovered she was pregnant.

Later, after the Bad Time ended in a protracted series of sputtering little agonies, she indulged in one instance of genuine self-pity, and—following the advice in one of the countless self-help books she'd accumulated—put the ugliness on paper:

> *Dear Larry,*
>
> *I don't know whether or not I'll have the nerve to mail this once it's finished, but according to most of these self-help books I've been reading (I've been reading a lot of them lately), it's supposed to be therapeutic to get your feelings down on paper. I feel like one of those characters in some corny play or movie who go to the grave of a loved one and talk to the headstone. I don't much like it.*
>
> *I don't know how to react to your card. I'd like to know who told you about it and why, after all this time, you felt you needed to contact me. I probably shouldn't be writing to you at all, but—impetuous, impulsive, spontaneous.*
>
> *You ask how I'm feeling. I feel angry, hurt, <u>very</u> misunderstood, and not close to apologizing to anyone in this world except myself for the mess I have made of my life. I need love and very much resent that I do. I*

can't find it in myself to trust anyone. I feel like a wounded animal in a cage. That's a bad simile, I know. I've been trying to figure out how to say the things I want to say to you—the things I should have said to you a long time ago—but I can't bring myself to write them down, it seems too cowardly. Mom understands, or seems to. It's kind of creepy at times, the way she knows what I'm thinking or feeling without me having to say anything to her.

I saw you a few days ago. You were coming out of the Sparta with some woman with red hair. The two of you seemed to be very close. Is it serious? Does the cook at the Sparta still make those wickedly delicious cheeseburgers? Do you ever think about what happened? I do. It was kind of weird, seeing you the other day. The moment I laid eyes on you, I felt grief. I looked at lost youth, innocence—mine! That evening on the hill for me was like a pleasant dream, an escape. But later— I suffered for it. Knowing the life I was in, the life I once had. Seeing you reminded me that I've lost the dearest thing in the world, the most precious thing I ever had.

I feel that I've loved many people in my life but very few have truly loved me. Some said they did, but words are cheap. Especially when they come out of the mouth of a man like you. Because of you I now find most men to be slobbering, indecisive fools to whom love and sex are equivalent. I worry that I'll feel that way for the rest of my life. I used to think that sex was a sacred thing, a joy, a fulfillment of life as God designed it to be. I'm still sure it was supposed to be that way— the purest physical connection a man and woman can make, echoing the spiritual connection, as well—but since that night I have learned what cruelty is, shame, *degradation, ugliness. For the first time in my life I look down at the ground when I speak to people. I won't look in mirrors. I feel dirty and inferior. I don't laugh and I won't smile. I'm aware that I'm not pretty, that I have a pudgy, sagging body, god-awful hair. My dad calls me a whore. He even points at whores on the street when we're driving and tells me the only way I'll ever snag a man now is if I dress like a whore and wear makeup like one. Lots of lipstick and tight clothes, he says. He's turned into such a bastard. You'd probably like him. Be the best of friends, you two.*

Everything about me that I always thought was good and kind or special has been ridiculed by him, scorned, criticized, and crushed. Still, I wonder why I've allowed myself to feel this way. To be compared by your own father to a common prostitute and come up lacking. Sometimes I almost believe his rantings.

I don't know if I want people near me anymore. I'm tired of the effort it takes to keep friends and loved ones. Yet I need love and friendship—and I fight that need. I want to drive everyone away. I don't want to be hurt again, not like that. I don't want what every other woman in this town has settled for, to be dominated by a man, to be told what to do and when to do it. If I ever subject myself to that again I'll scream. I scream inside now and can't wait for those times when I'm alone so I won't have to hold it in anymore.

And hate. I feel hate now as I never have before. Cold and calculating, not a normal heated rage that is spent quickly. A year of holding this rage inside has taught me well. Keep that guard up. I often find myself fantasizing about revenge. Mom says, "No, don't

*be like that. Read your Bible and be Christian." I
threw my Bible away. Christianity doesn't apply here.
I know that I'm wrong even as I write this, but don't I
hate as well as I love? The "old" me is so far away, so
distant—I don't think I'd recognize her if she were to
come around. She really believed she was loved, cher-
ished, and respected by everyone who knew her. She
didn't know that what I have lived even existed.*

*It's funny; I never used to feel sorry for the "bad"
girls, the "loose" ones that all the guys mistreated. No,
queen-angel Lucy felt they had it coming for their slut-
tish behavior. It wouldn't happen to me because I was
special. Ha! Talk about how the mighty have fallen.
Some women just have to get affection any way they
can. I wish I could find them, all of those girls I used
to look down my nose at, so I could apologize to them
for having felt superior. What they did, they did out of
loneliness, even if they didn't know it.*

*I want to escape from this thing I've become. I des-
perately want to start over—to be virginal again in
some way, any way. I want to change. I wish I could
afford total plastic surgery—nose, eyes, chin, boobs,
the works. And a name change, too. I want the old
Lucy dead, gone, her shame buried. I'm no longer that
girl. I'm what became of her.*

*Empty now. I just want to go to a strange place
where no one knows me. I don't know if I can feel anything of value now. Do I want to know? I can understand pain, fear, and rage intimately, even though I
don't want to.*

*Strange thing happened to me yesterday. I was go-
ing through all my old high school stuff and I came
across this paper I wrote for a psychology class. The
assignment was to write a letter to your unborn child,*

introducing yourself to them. The teacher told us to
pretend that our child was never going to see us, ever,
so we had to tell them everything important in this
letter.

The paper I wrote it on was really pretty.
I wish I could remember where I got it.
Thank you for the card.
Yours Truly,
Lucy

She never mailed it. It was too demeaning, mean-
dering, and empty-soul pitiful.

But she never threw it away, either.

That was after the end of the Bad Time.

This is how the ending began:

During the months following her hillside picnic
with Larry and his friends, Lucy's life became a long,
dreary, gray night, chiseled from gray stone and
shadowed by gray mist. More than a night of freezing rain, it was a tone—the kind that is part of the
province of loneliness and cannot be vicariously
conveyed to anyone who has not lived with the physical tension, stilled violence, and protracted anguish
of regret. Her father never spoke to her unless it was
to call her a whore, or a disgrace, or to remind her
that she wasn't anything special to look at and never
would be because all whores were ugly to God and
to all men; once in a while he would draw back his
hand to deliver a blow to the side of her face, which
never came because Mom, bless her sad heart, was
always nearby to intervene, to calm Dad and try her
best to maintain some semblance of love and famil-
ial compassion.

On those few occasions when she was able to catch

him at work, Larry either ignored her outright or made it clear that he was too busy to be bothered. She thought it would be easy to tell him about the pregnancy but there was always someone else around whenever she tried to talk to him; he seemed to make sure of that. Then came the afternoon when he'd stopped by the store for his check and found her waiting for him when he got back to his car.

"Ain't this supposed to be your day off?"

"I wanted to see you."

"Well, hey, y'know, I want to see you, too, but I'm kinda busy right now. Gotta get to the bank and—"

"Why won't you talk to me?"

" 'Cause I don't want everybody here knowing my business, that's why. They see us talking, just by ourselves, and they're gonna start thinking that maybe you and me got something going on."

"*Something going on?* You *fucked me,* Larry. It was the first time I'd ever been with a man like that and you act like it was . . . was—"

"You enjoyed it, didn't you?"

"While it was happening, yes, but everything since has made it seem so—"

"I don't need this shit from you, not today. You got something to tell me, then just say it, please?"

It was the "please" that did it, that should've said nothing at all but told her everything she needed to know, because when he said it a corner of his mouth twitched, curving slightly upward, a smile-in-progress abandoned at the halfway point, the syllables rising half an octave in pitch before they tripped over something caught in his throat and he coughed a false cough, looking down at his feet, and in that moment, because of those simple, telltale signs, Lucy knew it was hopeless, and saw in a flash what would happen if she were to tell him: he would start by denying that the baby was his, might even demand a blood test; then, when confronted with the truth, he'd try to defend himself by saying she'd wanted it just as much as he had, maybe even accuse her of having initiated the sex, and if the question of birth control came up he could always get Jim and Wanda to say that he'd wanted to put on a rubber but she'd been too hot to trot and how could she do this to him; even if he were to surprise her and accept his share of responsibility, the terrified look in his eyes and the tightness of his face told her he'd be an awful father, ignoring the kid, maybe even abusing it because it was the child's fault his youth came to a screeching halt just when it should have been gaining momentum; he'd hate the kid, he'd hate her, and she might even wind up hating herself worse than she did right now. God, how could she have been so stupid? To get involved with a guy who used his cock like a divining rod to guide him from one pussy to the next, doing whatever it took, saying whatever words were necessary to get the panties down and the legs spread wide . . .

She should have said no; it was that simple. Should have, but she'd been too caught up in being an object of desire for the first time in her life. This was now her problem; hers and hers alone. She didn't want anything to do with him, this man who might one day learn to regret the brash actions of youth but for now only looked upon her as another easy lay. There might be a note of fear in his voice right now betraying his bravado, a note that told her he knew what was coming, but in his eyes there was nothing but amused contempt, and she felt dirty and diminished for having shared her body with him.

"Nothing," she said, never taking her gaze from his face. "Just . . . nothing." Then she walked away. For just a second there she'd wanted to say "Have a nice life" or "Good luck" or something like that, something to let the man he'd someday become know there was no bitterness in her heart, but that wasn't true. She was bitter. And that made her too much like every other woman in this town.

It wouldn't happen to her. She'd have the baby, and she'd raise it like a good and loving mother should, and if that earned her the scorn of her father, so be it.

Even a whore knew how to show tenderness.

This is how the Bad Time ended:

It was a Wednesday night, right after dinner. Dad was still floating around in a constipated cloud of resentment and only looked at Lucy when it couldn't be avoided. When dinner was finished, he pushed away from the table and went into the living room to read the paper. Mom chattered away about everything and nothing, her voice the background noise of a radio playing in some distant room, tuned to a station no one ever listened to. Lucy busied herself clearing the dishes, then wiping off the table and kitchen counters. She was two weeks into her third month. The tension was killing her; between Mom and Dad and the people at work with their forced civility and snickering behind her back and whispers and disapproving glances, she felt like a leper. God, how she hated small-town minds. She knew she shouldn't let any of it get to her, and she tried to keep on keeping on, as the song said, but for the last several days her appetite hadn't been what it should have been, and she wasn't sleeping for more than a few hours at a time. The only real comfort she had was knowing that Dad would probably change his tune once he held his newborn grandchild for the first time.

As she was preparing to do this dishes, she thought back to her visit to her ob-gyn that morning, how she'd had that sudden attack of the weepies on her way out, and had sat down on one of the outside benches. There had been that little boy, Ronnie, who'd come over to talk to her, who'd asked if he could touch her and feel the baby, and that had damn near made her day—except for the moment where she could have sworn he'd muttered part of the "Mirror, Mirror" nursery rhyme—but that was probably her hormones shifting her imagination into overdrive. He'd been so sweet to her, had made her feel so much better . . . and there was something about his touching her that sent a . . . a tingling sensation through her. It was such a lovely moment. No woman in her right mind could feel depressed after that.

She was still thinking about Ronnie as she was adding dish soap to the water in the sink when she felt the smallest of twinges deep inside. She paused for a moment, waiting for it to pass, and was reaching for the first plate when the twinge returned, stronger this time, hotter, shooting into her back.

"Something's not right," she said to herself.

"What's that, hon?" asked her mother.

"Huh? Oh, nothing. I, uh . . . I have to go to the bathroom. Could you watch the water for me? Make sure the suds don't run over the edge."

"I been doing dishes since I was four, hon. I think it

might be okay to leave me unsupervised for a minute or two."

Lucy smiled at her, then left to do her business.

By the time she got to the bathroom, the twinge and heat had passed and she felt just fine—well, she needed to remove her bladder and slam it up against the wall a few times, but what else was new? She peed ten to fifteen times a day now, something her doctor and other pregnant women assured her was par for the course in the wondrous journey toward motherhood. If she could lay claim to no other epiphany resulting from this, she could firmly state that, in the past few months, she'd learned the truth about the so-called "radiance" of an expectant mother. It had nothing to do with her carrying the miracle of life in her womb; oh, no, that was a romantic myth best saved for the daytime soaps and cheap tearjerker novels. The truth was, if a pregnant woman appeared to "glow," if she took on a "luminous" quality, it was because she had just peed, or needed to pee and just discovered there was a bathroom nearby.

Lucy laughed a small laugh as she unbuckled her belt and unzipped her jeans and slid the works down past her calves as she glided down onto the toilet seat. This was another thing they never told you about— how a pregnant woman learns to turn the act of sitting down on the toilet into a beautifully choreographed ballet.

A breath, a sigh, a contended hum in the back of her throat, and the sweet waterfall sound of radiance filled the cramped bathroom.

For a few seconds, it was bliss.

Then an invisible hand rammed itself deep inside

her and dragged rusty steel hooks down the throbbing walls of her uterus.

For the rest of her life, she would remember the next sixty seconds in all of their terrible detail: first, the pain, wrenching and merciless; then the sound she made, somewhere between a shriek and a scream; next, the floor rushing up to meet her as the invisible hand wetly tore itself free and shoved her off the toilet seat; and then she was curled up on the floor, knees pressed against her stomach, feeling the blood seep from between her legs as she shuddered, then shook, her hands tightly clasped together and mashed against her vagina. She lay convulsing for what seemed hours before she heard the sound of the bathroom door being opened and then there was Mom, her warm, soapy hands cupping Lucy's face, tears streaking her cheeks, muttering "Oh, hon, my little girl" over and over as she gently helped her to sit up, and then embraced her, rocking her back and forth, stroking her sweat-soaked hair and whispering, "All right, it's all right now, shhh, there, there, it's over, it's passed, it's all right, I'm here, I'm right here, hon, you don't need to—"

"What the hell's all this racket in—?" Dad stood in the doorway, his eyes wide and furious, his jaw working as if words were still coming out of his mouth.

Mom turned toward him and said, "You just get on back to your paper. Leave us alone," then reached over and grabbed the edge of the door and began to close it in his face but Dad was having none of it; he bent his arm and slammed his elbow against the door, knocking it open again, then stormed into the bathroom, yelling, "You don't tell me what to do in my own house, woman! I'll not have . . ." And then the rest of it withered on his tongue and he fell silent.

Lucy pulled away from her mother, wiped the sweat and tears from her own face, leaving streaks of blood in their place, and saw that her father was staring into the toilet.

"Oh, my dear Lord," he said.

Lucy moved forward to look but then Mom was there in front of her, saying, "Don't, hon, you don't—"

Lucy pushed her out of the way and leaned over, her hands gripping the edge of the toilet bowl.

And there was her baby: small, like a bumblebee, like something you could balance on the tip of your thumb, Tom Thumb, that was its name, floating around in the center of the blood and urine and placenta and what remained of the amniotic sac, wriggling around as the force of its mother's beating heart against the porcelain created ripples in the water, little swirls, and as she stared Lucy could make out things, little things, microscopic Tom Thumb things like fin-flaps that would have been arms, knobs that might have been its hands, a bump that could have turned into a more flattering version of her own nose as Tom Thumb grew older, a dark pinprick of eye, all of it curving into a semihuman shape, *My child, my baby, swim to shore, swim like a good strong little boy, over here, I'm right over here*—

The lid slammed down on her fingers and she cried out, falling backward and yanking her hands free.

"I told you," said her father, his breath coming out in angry, wheezing bursts. "I told you God'd punish you for your shameful behavior."

"Stop that right now," said Mom.

"A common whore, that's what you was, and now look what you went and did! Poor little child never had a chance—*you* killed it, you know that, don't you? Killed it just as sure as if you'd gone to one of them murderin' sons of bitches that call themselves doctors and had it cut out of you."

Mom was getting to her feet now. "Get out of here. Do it now."

"I told you once, don't be"—he reached for the toilet handle—"ordering me around in my own house."

Mom's hand struck his wrist like a stone from a slingshot. "You can't flush it. She'll have to . . . to take it to the hospital so they can test it and see what went wrong."

Dad pulled back to strike her.

"Go ahead," said Mom, reaching over to snatch something off the shelf above the sink. "You go ahead and you hit me just as hard as you want." With a flick of her wrist the pearl-handled straight razor revealed its shiny contents. "But you try to flush this toilet again, I'll open you from stem to sternum, so help me God!"

Lucy reached up and took hold of her mother's free hand. She was shocked at how strong Mom's grip was, and how much her touch helped.

"P-please, D-Daddy," she said. "Please leave us alone."

One breath. For one breath she saw his face soften at hearing her call him "Daddy," then the Bastard came back, stronger than before.

"This's God's punishment on you, girl. I'll leave the two of you to do . . . what needs to be done. But you hear this: You ain't no daughter of mine anymore. I want you out of this house by tomorrow night."

"Then I'll go with her," said Mom.

"Suits me just fine."

"See how well it suits you at the end of the month when you won't have her paycheck coming in."

No words between them after that, only gleaming hatred from their eyes, only the ice pick in Lucy's throat.

Dad stormed out of the bathroom, then out of the house. A few seconds later the sound of his pickup truck roaring to life pierced the silence, followed by squealing tires.

"Write when you get work," said Mom. Then, "We gotta get you cleaned up and over to the hospital."

They managed to temporarily stanch the worst of the bleeding with a knot of Kotex pads; then Lucy's mother spent a minute mopping away the blood on the floor, all the time checking with her daughter to make sure the bleeding hadn't worsened.

"I'll go get . . . uh, a few things, hon. Why don't you come out and lay down on the couch?"

"No. I'll just . . . wait here."

"Do you think you ought to?"

"Yes."

"All right, then."

Mom quickly returned with a plastic ladle and a large, clear plastic freezer bag. "I poured some rubbing alcohol on the ladle so it'd be sterile and this bag's got one of them airtight seals, see? I figure something like this would be best." She opened the lid and knelt down.

"Mom?"

"What is it, hon?"

"I'd like to do it."

"Want me to stay here with you?"

"No, that's all right."

"You gonna be okay?" Her mother was on the verge of tears, so heartbroken was she over her daughter's pain and loss.

"I'll be fine," said Lucy, placing her hand against her mother's cheek. "Thank you."

Mom's eyes misted over. "You don't gotta thank me, hon. You're my little girl. I'd do anything for you. Don't you pay any mind to anything he said, all those names he called you. I'm not ashamed of you and never have been. You've never been a disappointment to me. I love you."

"I love you, too." She was stunned by the sudden, deep rush of affection she felt toward this woman who she'd secretly laughed at and pitied so many times. A rocking chair in the shadows at day's end with a glass of whiskey and some sappy Nat King Cole records being the measure of her happiness in the twilight of her life.

Lucy hugged her mother. "You were always there, weren't you?"

Mom shrugged. "Well, yeah. Why wouldn't I be?" She softly kissed Lucy's forehead, rose to her feet, then left, making sure to give one last smile before closing the door behind her.

Lucy knelt down, wincing against the pain and the bloodstone-knot of Kotex pads, took a deep breath, then did it quickly, making sure not to stare at the thing that would have been her child for too long. Everything went into the bag—fetus, placenta, blood, urine, amniotic sac—then with a quick *zzzzzzip* the bag was sealed.

She closed the toilet lid and sat on it, holding the bag near her chest.

Two minutes. She allowed herself to sit there and hold the bag and cry for two minutes, no more.

Mom filled Dad's metal lunch pail with ice and Lucy placed the bag inside, then secured the lock on the lid.

"I'm afraid you'll have to take a cab over to the hospital," said Mom, shoving a twenty-dollar bill in her daughter's hand. "We can't afford what they'd charge us for an ambulance—"

"It's okay, I think the bleeding's getting better now. . . . God, I'm getting kind of . . . of dizzy. . . ."

"I'd come with you, but I have to call Aunt Eunice and see if we can't stay with her for a few days, until your father calms down—and he will calm down. And probably be damned sorry once he does. You ain't gonna have to move out, I'll see to that."

"You sure he'll want us back?"

"You know it. For no other reason than he can't cook worth a damn. You wait. Six or seven days living on TV dinners does wonders for helping a man find humility. Can you make it by yourself? You're so pale."

Lucy felt as if she were folding in on herself; the pain was still screaming through her center, the nausea was still rising, and the shaking had only worsened. "I d-don't know. I think I c-could maybe use some help." Then came the dizziness.

The next few minutes were a feverish blur: Mom's voice, Mom's hands helping her to sit, to move, then the smell of exhaust fumes and a strange man's voice saying, "Is she gonna make it?" then a second pair of hands, hard and calloused and strong, helping her into the backseat, then motion, sick-making motion that caused her to leak all the more, so wet down there, so warm and wet; so why did she feel so cold?

. . . Voices and images, people in a drunken pain-dream swarming around her . . . bright lights, other voices, other hands, squeaking wheels and faster motion, her clothes taken away, sterile smells, pain still there, still leaking, her legs gently lifted, ankles into cold stirrups, a needle in her arm, a plastic mask placed over her mouth, numbness, my baby, oh Mom, empty, empty, *empty*. . . .

A previously undetcted defect in the fetus was the explanation the doctors gave to her. They were all very nice and showed the proper amount of sympathy and concern but, despite their words of comfort and their patient explaining of all the medical jargon and Mom's reassuring pats on her hand ("You can still try again, someday"), all she heard was *empty, empty, empty*. . . .

We don't need to dwell too long on what actually happened, do we? The doctors' explanation was—to coin a phrase—an old standby, an ace-in-the-hole, a backup used when the fact was they had no rational reason for what happened. Lucy was a young, strong, healthy woman with no physical or physiological abnormalities, no viruses, no environmental factors that could have contributed to the miscarriage—but of course you can't *tell* such a thing to a young woman who's just lost her first child, you can't just shrug your shoulders, shake your head, and say, "I have no idea what caused this"; so you make an informed guess, hypothesize and hope that will be enough.

What happened was: When Ronald James Williamson

laid his hands on Lucy, he felt a hurting beyond any he'd encountered before, one so black and hopeless and filled with physical suffering he almost cried out from the sheer agony of it, and knew that Lucy's unborn child was, at a very young age, going to suffer a death that would be slow and terrifying and too horrific for any human being to face. He couldn't allow that to happen, and so made his wish to stop the hurting.

But there was more to it than that, some new facet to his power that Ronnie didn't understand at the time. Something about this incident felt different from the others, and it would be several years before this new facet made itself clear to him; he would, in fact, awaken at four in the morning, soaked in sweat, alone in a motel room somewhere in Kentucky, knowing that he had only a small handful of hours to get back to Cedar Hill and find Lucy Holcomb (for that would be her name then).

Right now, though, we need to get back to Lucy.

She came back from the hospital dazed and tired, weak and enormously sad. She tried to remember if she had ever experienced such deep emotional pain before, then decided it didn't matter. The loss was great and complete in the way only death is. For the first few days she couldn't talk to anyone, but at the same time it hurt too much to be alone. She would just cry and cry without stopping; over this, she had no control. One of the clearest reminders that she was no longer pregnant was the speedy change her body went through. Within three days her breasts, once tender and swollen, were back to their normal size; her stomach, which had grown hard, was soft again. Her body was no longer preparing for the birth of a child. It was simple and blatant and cold. And then there was the bleeding. Her body would not let her forget. Mom and Aunt Eunice didn't know how to help, and she didn't know how to ask for it. They were much more comfortable talking about the physical and not the emotional side of the miscarriage. She needed to talk about both, but words seemed so pitifully inadequate to express her feelings. She understood the depth of the loss but realized she had never experienced the depth of the joy that should have been hers all along.

One night she imagined the baby was still inside her, and slept easier for the imagining.

Mom had been right. It took exactly seven days for Dad to crumple. When he showed up on Eunice's doorstep there were no apologies from him—the phrase "I'm sorry" had never been part of his vocabulary. He looked at Mom, then Lucy, and said, "You two coming home, or what?"

He insisted on helping Lucy to the car. "You're still pretty weak. I'll not have people saying you made yourself worse on account I wouldn't help out."

Things at home got better after that.

Not a lot. Just a little.

Sometimes Dad still whispered *whore* under his breath.

But things were a little better.

At least she was back home.

Although the child she'd lost was a boy, Lucy had always assumed she was carrying a girl. At no point during the three brief months (well, the ten brief weeks) she'd had a new life growing inside her did she ever want to know the child's sex; she wanted it to be a surprise.

It had been a boy, but she kept telling herself it was a girl.

So, in an effort to help "heal" herself (a word used time and time again in the self-help books that cluttered her bookshelves) she took the advice of one overhyped PhD and wrote a new letter to her unborn child:

My Dearest Daughter, Sarah:

Tonight, on the night of your birth, I wanted to write you a letter for your future—to tell you of my hopes and plans for you. They probably won't work out as I hope they will (a mother's plans rarely do, but that's the way of things), but I can't help trying to secure your future for you.

I'm glad you're a girl. I think I would have had trouble relating to a son. But I feel I can help you through your life.

I'm told that you'll ask what I was like. Well, most people who knew me will tell you that your mother didn't usually say much but she saw and listened to a lot. I was a quiet girl and hope that you'll learn the value of silence as you grow. Don't feel that you have to fill the gaps with meaningless words and pointless conversation; say only what is in your heart, and say it as well as you know how to. It may take a while but people will listen to what you have to say, so never be afraid to share your feelings and ideas with friends or people you hope will come to matter in your life.

I want all I have seen and learned and heard to be of help to you in the years ahead that will be more difficult, exciting, infuriating, and wonderful than you can possibly imagine. I hope you will believe in the equality of men and women, and will learn to look for the person inside, to be as sex-blind or color-blind or religion-blind as any person can be. What I mean is, I want you to be without hate. I look at you—so tiny, so helpless, so new—and wonder how so lovely a baby could ever learn to hate. But if so many others can learn, then so can you.

Your mother is an idealist, a dreamer. I hope for a perfect world. I see the mistakes I have made (you are NOT one of them) and hope that you will be wiser.

I love you very much, my dearest Sarah, and hope the enclosed picture of me will be enough for you to remember me by. I don't have much more time to write or room on these pages, so I have to choose only one thing to tell you about. I think I have chosen the most important.

The love between a man and a woman.

Someday you will meet a boy and you will have certain feelings for him, feelings that you've never had toward anyone else, and in parts of your body that have never made you aware of them before. You will be young and vibrant and curious about the angles and curves of the male body you have not seen before. His hand in yours will be like music to your soul. Just seeing him walk into a room will cause your heart to beat faster. And when he kisses you, you will feel more alive than you ever have before. The two of you will lay down together, and you will make love, and it will be wonderful. Don't be afraid to be playful when you do this; but don't be frightened of baring more than your body to him, either.

Don't ever let anyone tell you that this kind of love-making is dirty. Sex is not dirty in itself, but it can be *made dirty by people who don't value it properly. Treasure your sex, and his, and what they become when the two of them meet. Be truthful, but always remember to keep a private place inside of you just for yourself. Not a "secret" place—that means you are being deceitful—but a private place, a place to know the feeling of yourself, and what it means to be alone, and a woman, walking on two legs instead of four. If he loves you, he'll understand, because he knows there'll be a time when one of you will be gone, and what will happen to the one left behind if all of your I's have always been we's? Touch each other gently, and always speak truthfully, and remember to treasure every moment that you are together, even the ones that aren't so great (and there'll be plenty of those), so when you're old and the beauty of youth has faded, your love will burn warmly within you, like a candle on a winter's night, and your memories will hang around your neck like pearls instead of chains.*

The life ahead of you will not always be easy, but there will be many joys if your heart is true. I will always regret that we never knew each other, never sat down together for a cup of coffee, never went out and pointed at boys and men we thought were cute, and were never there to hold each other when tears and bad times came along, but I will love you forever, my daughter, my dearest Sarah, and I shall pray that these few scribbled words will help you on your way through life, with hope, smiles, comfort, encouragement, and much, much affection and love.

Be strong, my daughter. Be well, and happy.
With All My Blessings and Hopes,
Your Mother,
Lucy

* * *

A few nights later, having gotten up in the middle of the night to get herself something cool to drink, Lucy's mother, Henrietta, found her daughter sitting at the kitchen table, in the dark, quietly weeping.

"Oh, *hon*," said Henrietta, pulling out a chair beside her daughter and sitting down. "What's wrong? Wait—I know, I know, that's a dumb question, we both know what's wrong. I'm always doing that, aren't I? Asking a question I already know the answer to. It gets worse the older I get. I'm sorry, hon. I guess what I meant to ask is . . . is there anything I can do to help?" She reached over and took hold of Lucy's hand.

Lucy looked at her mother, smiled in the darkness, and then shook her head. "No . . . but thanks, Mom. I was just thinking about . . . oh, never mind."

"C'mon," said Henrietta. "You were just sitting down here thinking about what?"

"About the souls of unborn children."

"Well, now . . . that's maybe not such a bad thing to be thinking about, is it?"

Lucy shrugged. "Depends on the direction your thoughts go."

"So which direction are yours going in?"

"I . . . God, Mom . . . I really . . . I mean I don't want to . . ."

Henrietta's voice became softer, even more caring than it usually was when she talked to her daughter. "*Please* tell me about it?"

Lucy considered this for a few moments. Her mother was a very religious person; not fanatically so—her advice to "Read your Bible and be Christian . . ." was the closest she'd ever come to lecturing

Lucy about religious beliefs—but still, she said her prayers every night, went to mass every Sunday and on all Holy Days (especially at Easter and at midnight on Christmas Eve). While Lucy had always secretly considered herself an agnostic, she'd never told her mother because she did not want to hurt Henrietta's feelings; but in this case, right here, right now, with the emptiness and sadness still very much a part of her, diminishing her, gnawing at her, threatening never to go away or allow her a few minutes' peace, she felt not the least bit guilty about swallowing her concern for others' feelings and concentrating solely on her own.

"I've been sitting here for about an hour," she said to her mother, "and I think I finally figured something out. I think the Church has it wrong; stillborn or miscarried babies, embryos . . . they don't go to Limbo—they become angels. That's why angels look so terrifying—and they have to look terrifying, or else the angel that appeared to the shepherds on the night of Christ's birth would not have said 'Be not afraid' right away, you know?

"If the miscarried, the malformed, or . . . or the incomplete babies, the unformed ones, the ones that didn't grow into what they were supposed to be . . . if they go to heaven and keep the physical form they were in when they died, they'd be creatures no one would be able to look at if they encountered them on a city bus. Someone who doesn't live past birth is spiritually unblemished because they've never been hurt or hurt somebody else. They've never sinned, or been sinned against; they've never been selfish or unreasonable; they've never disappointed anyone, or been disappointed. They are pure, untainted, theoretical possibility—the souls who could become president, or an astronaut, or a genius, even if they do have messed-up genes or major chromosomal abnormalities.

"But because they've never lived as a human being, never laughed or cried or been surprised, never been beaten down by life, they are fundamentally inhuman . . . or maybe *un*human would be a better way to put it . . . I don't know . . . but because they're like they are, I don't see how it's possible for them to have genuine sympathy for the everyday human condition. My sitting here crying right now, you holding my hand, how much we love each other, how much we miss a child that was never born . . . none of this makes a damn bit of difference to the soul of my daughter. She's an angel now, and the angels, they have more important things to concern themselves with than an unmarried girl with the blues."

Henrietta stared at her for several seconds, then squeezed her daughter's hand. "I can't say I agree with everything you say, hon—I mean, I think every heavenly soul cares about the people they left behind, even them ones they didn't live long enough to meet—but I think you're right about the angel part. Don't that make you feel even a little bit better?"

"Not really, no." Then she saw the hurt in her mother's eyes and felt guilty; here the woman was, probably so tired she could barely stand, and she was trying to make her daughter feel better, and all her daughter could do was throw it back in her face. No wonder the woman hardly smiled anymore.

Lucy forced a smile onto her face. "I didn't mean that, Mom. This is helping a lot. I really appreciate you listening to me."

"You're my flesh and blood, hon, *of course* I'm gonna listen to you. I love you more than anything."

The tears she'd been holding back since her mother had come into the kitchen finally began flowing from Lucy's eyes. "I love you too, Mom. I really do." She leaned forward into Henrietta's embrace.

"You're going find yourself a good man someday soon," said Henrietta, "and you're going to be real happy, and you're going make me a grandmother—and I'll have you know that last one's an order, because I plan on being a *breathtaking* grandmother who'll spoil them kids rotten. And just so you know, I expect you to give me at least two. A boy and a girl. You want to give me more than that, well . . . that'd be all right, too. The more the merrier."

"Say that when it comes time to change the diapers."

Henrietta laughed. "I'm a world-class diaper-changer, hon. When you was a baby, I could change your diaper in less than a minute—and that was using cloth diapers and safety pins. These disposable diapers they been comin' out with, them ones with the tape—hell, twenty seconds, tops. And that's *including* having to wipe off the baby and use baby powder."

Lucy laughed. "Think a lot of yourself, don't you?"

Henrietta kissed her daughter's cheek. "Just wait 'til you see me in action. You'll eat your words."

"Eat *what* words? I never said I doubted you."

"Oh, I know. But I can't wait to see the expression on your face when you see how fast I am. Like ridin' a bike—you never forget."

"Will you teach me how to do it?"

"If you're nice to me . . . maybe."

Now both women laughed, and it was a fine sound, a happy sound, a sound of healing.

Lucy did feel better eventually, and she did find a better man than Larry Parre (who was shot to death before his twenty-ninth birthday during a botched liquor-store robbery attempt, unemployed and trying to get enough cash together to pay for an abortion for his girlfriend). She and her new husband, Eric Holcomb, gave Henrietta a beautiful granddaughter who she named Sarah, after all, and who Henrietta, true to her word, spoiled rotten every chance she got.

And, yes, she did show Lucy her diaper-changing method, which left Lucy awestruck.

At the moment of Sarah's birth, the best six years of Lucy's life had begun.

CHAPTER THREE

During the ensuing years, things weren't all that bad for Ronnie, either. Though he had to take the hurting away from more children than he would have liked, he also took it away from several animals, as well, and each time found that he was gifted with the memories of each and every animal and child, as well as the visions of what *would* have happened to them had he not come along to save them.

The first and most painful of the children had been the eleven-month-old baby outside the Kresge's department store two weeks before Christmas when Ronnie was ten. The infant's mother had come outside, weighted down with packages, and realized that she'd left her purse on the checkout counter. Setting down the boxes and bags, she went back inside and left the baby alone in its stroller. Ronnie (who'd been downtown doing his own Christmas shopping with the twenty-six dollars he'd saved from his allowance) walked over to the stroller and looked down at the baby, then made the puffy face that always caused babies to laugh. But this one didn't; it just looked at him, expressionless. It didn't even so much as smile and make the *goo-goo* noise. This was not right. The puffy face always worked. *Always.*

Ronnie looked around to make sure no one was watching him, then bent down, reached inside the stroller, and took hold of one of the baby's hands.

And knew.

Knew so very clearly.

God, how he knew.

He knew that this baby's name was Suzanne, and that she was loved—she was *so* loved; he knew that Suzanne's mother had never before gone off and left her alone like this in public, and that she was already cursing herself for having done so, but she had nearly two hundred dollars in her purse and needed to get it back immediately; he knew that both of Suzanne's parents worried because she was such a quiet baby, and that her pediatrician was a secret alcoholic who would one day come close to killing one of his patients because he would prescribe the wrong antibiotics; but mostly what Ronnie knew was this: that Suzanne was such a quiet, unsmiling baby because there was a tumor pressing on her stomach, a tumor that had not yet been diagnosed, and he knew that by the time it would be diagnosed, it would be too late; that even if Suzanne's mother were to come out of Kresge's right this second and take her baby directly to the hospital, it would do no good. The tumor had already caused other, smaller tumors to grow all over Suzanne's insides, so even if the doctors were to cut out the tumor on her stomach and give her months of cobalt treatments, more would come along to take its place and Suzanne, the quiet, delicate, unsmiling baby, would not live to see her third birthday. And she would be scared and in great pain right up to the moment of her death—with neither Mommy nor Daddy there to hold her because both had been awake at her hospital bedside for nearly three straight days, and both had fallen asleep in their chairs, and Suzanne wouldn't have the strength to cry out and wake them.

She would die alone, without another's loving touch on her skin, and she would be in agony, and she would be so very, very afraid.

Ronnie's eyes filled with tears and he began crying like a little baby himself, because he knew that he was the only person who could take Suzanne's hurting away. He hadn't even planned on going by Kresge's today—he was planning on going to Carol's department store instead—but something had turned him in this direction, and he knew that it had been because Suzanne would be here.

He had to do it.

And he had to do it fast, before anyone noticed him, and before Suzanne's mother came back outside.

He leaned farther into the stroller and kissed Suzanne; first on each cheek, then on her mouth. When he began to pull away, Suzanne reached up and gripped one of his fingers—his left index finger—and gave it a squeeze as a smile came to her face and her eyes began to sparkle. It was like she knew, as well, and understood what he was going to do, and wanted to thank him for it.

"I love you," said Ronnie. "And I'm so *sorry*. . . ."

Suzanne giggled and squeezed his index finger again, then closed her eyes and let go.

He cupped her head between his hands, spluttered out another burst of grief, and did what had to be done.

Like with the bird, it was quick and painless. Suzanne had already known enough pain. She was with Jesus and the angels in heaven now. She was happy, giggling, flying around with her new wings.

I love you, she whispered to Ronnie. *You don't have to be sorry. Thank you.*

He was almost to the end of the block, lost among the throngs of shoppers, when Suzanne's mother released a scream so loud, so shrill, so inhuman and raw in its shock and terror and grief and pain that it seemed like the entire city came to a stop because such a terrible, overpowering sound demanded that everything stop, and listen, and mark the moment, and always remember.

In the years to come, it would always be Suzanne to whom Ronnie would turn after taking the hurting away from another child; it would always be Suzanne who would be there smiling at him, whispering how much she loved him, how it was okay; it would always be this quiet, fragile baby (who now couldn't *stop* smiling) who would forgive him, each and every time.

By the time Lucy Thompson had met her future husband and married him and given birth to her daughter, Ronnie was sixteen and living in a group home near the east end of Cedar Hill. By then he had taken the hurting away from seven children, all of them in pain, or living in fear—beaten by their parents, abused by relatives, raped by friends of the family . . . the horrors were numerous, and never-ceasing. With all of them, he knew of no way out, and that each of them had been ruined forever. With each child Ronnie wept, and asked for both the child's and Suzanne's forgiveness; and, always, he received it.

After Suzanne, it occurred to him that there might be some people left behind who genuinely loved and cared about these children (although not enough to do anything to help them, assuming they even knew what was going on), so he began leaving notes with the bodies: *I'm sorry.*

And he signed every note: *With Love, Uncle Ronnie.*

"D'ya think it's okay to do that?" he asked Suzanne. *Does it make it easier for you?*

"Yeah, I think it does. I think . . . I think they need to know that I wasn't being mean or nothing like that, ya know?"

I do, and I love you all the more for it. All of us love you, Ronnie. You made our hurting stop.

"I wish I'd left a note for your mommy."

Shhh, Ronnie; you don't need to worry about that. I talk to her every night in her dreams. She knows I'm fine now. She's not sad anymore, and neither am I. None of us are. You have to remember that, okay?

It helped—not much, but some. Despite the forgiveness and his talks with Suzanne and the others, his soul did not commune with the angels, did not fly on wings of song, did not feel cleansed or heroic or purified, but rather sat—as did he most of the time—in a sad, still, lightless, isolated silence that could not be penetrated by any kindness or gesture of tenderness.

Sometimes there were rare moments when the words of Suzanne and the others made him feel better, less evil, less like some kind of monster you saw in the movies on Chiller Theater on Friday nights.

But then he'd touch another child and feel their hurting and see what was going to happen to them and know there was no way to change it or make it better and he'd do what had to be done and then get sad and sick all over again.

Which is why, when his parents put him in the group home, he decided that he was never going to touch another human being again for as long as he lived.

No one ever suspected that he was Uncle Ronnie, the horrific child-murderer responsible for the deaths of seven children in as many years (they never knew that he'd killed Suzanne, so she was not included in the thick files that contained information on all his "victims"). The assumption on the parts of the police and FBI had been that they were dealing with an adult who had been severely abused as a child. It never occurred to any of them to look for a teenager.

Many of the people living in the home with Ronnie thought he was unfriendly because he never touched anyone, or wanted to be touched by any of them; but he was always willing to talk to them, or listen to them, or quietly sit by as they cried because once again their parents had failed to come to see them on visiting day. (Ronnie always thought of a way to make these others laugh and feel better when this happened to them—and it happened to a *lot* of them, the group home being the place where ree-tards and speds were tucked safely away where they couldn't annoy, inconvenience, or embarrass their families.)

And then came the night of the Valentine's Day dance.

Ronnie had never been so terrified in his life. He volunteered to serve punch or help with the records that were going to be played—*anything* that meant he wouldn't have to touch someone—but the social worker who'd been assigned Ronnie's case (a lovely, short, compassionate woman named Ruth) wouldn't hear of it.

"Ronnie," she said to him, "the whole point of this dance is for all of you to work on your social skills. Understand?"

"But I do good in the workshop," he replied. Which was the truth. Ronnie—like everyone else who lived in the group home—was bussed five days a week to a sheltered workshop run by the Central Ohio Department for the Developmentally Disabled—better known as "Sped Central" by those who thought assigning it a mocking moniker to be clever.

Ronnie worked in Cell #5, one of the more advanced cells of the workshop—meaning that he was permitted to use tools such as hammers, nails, saws, and screwdrivers. Ronnie's cell was always assigned the more complicated jobs, such as a big one they'd had a few months back assembling wooden shipping crates for a local manufacturer of small farming equipment. Because the work done at the sheltered workshop was considered by the state of Ohio as "training," each person was paid a "training rate"—not by the hour but by the completed piece; in the case of the shipping crates (one of the best-paying jobs the cell had all year), twenty cents apiece.

The habilitation supervisor in charge of Ronnie's cell was a former Marine sergeant named Pierce, who ran a very tight ship and was damned proud that his cell consistently had the highest output-without-returns ratio of any in the workshop. If you worked Pierce's cell, you worked straight through, nonstop, no chatting, made sure you were back before either of your ten-minute breaks were done, and took no longer than twenty-five minutes to eat your lunch. Ronnie loved it, because it gave him something else to think about besides the hurting.

But Pierce wasn't going to be around to help Ronnie—oh, Pierce would be at the dance, all right, but odds were he'd *make* Ronnie dance with a girl if he tried to hide behind a punch bowl or the record player.

And so Ronnie dipped into his savings and took out enough money to buy himself a new tie and pair of shoes ($24.97 altogether) and spent the first thirteen days that February in a constant state of near-panic.

He also started to get angry—not that he yelled at anyone, or treated others with discourtesy, or was snappish, nothing like that, no; he began to get angry at the *unfairness* he saw all around him.

It struck him as unfair that everyone in his cell worked nine hours a day, five days a week, always on their feet (some of them skipping both their ten-minute breaks *and* lunch because they wanted to make more money), and for all that work, all that effort, for all their sore feet and bloodshot eyes and tired backs, they would be handed a pay envelope every two weeks containing maybe, *maybe* twenty-five dollars if they'd really gotten it "the hell in gear" as Pierce was fond of saying (twelve dollars or a little less was the usual amount, a whopping twenty-four dollars for a month's labor); it struck him as unfair that everyone who lived in the group home hardly ever had any visitors, and that the social workers who came to take them out to the movies or for pizza twice a month always seemed distracted, as if there were something else they'd much rather be doing; it seemed unfair to him that *anybody* felt lonely or stupid or unloved or unwanted; and it really, *really* struck him as unfair that each and every child from whom he'd taken away the hurting had *somebody* in their lives who *could have* done something to help, to make it better, but for whatever reason didn't.

But what made him the angriest, what tore him up whenever he thought about it for too long, what gave him bad dreams and stomach cramps and dark circles under his eyes, what haunted him most of all was the knowledge that the people who had inflicted this hurting, who'd brought so much pain and misery into the world, who'd treated the children worse than they would have treated a stray dog, these people went unpunished and probably smiled a lot like everything was just fine and went to sleep at night to find nice dreams waiting for them.

And so Ronnie began to think of ways he could punish them; all of them.

And the worse the punishments he imagined for them, the bloodier, the more painful, the wider his smile became.

"Someday," he whispered to Suzanne one night, "I'm gonna make all of 'em real sorry for what they did. I don't know *how,* exactly, but I'm gonna do it."

My Ronnie doesn't talk that way. He doesn't think those things.

"But it ain't *fair!*"

That's not for you to decide, Ronnie. Can't you just be happy that you've saved us? We're happy here.

"I wanna be happy, too," he said, starting to cry and hating himself for it. "I don't wanna have any more bad dreams or remember everything that I've done to all of you or . . . or watch how the other kids here get all sad when nobody comes on visiting day."

Stop worrying about everyone else for one night, okay? You look very handsome in your new tie and shoes. Every girl there will want to dance with you.

Ronnie didn't say anything to that.

Every girl there will want to dance with you.

That was precisely what he was afraid of.

The Valentine's Day dance was a tradition at the Central Ohio Department for the Developmentally Disabled. Each year "clients" (that's what they were called; not "patients" or "students" or "subjects") from every group home, sheltered workshop, and special education school in the county were invited ("required" would have been the more appropriate word, but the Special Education Board felt it held too many negative connotations, so "invited" it was) to attend a "gala" celebration in the main ballroom of the Sheraton Hotel in downtown Cedar Hill. For an entire week before the dance, classes from various schools and cells from assorted workshops gathered together to decorate the space, making it look as romantic as possible. This year's theme was "Evergreen," after the Barbra Streisand song from the movie *A Star Is Born*. (Everyone else was putting on dances celebrating the bicentennial, and a person can only take so much red, white, and blue before they start getting a headache—or at least Ronnie could only take so much, so even though he was terrified of the dance, he was at least glad they'd chosen other colors.) The drama department from Cedar Hill Senior High School donated a box of colored gels and also loaned out a few of their spotlights so the ballroom would look extra classy.

Coupled with the opulent chandelier hanging from the center of the ceiling, the ballroom looked like something out of a fantasy movie, and made all the attendees, even Ronnie, feel like real movie stars, maybe Al Pacino or Robert Redford or that guy who played Rocky, and all the girls felt like Jane Fonda or Sissy Spacek.

It was actually kind of cool.

Ronnie did his best to monopolize the punch service, until one of the lady supervisors pulled him out from behind the table and made him dance with her. Ronnie was shocked to find that he felt *nothing* while doing this—at least, nothing bad. The supervisor was in a good mood and thinking only about happy things.

She then asked Ronnie if he'd go over and ask Vicki Flowers to dance with him. Vicki came from a different workshop and group home but Ronnie had seen her at a couple of events this past year, and she seemed nice even if she was a bit on the short and plump side.

Vicki had Down's Syndrome and didn't talk much, but she was always very sweet to people, and it made Ronnie feel good to see the way she smiled when he asked her to dance, like she'd been waiting all night for someone to invite her to come and join in on the fun. What made it even better was that, when he touched her, he saw her whole life as it had been, as it was, and as it would be . . . and it was *great*. Her parents (both in their early sixties, Vicki being a late-in-life baby) loved her more than anything and always hugged her and took her out to movies and for pizza and always made sure she had friends to play with and kept her clothes clean and made sure she had enough to eat, and it almost made Ronnie happy, seeing what a wonderful life Vicki had and was going to continue to have.

He was so relieved that, for the first time in years, he let his guard down and just decided to have a good time.

He danced with Vicki for most of the rest of the night, ignoring the little snickers and whispers of "Vicki and Ronnie, sittin' in a tree . . ." because this was the best he'd felt in . . . well, *ever.*

So he danced with her, and didn't care what the others thought.

With about forty-five minutes to go before the dance would be over, Ronnie knew (without her having to say so) that Vicki needed to go to the bathroom, so he took her by the arm and walked her over to the doors and stood waiting while she went in. As he was standing there, another supervisor came over and asked him if he'd ask Arlene Sanders to dance— it seemed that almost nobody had asked her to dance all night, and she'd spent most of her money on a new dress.

Arlene worked in Cell #3 at Ronnie's workshop, was kind of plain, and very, very shy—almost afraid of everyone. Ronnie was feeling pretty good at this point, so he walked over and offered his hand to Arlene (who was sitting in a folding chair along the wall, nobody sitting anywhere near her) and asked, "Would you dance with me?"

Arlene's face didn't exactly light up, but she looked happy enough. She didn't take Ronnie's hand right away, but rather stood up and followed him out onto the dance floor as the DJ began playing "Evergreen" for the third or fourth time that night (Ronnie had thought about maybe sneaking over there and breaking the darn record when the DJ was on a break, but then figured most of the girls here seemed to really like the song so it was probably a bad idea).

Ronnie turned to face Arlene, one arm at ten o'clock, the other at three (the way a gentleman danced with a lady) and Arlene—not meeting his gaze—stepped up to him and they began to dance. . . .

And no sooner had they made physical contact than Ronnie felt all the rage and sickness and sadness and hurting slam into his gut like a sledgehammer, and he almost fell over but took a deep breath and pretended he'd just lost his balance, even tried making a joke out of it so that Arlene might smile, and she almost did, almost, but it took all of Ronnie's self-control to keep a smile on his face and hold his body steady because there were these waves of fear coming from Arlene, fear and shame and misery and depression and loneliness and hurting—*God*, so much hurting . . .

And all because of Mr. Pierce, Ronnie's supervisor in Cell #5.

Mr. Pierce did things to Arlene that he wanted to do with his wife, but his wife thought they were sick and perverted, so he found himself a ree-tard, a sped who never talked much anyway and who had few friends and he did these things to her. He put himself inside her, in her mouth, between her legs, "doggy-style," but there was more: objects, ropes, belts, marks he left on her that she had to cover up (Ronnie always wondered why she wore long-sleeved shirts, even in summer) and other things that involved peeing and pooping and for a moment Ronnie couldn't take it anymore. He let go of Arlene's hands and stepped back, trying to force the hurting away from him, and for a moment, just a moment, Arlene's eyes looked directly into his and he knew that she knew that he knew, and it was real confusing because this had never happened before, but he didn't look away from her—nothing could have made him look away from her—because this was the first time in over a year (since Mr. Pierce had started "visiting" her, or taking her along during "special errands" during regular workshop hours) that she'd felt any real connection with another person, and Ronnie wasn't going to deny her, so he pulled in a deep breath and stepped forward and took hold of her again, more firmly this time, because he wanted to share as much of her hurting as she was willing to show him, and Arlene held nothing back, she couldn't, everything flooded out of her and into Ronnie and she started crying and lay her head on his shoulder and he held even tighter to her, no one was going to pull them apart, not yet, and after she'd shown him every moment of her hurting, everything that had been done to her, everything that she'd tried to hide from the world, Ronnie let himself go the rest of the way and see what her life was going to be like if he didn't take the Hurting away. . . .

And something new occurred to him, something that might have been there all along (or maybe not, it was kind of hard to tell): except for what Mr. Pierce had done, was doing, and would *continue* to do to her, Arlene had a good life, with parents and brothers and sisters who loved her, and friends who came over a lot, and nobody else had hurt or *would* hurt her; if it weren't for Mr. Pierce, she'd be just as happy as Vicki Flowers.

Ronnie staggered a little bit with the realization that he wouldn't have to kill Arlene; he could take the hurting away by killing Mr. Pierce.

He could save her.

He wanted to save her.

He *would* save her.

And looking into her eyes, he also realized that she'd shared his every thought since the moment they'd touched; his guard had been down, he'd made a connection with her that he'd never made before (or maybe he had and just didn't know it . . . it was still confusing), and Arlene wiped her eyes and then actually *smiled* at him.

"You can't never tell anybody," he whispered in her ear.

"I promise, R.J. Cross my heart and hope to die, I promise."

R.J.

She'd called him R.J., just like he'd always wished someone would.

That was all he needed. He leaned down and kissed her on the forehead. Then, once the song was over (it wasn't such a bad song, after all, he thought) he escorted her back to her chair just like a gentleman was supposed to, and she was smiling and laughing, and because she was smiling and laughing another boy came over and asked her to dance, and she said yes, and seeing her out there with another boy, laughing and spinning to the music, Ronnie felt something in his heart that he hadn't felt in years, if ever.

Hope.

Vicki came out of the restroom and he took her hand and they danced for two more songs, then the DJ announced a five-minute break and then he'd be back for the last three dances of the night, all of them ladies' choices.

Vicki went over to sit next to Arlene while Ronnie made his way over to the punch bowl. He wasn't thirsty but he needed to be someplace where he could see the whole room. Mr. Pierce was here someplace—had, in fact driven the van that Ronnie and several other boys had ridden in from the group home—and Ronnie was going to find him.

It took less than thirty seconds. Ronnie spotted Mr. Pierce going out one of the side doors that emptied into the parking lot. He was probably going out for a smoke. Even though people were allowed to smoke inside, the supervisors had made it clear that no one was to smoke in the ballroom because the smell would get into everyone's clothes and some of the clients had spent most, if not all, of their money on their dance clothes. So it was agreed that anyone who wanted to have a smoke had to go either to the hotel bar or outside.

Ronnie scanned the ballroom to make sure no one was watching him.

He put down his punch cup and began to walk in the same direction as Mr. Pierce, then suddenly turned and headed toward the bathrooms.

Suzanne had told him to do this.

I don't want you to do this, Ronnie, but if you're going to anyway, then I don't want you to get caught. Go to the bathroom and climb out one of the windows. That way, everyone will think you were using the bathroom.

He made a point of saying hello to a couple of the workshop supervisors on the way, going so far as tell one of them that he'd "had way too much punch" before going through the doors that led to the bath-rooms.

Suzanne had been right; two of the toilet stalls had windows high up on the walls inside, and it was easy for Ronnie to open one of them and climb through. It was pretty cold outside, so he hoped that no one else came in and found the opened window while he was gone. He lowered it just enough so that he could get his fingers underneath and open it from outside, but it was still pretty drafty.

Then he decided that he didn't care.

He quickly walked around the side of the building leading to the parking lot, and saw Mr. Pierce standing next to the van, smoking.

The sidewalk and parts of the parking lot were pretty icy (winter always came late to Cedar Hill), so Ronnie was having a hard time getting over to the su-pervisor, what with his new shoes and their smooth soles . . . and then he realized that he could use this.

He made himself fall down; not *too* hard, but enough that, from where Mr. Pierce was standing, it would look like it hurt.

"Ronnie?" called Mr. Pierce from beside the van. "Are you all right?"

"I'm sorry, Mr. Pierce," Ronnie called back, making his voice sound as weak as possible. "I think I busted something. I'm sorry."

Pierce sighed loudly, took a final drag from his cig-arette, and carefully began making his way over to where Ronnie lay on the ground. "Jesus Christ, Ronnie—what the hell were you thinking, coming out here, anyway? It's cold and—"

He was bending down to help Ronnie get to his

feet when Ronnie's right hand shot up and clamped around Pierce's throat. Ronnie was very strong, had perhaps the strongest grip of any client in Cell #5. Even using both of his hands, Mr. Pierce couldn't loosen Ronnie's grip.

Ronnie rose to his feet while simultaneously pulling Mr. Pierce down toward the curb, face-first. When the supervisor was flat on the ice, his mouth pressed firmly against the cement curb, Ronnie stood up and pressed his foot against the back of Pierce's head.

"You don't get to hurt Arlene anymore," he said.

And pressed down with all his strength.

Pierce made a sound somewhere between a groan and a scream that was muffled by the ice and the pressure of Ronnie's foot, and then his teeth began to shatter and fly backward down his throat, but Ronnie didn't stop there, he pulled back his foot and this time *stomped* as hard as he could right on the crown of Pierce's skull, directing the force toward the supervisor's jaw, and Pierce spewed blood from his mouth and face and ears, and Ronnie knew the third one would be the last, and he smiled as he came down even harder than before and pulped the back of Pierce's skull while at the same time separating the man's jaw from the rest of his head.

God, was there a lot of blood. And several bits of shattered teeth. And something that looked like a chunk of the man's tongue.

Ronnie looked around and saw no one else in the parking lot, and then knelt down and took Mr. Pierce's wallet and the cash in his pockets, as well as the keys to the van. He ran back to the opened window—making sure to step in a puddle to get any blood off his shoe—and climbed back inside, making sure to close the window behind him.

He walked over to one of the urinals and flushed it just as the door opened and another male supervisor came in, and the urinal (this made Ronnie so happy) overflowed onto his shoes.

"Oh, Ronnie," said the supervisor, Mr. Ireland, "step back before you ruin your new shoes, why don't you? Here, let's get some paper towels and see if we can't save them, okay?"

Ronnie smiled. "Thanks, Mr. Ireland. I sure don't want nothing to happen to these."

"Don't want *anything* to happen to them," said Ireland, correcting Ronnie's almost always questionable grammar. "Here, let's wet down a couple of paper towels and see what that does."

The last twenty-five minutes of the dance were among the happiest of Ronnie's life. For the last dance, both Vicki and Arlene picked him, and they made a circle and held hands and spun around and around and around to "Gonna Fly Now," all of them laughing as they got dizzier and dizzier, the multicolored lights soaring around them like something out of a dream.

When it was over, both Arlene and Vicki kissed him good night, one taking each cheek. His face turned so red it looked like an apple.

Mr. Pierce's murder was a shock to everyone and big news for several weeks. The police came and questioned everyone who'd been at the dance, but no one had seen anything. The *Cedar Hill Ally* ran a long obituary with photos mourning the loss of this "compassionate community member who served his country, as well as the less fortunate."

Everyone from all the workshops and group homes attended the funeral. Ronnie and Arlene kept looking at one another and smiling—but not *too* widely, so no one would know or suspect.

No arrest was ever made in the robbery and brutal murder of James Leonard Pierce.

What was never made known about Pierce—not even by his wife, who knew some things for a fact and suspected several more—was that he liked to drive to Columbus every few weekends and frequent brothels, both high-class and low-life (his sexual tastes were, to put it mildly, extremely varied). He had, in fact, been planning such a weekend the night of the Valentine's Day dance (Arlene was beginning to bore him) and so had nearly two thousand dollars in cash on him at the time of his death.

Ronnie was very careful to hide that money, because he knew he was going to need it.

There was no way he could stay in Cedar Hill much longer. Not after this.

Ronnie's mother died unexpectedly a week after Pierce's funeral. She had a heart condition that she never told Ronnie or his father about; her death, if it can be said of any death, was as peaceful and painless as it could have been, coming in the middle of the night, in her sleep, deep in the "wee hours" (as she liked calling them). She simply kissed her husband and her son good night (this was a weekend when Ronnie was staying at his parents' home), went upstairs, fell asleep, and stayed that way.

Her funeral was well-attended, and Ronnie couldn't stop crying; he never realized that his mother had so many friends.

He didn't even bother going back to the house afterward. He walked downtown, bought a bus ticket to Indianapolis and, once there, quickly vanished into the city.

It took his brothers, sisters, and father several hours to notice that he was missing.

Though he never did—as the doctor predicted—grow beyond the age of eleven years old emotionally, he was nonetheless a smart and exceptionally resourceful eleven-year-old. Armed with the two thousand dollars he'd taken from Mr. Pierce, he found it easy to find inexpensive rooming where no one asked any questions once they saw the money up-front. He ate three meals a day, no snacks, and took great care to make sure he got full use out of the various clothes and toiletry supplies he had to purchase.

Once the two thousand began to run low, he took to hanging out in front of temporary employment agencies where every morning around four, several trucks would pull up, a man would open the passenger door and stand on the running board, his eyes scanning the dozens of men who stood patiently enduring this often degrading inspection; then the man would begin pointing to certain individuals—"I'll take you . . . and you . . . and you over there. . . ."— until he had his quota of workers (usually a dozen), and Ronnie, who by now was big for his age and quite strong-looking, would always be picked. He'd then climb into the back of the flatbed truck with his other coworkers for the day and they'd be driven to a field to pick fruit, or dig ditches, or help with landscaping projects, or sometimes to just haul trash or bricks or old furniture from the sites of demolished or condemned buildings.

It was always hard work, and Ronnie was usually exhausted by the end of the long days (fifteen hours was the average work time), but the jobs paid in cash at the end of the day, and the trucks always drove the men back to the front of the employment building when things were done. The money wasn't as much as he would have made if he'd gotten a regular steady job, but Ronnie didn't have any official identification—and, besides, he didn't want anyone to know his real name, anyway, just in case one of his brothers or sisters had reported him to the police as missing.

He also discovered the fine art of pool-sharking, albeit by accident.

After a particularly long day hauling railroad ties for a huge private landscaping project, some of the men decided they wanted to go grab a few brews at a local bar, and Ronnie—without being asked—went along.

He was feeling sad and sick because the night before he'd had to take the hurting away from a seven-year-old boy he'd found lying beaten and bloody in an alley not far from the motel where he was staying. He'd been coming back from the previous day's work (railroad ties, all week long it had been the same landscaping job with the railroad ties) when he heard a trash can bang up against another one and turned to see a small arm flop out into the mud.

The alley had only a single source of light—a dim bare bulb suspended over the kitchen door of a Chinese restaurant—so at first Ronnie was uncertain if he was seeing a real arm or if it was just piece of trash from the restaurant that *looked* like an arm.

You should take a look, Ronnie, whispered Suzanne.

For a moment he just stood there, staring down into the dim, dank, dark alley, not wanting to move any closer.

What is it?

—It's been so long, Suzanne. Almost a whole year. I dunno if I can . . . if I can . . .

Shhh, there, there . . . maybe it won't be anything.

—Maybe.

But you're my Ronnie, aren't you? You love me, you love all of us. Our *Ronnie wouldn't just walk away, now, would he?*

He closed his eyes and took a deep breath, held it, and then released it in a slow, steady stream. Sometimes—not very often, just sometimes, every once in a while—it really bugged him when Suzanne said those kinds of things. *We all love you . . . Our Ronnie . . . You're my Ronnie . . . We all know we can depend on you to do the right thing. . . .* But he'd never let her or the others know that. He never wanted them to feel bad or guilty for having to sometimes give him a little push to do the right thing. Still, sometimes, like now, *right now,* it did make him feel guilty, because he was never sure if he was doing it because he knew it was right or if it was because he didn't want to disappoint Suzanne and the others or if . . .

Oh, well, *darn it!* Who was he kidding? The truth was it *had* been almost a year since he'd last had to take the hurting away from another kid, and in all these months Ronnie had been sleeping better than he could ever remember. He'd been getting out of bed every morning looking forward to the day, not dreading what might happen *if.*

But that was selfish, wasn't it?

Yeah, it sure was.

Ronnie?

—Huh? Oh, sorry.

And he walked into the alley, pulling his flashlight from his jacket pocket. He'd discovered after the first week that it was a smart thing to carry a good flashlight with you in the morning. It made it easier to see all over the field or big yard or building site where you were going to be working when you first got there, and also because a lot of the guys brought along newspapers to read during the ride but there wasn't a lot of light to read by at four fifteen in the morning (the streetlights were spaced too far apart to be much good; that's what one of the guys told Ronnie when he asked to borrow the flashlight), so a flashlight went a long way toward making Ronnie fast friends on those rides.

He turned on the flashlight but cupped his other hand around the front so that it didn't make a great circle of light—a big old spotlight might attract someone's attention, and Ronnie had become very good at *not* attracting attention to himself—and slowly walked forward, guiding the light to the spot where he thought he'd seen . . .

And there it was. A child's arm—bruised, with a few streaks of blood running down the forearm, the hand turned upward with its fingers curled like some kind of claw.

Take a deep breath, Ronnie. You know what to do.

—I love you Suzanne, I love all of you . . . but could

you maybe please not talk to me for a minute or two? I'm not mad or nothing, but . . . you know . . .

The reply was silence.

Looking back over his shoulder to make sure the street behind him was still empty, Ronnie moved toward the arm, pointing the flashlight's beam at the muddy ground. He walked around the row of trash cans, stepped over the one that had been knocked over, and then knelt down, taking care to set the overturned trash can upright in order to hide himself.

This was the worst part, coming across one at night like this. Ronnie had never really liked the dark—not that he was *afraid* of the dark like some kind of crybaby sped ree-tard, no . . . it just seemed to him that the dark always made people think about dying, how dark it was in the coffin, buried under the ground, and maybe being reminded every night that you were going to die was kind of mean. He wondered how long the child's body had been out here. If it had been left less than two or three hours ago, it still carried some ghost, some remnant of its final minutes, and Ronnie knew that he didn't need even that much; all he needed was a few seconds, or one—a single second of memory contained unseen threads connecting it to the countless memories and sensations that the child had carried since the moment memory and sensation had first registered. One second of memory unfolded countless times, revealing the entirety of their existence. So much hidden inside so little.

He moved the flashlight's beam toward the child's face, or what was left of it.

The beating had been brutal, monstrous, and vile.

The little boy's head was almost pushed in at a couple of spots, and both his hair and skin were lacquered with blood. And he was still alive.

Ronnie lay down the flashlight and flexed his fingers, wincing as he heard the tiny bones crack.

"It's gonna be okay," he whispered to the little boy.

One of the child's eyelids spasmed, then began to lift, making it only halfway. Beneath was an eye so filled with blood that it appeared almost black, except for the smallest, thinnest ring of white right in the middle. Ronnie had watched a cop show on TV one night and heard one of the characters refer to this as an "eight-ball hemorrhage" (at least, that's what it sounded like); it had sounded funny at the time, because the only eight ball Ronnie had ever seen was the Magic kind, the kind you asked a question and then shook real hard and then turned upside down to read the answer. But there was nothing funny about this.

He reached down and took hold of the child's upturned, clawed hand.

"I'll stay right here," said Ronnie.

The eight ball quivered in its socket. *Please* . . .

The child's hand closed on Ronnie's.

And Ronnie knew.

Oh, it took a few seconds before the knowledge started to filter into him; there was such a thick, sour thrumming and a heavy miasma of cold wet pain that almost led to Ronnie losing consciousness, but he hung in there for Jimmy's sake, for that was his name, this blood-lacquered broken mass of meat and bone. Jimmy Stiles, and today had been his seventh birthday, but Daddy had come home drunk this morning without any presents or the cake Mommy had ordered from the bakery, and when Mommy started yelling at Daddy (*"What? You spend all night buying drinks for your buddies or did you lose it hustling pool games again?"*) he'd hit her jaw with the back of his hand (*"I don't need this shit from you, you fat-ass, miserable, ball-breaking, castrating, son-of-a-cunt bitch!"*) and she'd hit back, and then Jimmy, he'd started crying because he hated it when they yelled and hit each other, that's why he didn't have any friends, nobody ever wanted to come over to his house because of his parents, and most of the time that was okay, it really was, because he had his drawing pad and his charcoal pencils and his watercolors and comic books and his records and record player, so he'd draw friends and set their pictures all around and then they'd listen to music together and later everyone would ask him to read from the comics, and they all said he was a good reader, that he ought to be an actor on TV or in the movies, and that made Jimmy feel good, so he'd drawn a whole *bunch* of friends for today's birthday party, even drew goofy hats for all of them, so he was real disappointed when Daddy didn't come in with the cake or a present—all he'd wanted were some new comic books to read to everyone after they'd had cake—but he couldn't say anything, especially now that Mommy and Daddy were *really* screaming and hitting each other—fists, now, and there was a little blood at the corner of Mommy's mouth—but he couldn't help himself, Jimmy couldn't, and he started crying because he'd been looking forward to a nice birthday and now he was gonna have to hide up in his room with his head buried under the pillow trying to make the yelling and screaming and thumping and sounds of breaking glass and all of it go away. He'd gotten real good at doing this, even though it scared him because he never knew what he was going to find after it was all over and everything was quiet for a while and he chanced to sneak downstairs to see what had gotten broken or snapped in pieces or see if maybe Mommy needed him to help her patch up her face or if there was blood on the rugs that he was gonna have to help wash out. For a little while he could make most of that go away with the pillow over his head and pressed against his ears while he hummed "Hello, Goodbye," his favorite Beatles song ever—but right now he wasn't scared, or even angry, he just felt *bad*, felt *awful*, like this was all his fault, and so he ran into the room and shouted, *"I'm sorry! I'm sorry! Please don't yell, I don't need a cake or anything, we can just have mac and cheese, that'll be a good birthday, it will!"* and both Mommy and Daddy stopped and looked at him and Jimmy saw it in their eyes, saw that all of this *was* his fault, all of it, every fight, every scream, every slap and punch and broken dish and the crying and the bruises, it was all because of him, and it scared him so much he couldn't move, couldn't turn to run upstairs to his room and lock the doors and make it all go away with the pillow, and the next thing he knew Daddy had let go of Mommy's throat and Mommy just sort of dropped to the floor, her eyes staring at her son, not blinking, and Daddy reached under the sink and pulled out the big pipe wrench he kept down there to fix the plumbing when it started to leak, 'cause it always leaked under the sink, Jimmy had helped Mommy clean up water from the kitchen more times than he could count, and Daddy walked over to him and smiled and said, *"A birthday boy gets birthday smacks before cake and presents, remem-*

ber?" and he lifted up the wrench with both hands like a baseball player with a bat at home plate and then Daddy swung down and then . . .

Ronnie felt the tears running down his face as he squeezed Jimmy's hand, because he knew that this time was different, this time he had to take the hurting away like a sponge absorbing water, slow and steady, not with a quick bird-snap. Jimmy was moving beyond the pain now, he couldn't feel anything except Ronnie's hand in his, and it was good, this feeling, it was nice and warm and gentle, it made him happy, but he was getting cold, so Ronnie sat down in the mud and cradled Jimmy's head on his lap, stroking the boy's blood-slopped hair back from what was left of his forehead, rocking him back and forth, back and forth, a mother with her newborn in a rocking chair, back and forth, back and forth, shhh, there, there, it'll be okay, it'll be gone soon, you won't hurt anymore, just close your eyes and I will sing you a lullaby . . . but then Ronnie realized that he didn't know any lullabies, no one ever sang lullabies to unwanted sped ree-tard babies, so he did the next best thing: he leaned down and pressed his lips close against Jimmy's remaining ear and began to hum "Hello, Goodbye" hoping that he stayed in tune because he'd never been much of a singer, and for a few brief moments they remained that way, the two of them in that cold, muddy, dark, filthy alley, surrounded by garbage and rats and the deepening shadows of the uncaring night, but neither of them were a part of it now, they were untouchable, separated from the hurt and loneliness, outside and above all harm: one ree-tard sped humming an old Beatles song (in tune) and a little boy who closed his eyes a few minutes before midnight on his seventh birthday, feeling no pain, not afraid, not anymore, and trying to smile because it was nice to have a friend who wasn't just on paper, and that made this the best birthday ever.

Ronnie continued to sing and to rock Jimmy for several minutes after the boy had died before he simply . . . stopped, just sitting there, the two of them a tableau amidst the trash.

There were still tears in Ronnie's eyes, but these were different than before; where before he'd been weeping from the overwhelming pain and loneliness he'd felt from Jimmy, now Ronnie wept in rage, for the very last thing he'd seen as the hurting passed from Jimmy to him was the face of Jimmy's dad. And it was a face that was going to be easy for Ronnie to remember, because he'd seen it before. *("Excuse me, friend—can you shine some of the light over here so's I can read this goddamned paper? Or maybe I could borrow it for a few minutes? Yeah? Hey, thanks. I owe you a beer.")*

Three days in a row he'd worked alongside Jimmy's dad, and it was Jimmy's dad who was always suggesting to everyone that they go "grab a few brews" after work.

Tomorrow night, Ronnie was going to go along whether he was invited or not.

"I love you," he whispered in Jimmy's ear. "And I'm sorry." Then he kissed the dead child's cold forehead, rested the boy's head on a pillow of mud, and rose to his feet.

—Suzanne?

He just got here, Ronnie. He's fine—he's a little confused, but he's fine.

—Please tell him I'm sorry he didn't have any cake.

I will, Ronnie, I promise.

—Does he look happy?

Oh, he sure *does. He's got so many new friends to meet. He looks like such a nice boy.*

—Don't never let him be lonely, okay?

No one here is lonely, Ronnie. We've got you to thank for that.

—I love all of you *so much.* You know?

Of course we do, Ronnie. And we love you, too. Now, if you'll excuse me, we've got a belated birthday party to throw for a certain someone. . . .

And so here Ronnie was, part of the gang (along with Jimmy's dad, who acted no differently tonight than he had last night or the night before), heading into the bar down the street.

Ronnie thought he might actually have an extra beer tonight—not that he had beer all that often, but this place didn't ask for ID and, besides, Ronnie could pass for twenty-one even though he'd just turned seventeen.

He sat at a large table with Jimmy's dad and the other men from that day's crew and listened to them talk about the fucking economy and the fucking energy crisis and the fucking gas lines and that fucking Carter the fucking peanut farmer president and their aching fucking backs and how they'd like to fuck this waitress or that one who was serving them.

"Doggy-style," Ronnie said, because it seemed polite to join in the conversation. All of the men burst out laughing, a few of them slapped him on the back and said things like, "You're okay, kid," or "I like the way you think." Jimmy's dad—everybody called him Slugger, but somehow Ronnie figured that wasn't his real name—put an arm around Ronnie's shoulder and slurred, "Damn straight, doggy-style—that way you don't have to cover their head with a paper bag."

Ronnie smiled because he wanted everyone to think he felt like one of the guys.

In a way, it made him sad that he'd never see any of them again after tonight. A couple of them had been real nice to him.

After about an hour most of the men left, but Ronnie stayed behind along with three or four others, including "Slugger" Stiles, who was now on his second game of pool. For this game, he'd gotten the biker-type he was playing against to make a "small wager—just to make it more interestin', ya know?" Both men had placed twenty-dollar bills on the edge of the table.

One of the other men tapped Ronnie on the shoulder and leaned in. "Now, you watch this asshole fall for old Slugger's hustle. See how Slugger's kinda wobbly on his feet? He's a bit drunk, but he ain't *that* drunk. He's gonna lose this game—not by too much, mind you, but enough that the other fellah's not gonna think twice about upping the next game to fifty bucks. I seen Slugger come in here on a busy night like this and walk out of here at closing time with damn near a thousand dollars in his pocket."

Ronnie smiled and nodded, and then watched as Stiles did, indeed, lose to the biker, but in such a way that you'd have to *know* he was setting up the other guy. The biker turned to his friends and laughed behind Stiles's back, then faced Jimmy's dad again and said: "I feel bad about taking your money. What do ya say we grab a piss-break and play one more? Double or nothing, winner takes all."

Stiles blinked, wobbled a bit more, then said, "That's . . . w-what? Shit, never could do math in my head once I got that second pitcher started . . . lemme see, that'd be . . . *eighty dollars?*"

"Sounds about right."

Stiles looked confused, then said: "How 'bout making it an even hundred?"

The biker looked at his friends and gave them a quick wink, then faced Stiles again. "A hundred sounds even better."

The men shook hands, the biker heading for the restroom, and Jimmy's dad heading out the back exit into the alley.

"Where's he going?" asked Ronnie.

"This's part of the hustle, kid," replied the other man at the table. "See how he made sure the biker's friends saw him stumble out the door? In a minute, he's gonna start making sounds like he's back there puking his guts out, then sit down and have a smoke. Biker comes back from the restroom, his friends are gonna tell him that Slugger's out back being sick, and the biker, he's gonna take it for granted that he's already won the next game. Won't play as well as he did the last time 'cause he figures Slugger's too sick and too drunk to give him any kind of game." The guy pressed a fist against his chest, let fly with a loud, wet belch, then finished off his glass of beer. "Speaking of taking a piss, seems the lizard needs draining. Do me a favor, will ya? Order us up another pitcher while I'm in there. I think I may be a few minutes—that damn Italian sub I had for lunch has finally found the escape route." He patted Ronnie's back. "Be back in a few." He rose from the table, weaving and zigzagging through the crowd.

Ronnie was glad the place had gotten so crowded.

He flagged down a waitress and ordered two more pitchers of beer and some onion rings, gave her a five-dollar tip, then asked the remaining guys at the table to save his seat.

Making his way through all the people, Ronnie walked past the pool table and the cue rack. No one was paying any attention to him or the table area, so he grabbed the opportunity to take a couple of items. No one noticed. The biker's friends were too busy talking about the "stupid motherfucker" who was "puking up his lunch in the alley" and how Oz (that must be the biker's name) was going to "clean him out" when they played the next game.

Ronnie guessed that Jimmy's dad must have been doing this for a long time, and that he was pretty good at it . . . at least most of the time. *("What? You spend all night buying drinks for your buddies or did you lose it hustling pool games again?")*

Ronnie stepped out into the alley, making sure to close the door behind him—but not too fast, and making as little noise as possible. Not that anyone could hear it over the loud music from the jukebox.

Jimmy's dad was at the far end of the alley, half in shadow, sitting on a crate that was just barely outside the glow of light from a single bare bulb hanging over another door across from the back of the bar. He was smoking a cigarette and humming to himself.

It wasn't until Ronnie was closer that he realized what song the man was humming, and when he did realize what song it was, the burning fury that had been roiling in his stomach and chest all day long became suddenly cool, comforting, almost peaceful.

"What song is that?" asked Ronnie as he came a little closer.

"What? Who's—? Oh, hey, it's you. The song? I dunno. Some goddamned Beatles song my shit-for-brains kid used to sing to himself." And then he laughed.

It was the "used to" and the laugh that did it. Ronnie dropped the second object he'd taken from inside the bar and wrapped both his hands around the skinny end of the pool cue, pulling back like a baseball player at home plate readying to take a swing. "Hey, Slugger."

Jimmy's dad had crushed out his first smoke and was lighting another. "Yeah?" he turned and saw the raised pool cue. "Hey—what the fuck you doin' with that?"

"Jimmy wasn't dead when you left him in the alley."

Stiles's eyes narrowed for a moment, and then grew wide as he jumped to his feet and raised his arm to ward off the oncoming blow, but that was exactly what Ronnie wanted him to do because instead of swinging down, Ronnie faked to the side and then swung upward with all he had, smashing the fat end of the cue right into the center of Stiles's Adam's apple and enjoying both the sound it made and the look of shock that froze Stiles's face into an expression of complete and utter terror.

"You know what? He *loved* you, Jimmy did. He really loved you and your wife. Is she really dead?"

Stiles tried to make a sound but all that emerged was a soft, wet, strained gurgling noise. He staggered forward, both hands now clutching at his throat, then dropped to his knees.

Ronnie flipped the pool cue around so that he was now gripping the fat end. He didn't speak again for the rest of it.

Taking a deep breath, he pulled back the cue, got his footing, and then ran forward like those knights always did in the movies when they were having a jousting battle. The business end of the cue went straight through Stiles's left eye and pushed another inch or so into his skull before the man fell back. Once he was on the ground, it was easy for Ronnie to just stand on the man's chest and put all of his weight into pushing the cue even deeper. It was a lot harder than he thought it would be, ramming the thing all the way through Stiles's head, but Ronnie kept at it until he felt the end of the cue burst through the back of Stiles's skull and hit alley-floor mud. Yanking the cue out of the bloody mess, Ronnie threw it aside and then retrieved the second item he'd taken from the bar.

This time he sat on Stiles's chest, one leg on either side of the dying man. Before finishing things, Ronnie grabbed Stiles's left hand and took something from him—he'd always suspected that he might be able to choose what he took and what he didn't, but he'd never tried before because with the kids, he wanted to take it all away.

With Stiles, he didn't care if the man's final moments were filled with hurting.

Once he took what he wanted from Jimmy's dad, Ronnie used his fingers like an ice cream scoop and worked all the glop and blood and tissue and bone fragments out of the eye socket, and then placed the gleaming black eight ball over the chasm—which still wasn't large enough.

Looking around, Ronnie spotted a brick lying amidst the junk back there, and he grabbed it, and— being careful not to shatter the eight ball—used it to tap, press, and pound the ball into place.

"Now *that* looks like an eight-ball hemorrhage," he whispered to himself, and then laughed.

He found a hose and used it to wash the blood from his hands, then pulled off Stiles's coat and—seeing that it hadn't gotten too much blood on it, and it was black, anyway—decided to wear that. For good measure he went through the dead man's pockets and took all of his cash—nearly five hundred dollars.

"You had plenty of money to buy him a gift," he said to the corpse, and then kicked it.

As he was walking out of the alley, he stopped for a moment when he heard the laugher of several children.

—Is the party going good?

Oh, it's wonderful, Ronnie, replied Suzanne. *Jimmy is having the time of his life.*

—That's good. That's real good.

Where are we going now?

—I don't know yet. I have to go back to the motel and get my stuff.

Don't dawdle, Ronnie. In a minute or two, Oz or one of his friends is going to come out into the alley looking for you-know-who.

—I know. I'll be quick.

Are you done hiding now? Are you done running away from the hurting?

—Yeah, I guess so.

And he heard all the children shout: *Yay! Uncle Ronnie's back!*

"I guess so," he mumbled to no one in particular as he walked out of the alley and started toward the motel.

At least he had another way to make money now. Thanks to Jimmy's dad.

* * *

Over the next six years, Uncle Ronnie claimed seventeen more victims, all of them between the ages of two and thirteen. He tried to search for a way *not* to take the hurting away from the children, not to kill them, but the truth was that even if he had killed those who had been inflicting such pain on them (as much as he'd enjoyed killing Jimmy's dad, the opportunity to repeat that with someone else had not presented itself), the children themselves were ruined beyond hope, repair, or prayer—emotionally, psychologically, and spiritually. They would never know a day without pain, without sadness, without dread or anger or heartbreak.

He had no choice.

But in those moments of communion when he took away the hurting, Ronnie made it a point to memorize the names and faces of those who had brought this onto the children; he made a connection with them that could never be broken, a thin, silver thread of consciousness that would enable him to always, *always* find them when he wanted to.

And someday he would; he'd find each and every one of them, and he'd make them pay, just like he'd done with Jimmy's dad.

Suzanne and the others looked on, and whispered to him, but he found the more children he took unto him, the more their voices drowned each other out. What he could hear, though, what kept him going, were the cumulative tones of love and gratitude. Without that, he would not have lasted as long as he did.

Four days after his twenty-third birthday, Ronnie awakened in a motel room in Lexington, Kentucky.

He was drenched in sweat, his heart was trip-hammering against his chest, he could hardly pull enough oxygen into his lungs to breathe, and he was more terrified than he had ever been in his life, because he awoke knowing that, several years ago, he'd made a terrible mistake.

And the thin silver thread that still connected him to a woman whose name he could not remember, the thread that had become slack and nearly forgotten over the years, instantaneously pulled taut and inflexible, becoming an increasingly constricting noose around Ronnie's neck.

He managed to pull himself into a sitting position just a few seconds before some of the pressure around his throat and in the center of his chest eased, unclenching his stomach and its surrounding muscles. Jerking to the side, he managed to grab hold of the metal wastebasket and pull its over to him just in time. He vomited very little (he'd not been eating much the past few days) but it felt as if he were emptying his stomach of everything he'd eaten since the age of three.

Afterward, he dry heaved for a few minutes more, then slowly pushed his legs off the bed until he felt the cold floor rise up to meet first the sole of his left foot, and then that of his right. He paid careful attention to each and every movement. No gesture, no step, no touch could be wasted. The silver noose around his neck vibrated but did not choke him this time; instead, it guided him, and *would continue* to guide him.

Because he'd made an awful, terrible, *horrible* mistake . . . but there was still time.

He rose from the bed while reaching for his watch

and wallet on the nightstand. He'd been sleeping in his clothes for the last few days, so there was no need to pack—he had only to grab his knapsack from its place beside the door as he left the room.

He used the bathroom, drank a glass of cold water, and put on his shoes.

—Suzanne?

I'm here, Ronnie.

—I didn't imagine it, did I?

No, Ronnie. I heard it, too. We all did.

—I made a mistake, Suzanne. I made a bad mistake.

I know, but it's not too late.

—I sure hope you're right.

He stumbled only once as he headed for the door, regaining his footing as he grabbed his knapsack and closed the motel room door behind him. Checking his watch, he saw that it was only a little after five A.M. If he hurried, he might be able to bum a ride from one of the truckers who frequented the diner/gas station/bus depot across the road. If not, he could at least buy a bus ticket back to Ohio . . . and hope that a bus going that way came through soon.

He went out through a side exit of the motel because it was on the side closer to the diner, sprinted across the motel parking lot, paused, and then broke into a run again when he saw that the road was clear. There were at least seven large semis parked in the lot, and two buses on layover. One of them had to be heading to Ohio.

Ronnie said a prayer to Jesus in heaven, asking Jesus to help him find a ride really, really fast.

"I don't wanna be too late," he prayed to Jesus. "Please, Jesus, help me get back home."

He heard you, Suzanne whispered.

—You sure?

Uh-huh.

—Promise?

Promise.

Ronnie took a deep breath as he zigzagged through the parked vehicles and then made a beeline for the diner's entrance.

—Suzanne?

What is it, Ronnie?

—Does Jesus hate me? I mean, I done so many bad things.

Jesus hates no one, Ronnie.

—It's just . . . I dunno . . . maybe he only *told* you he heard me. I had a lot of people do that, ya know? Tell me something just to make me go away or shut up and leave 'em alone.

Jesus isn't like that, Ronnie.

—What about His dad? Does God hate me?

I have been told to inform you that we do not answer silly questions.

—Who told you to say that?

Someone who doesn't hate you.

—I just worry, ya know?

There's one other thing I've been asked to tell you. At the counter in the diner, there's a man sitting way down at the far end, near the pay phones. He's got a lot of gray hair in his beard and he's wearing an old jean jacket and an OSU Buckeyes cap.

—What about him?

I don't know. I was just supposed to point him out to you.

The man's name was Floyd Hopkins, and he was driving his rig as far as Pataskala. "But I'll bet you anything we'll find you a ride into Cedar Hill before the waitress comes for your lunch order," he said after he and Ronnie finished their breakfast and were heading for his truck.

A little over three hours later, at the grocery store where Floyd was making his delivery, another trucker who was just finishing his delivery told Floyd that he had another delivery to make in Hebron, which meant he'd have to drive near Cedar Hill, and Ronnie was welcome to ride along.

Ronnie had walked out of the motel in Kentucky at five fourteen A.M.

He set foot in Heath, Ohio—less than five miles outside Cedar Hill—at nine thirty-five.

He allowed himself to feel relief only for a minute, and then he had not one, but two problems to deal with: making sure that he didn't run into any members of his family once he got into town, and, most importantly, finding the lady whose name he couldn't remember and correcting his mistake.

Correcting the part that *could still be* corrected, that is.

He took a deep breath, made himself aware of the silver thread, and began following it.

Ronald James Williamson and Lucy Thompson were about to meet for the second time.

INTERLUDE
The Hangman, 11:00 P.M.

1

Grant McCullers looked across the bar at Sheriff Ted Jackson, who was shaking his head as he and the Reverend exchanged unreadable glances.

"Am I missing something here?" asked the man they were still referring to as 'Henry.'

"No," said the Reverend. "It's just . . . well you must admit, you're offering certain details that some might construe as . . . that is, I mean to say—"

"You're telling us stuff there's *no way* you could know," said Jackson.

"I wouldn't be so sure," said Grant.

Jackson looked at him. "First of all, I need a refill on the popcorn and my soda, and, second—you wouldn't be so sure of *what?*"

Grant smiled as he refilled Jackson's Pepsi. "I'm just saying, we shouldn't be trying to poke holes in the story until we've heard the entire thing." He gestured to the long shelf of knickknacks that ran the length of the bar. "Pick any item from up there—say, that busted guitar neck—and try to tell the story behind it and see how *you'd* feel if someone stopped you halfway through to start nitpicking about what you could have known or what you couldn't have. *Anybody'd* sound crazy if you stopped them halfway through."

Henry looked up at the shelf. "So you're saying that *everything* on that shelf has got a story behind it? A story like mine?"

"There is no story like yours," replied the Reverend. "Each one is unique. Some more so than others."

"Like that busted guitar neck? Or that model ship and lighthouse?" asked Henry.

"You'd have to hear the stories first and then judge for yourself."

"Oh."

Grant set two fresh bowls of popcorn on the bar, made sure they all had fresh drinks, poured himself another cup of coffee, and took his seat once again. "Have we gotten to the part yet where the doctors usually pull out their prescription pads and start scribbling away?"

Henry tried smiling and almost made it this time. "Depends on which doctor."

"Ah."

"So, you guys . . . you don't think I'm nuts?"

Jackson shook his head. "I haven't had my yo-yo alarm go off yet. You two?"

"I'm going to pretend that question was never even asked," said the Reverend.

Jackson put a hand on Henry's shoulder. "Look, it's not that I don't believe you, okay? I'm just—I mean, c'mon, look at me! I wear a badge, ya know? It's a force of habit to look for holes in someone's story. If I do it again, ignore me. Or you could do what my wife did and leave. But I hope you finish the story first."

"Okay," said Henry.

"So," said Grant, "if no one needs to take a bathroom break, I think we can let Mr. Henry continue." He looked at Henry and nodded. "I believe that Ronnie was about to meet Lucy again, right?"

Henry looked down at his hands, flexed his fingers, and released a slow breath. "Well, yes and no."

"Oh?" asked the Reverend. "A slight detour in the narrative?"

"You might say."

"What *kind* of a detour?" asked Jackson.

"I need to jump ahead a little bit, if that's okay."

Grant offered a glass of ice water. "It's your story, Henry. We're just listening."

Jackson rubbed his eyes. "And I evidently haven't been listening as well as I thought. You said that Ronnie and Lucy, they met a total of three times?"

"Yes."

"But only one of them recognized the other?"

"Right."

The Reverend sighed. "Yes, Theodore—look at that expression. He hates it when I call him by his Christian name. All right, all right—*Ted*. Before you ask another question of the 'duh' variety, I think we're all in agreement that it was—or rather, *will be*—Ronnie who did—*does*—the recognizing." He looked at Henry. "Am I correct?"

"You are."

"See? Some of us know how to give our *undivided* attention to a tale and he who tells it."

"Bite my bag," said Jackson.

"I knew you'd return to that old standby eventually."

Henry grinned; it wasn't quite a smile, but the guy was getting closer with each try. "I really appreciate this, you guys. I really do. Having someone listen and not . . . well, you know." He took three deep swallows of the cold water, set down the glass, and said, "Lucy Thompson . . ."

2

The sun shone mercilessly upon the mountain of gold, its brilliance hypnotizing him as he moved farther upward in slow, agonizing degrees. The mountain was everything to him now—mother, sister, wife, lover, torturer, redeemer, the schoolyard bully who used to pick on him in grade school, the muscle-bound beachcomber who took sadistic glee when kicking sand into the ninety-pound weakling's face—and he continued on both for and in spite of all the mountain was to him now.

I know you're up there . . . somewhere. . . .

He could feel the blisters on his feet and heels swell, then burst in searing liquid pain.

The sun beat down upon his back, scorching the flesh underneath his shirt.

He would not stop.

He didn't care if he had to climb until he died; at least he would die doing something, making the effort, striving to free himself of the doubt and nightmares that had haunted him all his life.

I'll find you. God help me, I'll find you.

I know you're there.

I know you're real.

You have *to be.*

Taking hold of a firm root in the mountainside, he pulled in a deep breath, counted to three, then released it as he pulled himself up another nine inches.

PART TWO

THE MOUNT OF THE MOON

"Violence shall synchronize your movements
like a tune,
And Terror like a frost shall halt the flood of
thinking."

—W. H. Auden
Letter to Lord Byron

"The only reason I stopped shooting was
because I ran out of bullets."

—Bernhard Goetz, in his statement to Concord,
  New Hampshire, police on December 31, 1984

CHAPTER ONE

Lucy Thompson, feeling the buzz kicking in from the two drinks she'd had before coming, sat very still among the other members of the grief support group and watched the man who stood at the podium. A detective, he was, first-class, with the Cedar Hill Police Department. He spoke very well, very clearly, as he explained to them various precautions they could take to make sure their children (*the ones you have left* remained unspoken but was nevertheless understood by all in the room) would remain safe and informed while at the same time still able to enjoy all the wonders of childhood without believing they had to look over their shoulders every ten seconds.

"Nothing is worse," he said, "than to let fear infect your children. Now, I'm not saying that you should not make them aware of the dangers out there—far from it—but it's important that you know when to pull back, when to draw the line. There *is* such a thing as too much information, especially when you first begin talking to your children about something like this. Let them see your concern, of course, but never let them know your fear."

Never let them know your fear, Lucy repeated to herself in silence.

Then: *But what if that fear could have been the thing that saved them?*

"Excuse me?" said the detective, whose name Lucy suddenly couldn't remember. "Is there a question back there?"

Jesus! Had she actually said that *out loud?*

She felt her hands ball into fists, which she pressed against her legs; she figured that once she heard bones crack she'd stop.

Several people were turning to look at her.

"Sorry," she managed to get out. "Just thinking out loud to myself." Please, God, let him buy that and move on.

"But that's an interesting point, Ms . . . ?"

"Thompson," she said, the word, slightly slurred, crawling from her throat as if it were afraid of the light. "No *Mrs., Miss,* or *Ms.* Just Lucy. Lucy Thompson."

The detective stared at her for a moment, then looked over at the counselor who ran the meetings; she gave a slight nod of her head, and the detective—Bill Emerson, that was his name—said, "Your question—if I heard it correctly—is whether or not instilling fear into a child might help save them?"

She could barely swallow now. "Yes."

Detective Emerson appeared to think very hard for a few moments before answering. "Look, every last one of you is here because you've lost a child. Whether it was from violence or because they suddenly went missing doesn't matter at this moment; what does matter is that the emptiness and grief has become more than you can handle on your own. But many of you still have other children that you can protect—and I don't mean to imply or for you to infer that you *didn't* protect your lost children. Yes, making them afraid would probably help protect them to some degree . . . but at the same time, it can also foster paranoia in them. So, again, I have to come back to my original point: Infecting them with that degree of fear may make them wary of strangers, it might emphasize the importance of never being alone after dark, and it would probably guarantee that they'll walk home from school with friends, but where's the room left for childhood? If they're so frightened of what might happen to them in the outside world that all they do is stay home and tell themselves at least they're safe, at least what happened to their brother or sister won't happen to them, aren't they then being robbed of a *child's life* just like their absent siblings were?"

"But what other choices do we have?" asked a man sitting near the end of Lucy's row. "My God, we can't . . . we can't watch over them every second of every day, no matter how much we want to."

"I know," said Emerson, his voice full of sympathy. "And no one with the common sense that God gave an ice cube would expect you to watch over them twenty-four/seven. It just isn't humanly possible. So you find people you can trust—an older sibling, a friend you've known for ten years, neighbors with children of their own—and you make them part of your child's social circle. Teachers, the person who drives their school bus . . . you'd be surprised, if you take the time to sit down and make a list, at just how many people there are in your world that can be trusted with sharing in your child's welfare. The trick is not to give your grief and fear the upper hand. And one way of making sure that doesn't happen is to instill caution and knowledge in your child and *not* resort to scare tactics."

A middle-aged woman near the front raised her hand. "But that doesn't make sense, Detective. Most of the cases you hear about . . . I mean, *it seems* like most of the cases you hear about, it involves someone the family *thought* they could trust, just like you said. How . . . how's a person supposed to know that they aren't asking some pervert to help watch over their child?"

Several people in the room mumbled their agreement.

Emerson rubbed at his temple, looked through his prepared notes, then sighed. "I don't know," he said, looking back up at the room. "I wish there was something in all this material to answer that question, but there isn't. You see all these horrified, shocked faces on the news—faces of mothers who thought their nephew was a good kid, so it was okay to leave little Jenny in his care for a few hours, faces of parents who can't understand why their older daughter would do such a thing to her newborn brother, families looking on as aunts or uncles or the bus driver who everyone thought was a wonderful person is hauled off in cuffs while a sheet-covered body is brought up from the basement . . . I don't know. I'd go back and say, 'Trust your instincts,' but, then, how many people trusted their instincts only to have their child taken from them as yours were from you?"

"You don't have to be so apologetic," said another man in the room. "Hell, it's nice to hear someone in law enforcement admit that they don't know the answer to something. I got so goddamned sick and tired of the police and FBI always having a quick response to every question me or my wife had, and every last answer said the same thing, more or less—'We got it under control and you'll have your child back with you soon.' I mean, they never said that *directly,* but every answer they gave us had that . . . that *undercurrent* to it, you know?"

"I do," said Emerson.

Lucy began to tune out Emerson's voice and those of the group members who asked the detective questions.

She fused her fists into one ten-fingered, white-knuckled knot, and continued to press down on her lap. The pressure was a distraction at this point, and that was good, that was fine, because as long as she remained distracted she—*turns around for only a few seconds, maybe ten, maybe twenty, but it isn't that long, Sarah right next to her, holding her hand, and Lucy doesn't think twice when Sarah says, "I need my hand, Mommy," so she lets go of her daughter's—*

Her hand came up slowly and began rubbing her temple. *Stop it,* she thought. *Just stop it, don't think about it, keep yourself distracted, keep that distance and you won't—*

"Where'd she go?" *she says to the woman she's been talking with.*

The other woman looks over Lucy's shoulder; her eyes narrow and her brow wrinkles with confusion. "I don't know, Lucy, she was right there a second ago."

Lucy turns and shouts Sarah's name—it has only been a few seconds, that's all, so she can't have gone far—but when her call goes unanswered the first thing she feels is irritation at her daughter's running off like this. Okay, sure, it's a small parking-lot carnival and kids love these things (Lucy loves them herself, there's something so sad and tacky about them but all the kids see are the rides and the games and the candy and fun fun fun) and anyone who thinks they can keep a child standing still for more than a minute at one of these things deserves the sore feet and headaches they get, but Sarah—who, at age I'm-practically-six, is already a parking-lot carnival veteran of some two dozen excursions—knows better than to do something like this. Lucy had told her she only wanted to stop and talk to Mrs. Shaw for a second, and Sarah said, " 'Kay," and went back to playing with her balloon and that hand-sized wooden rocking horse she'd won at the bottle-toss booth while Lucy asked Mrs. Shaw about the new teacher at Sarah's preschool, Mr. Kessler, and Mrs. Shaw, who was in charge of the preschool, held tight to her six-year-old son's hand and said that Mr. Kessler came to them with exceptional references and the kids all seemed to like him, why, even Sarah had remarked that he was more fun than most grown-ups, and that's when Lucy turns around and finds herself facing a huge, cold, and frighteningly empty space where her daughter had been only twenty or so seconds before, so now she's walking away from Mrs. Shaw without saying so much as "Excuse me," because the irritation is giving way to anger and she knows that the anger is only a whitewash over the terror that she feels rising from her gut, and she's calling Sarah's name again, much louder this time, and doesn't hear the note of hysteria that's creeping into her voice until Mrs. Shaw comes up behind her and grabs her arm and says, "It'll be all right, Lucy, come on, we'll keep looking on our way over to the security officer—see, he's right over there—and we'll find her, don't worry, this isn't a big carnival, she can't have wandered far," but there's something in Mrs. Shaw's voice that's a just a little too *con-*

trolled, and like an instantaneous explosion in Lucy's brain the music from the carousel is just a little too loud, the twinkling lights over the game booths are far too bright—blasts of aura-light before a really bad migraine—and the smells from the food vendors and cotton candy machines are taking on a rancid quality as she breathes them in and it seems like it's taking forever to get to the security guard, but then he turns and looks at them and that's when Lucy realizes that she's still shouting her daughter's name, and for a second, only for a second, just one, that's all, her shouts become the scream of a million babies doused in gasoline and set aflame because now a bunch of people are looking at them and she forces herself to swallow it back, to bite down hard, to pull it all into a tight knot that will come gloriously loose when she finally holds Sarah in her arms again, but then Mrs. Shaw is talking again and that too-controlled thing in her voice is stronger now, which makes it worse, so much goddamn worse because hidden somewhere between the control in Mrs. Shaw's voice and the actual words she's speaking is a cold spot that catches the wind and flies toward Lucy, shrouding her, and within that cold spot is a rift, and behind that rift is a demon, one of unspoken things, hunchbacked, long-clawed, and chortling sulfur, imparting to Lucy the knowledge that she's never going to see Sarah again, but she does her best to ignore it and soon it's gone and there is only the search, the people, the police and volunteers, her reaching into her wallet for a recent picture of Sarah and thanking God that she'd decided to stop at that tacky photographer's booth at Sears and have a Halloween photo taken of her daughter, and as she's handing the photo over to the police officer who will have leaflets made within the hour she is suddenly struck dumb by the suspicion that perhaps every parent keeps a recent photo of their child with them not so much to preserve a moment of childhood but be-

*cause there is the quiet, constant, gnawing fear in their gut
that someday the pit will widen and something like this will
happen and their child's life might depend on whether or
not they have a memory recently preserved and what in hell
are you supposed to do if this is the* final *memory of your
child and soon the leaflets are being distributed and more
police are coming in and someone says something about the
Ohio branch of the FBI having been called but all Lucy can
hear is the sound of her own voice, so tiny and weak and
ineffectual as she walks through the crowd and hands out
the leaflets and asks stranger after stranger, "Have you
seen my daughter? Have you seen her? Have you?" and all
of the people, they're so concerned, like Sarah is* their
*daughter, not Someone Else's Kid—one young man even
runs up to Lucy and grabs her by the shoulders and says,
"Is there any word? Have they found her yet?" and when
Lucy says no the young man looks like he's going to start
crying, but he doesn't, only pulls Lucy into a quick embrace
and whispers, "I'm sorry," before dashing off to join in the
search, and as helpful and concerned as everyone is being,
Lucy tries not to notice the pity in their eyes or the way
they're suddenly clutching their own children much, much
closer. . . .*

*And somewhere around eleven thirty they find the small
wooden rocking horse—its tail snapped off and a few heavy,
dark streaks covering its snout—in some bushes just outside
the carnival grounds . . . along with one of Sarah's shoes
and both of her socks, all three torn and covered in mud. . . .*

*And just when Lucy thinks it can't possibly become any
more nightmarish, one of the volunteers shines her flashlight
into a patch of foliage a few feet beyond the bushes and finds
Sarah's other shoe . . . along with her* Sesame Street *underwear, which has her name written inside the waistband,
and all Lucy can think of when one of the detectives asks her*

*to identify the item—being careful not to tell anyone about
the thing she herself found—is that Sarah will be so upset
when she finds out that the splotches of blood have forever
bound Big Bird's wings and blotted out Elmo's grin, sunny
day, singing my cares away, can you tell me how to get, how
to get to . . .*

". . . a few things we need to discuss before breaking up this week," said Dr. Astbury, taking her place
behind the podium as Detective Emerson smiled at
the polite applause the group offered.

"Here it comes," whispered Lucy to herself. Time
to see if the rumors were true.

Detective Emerson looked to Dr. Astbury and, at
her prompting, said, "I'm sure that most of you have
read about Timothy Beals in the paper recently. As
you may or may not know, Mr. Beals was charged with
second-degree murder thirteen years ago in the
death of his three-year-old daughter—"

"And he was released a month ago after serving
twelve years of a twenty-five-year sentence," snapped
Lucy. Everyone in the room turned to look at her.

"Yes," said Emerson. "He's currently residing in the
Spencer Halfway House. One of the many conditions
of his parole is that he attend therapy sessions twice a
week. One session is private, one-on-one, but the
other needs to be in a group environment."

"I think," said Dr. Astbury, "that it might be good
for both him and us if that group were to be ours."

Shocked silence. How dare they suggest that a
child-murderer become part of this?

"Look," said Emerson, "I know this seems . . . well,
thoughtless, under the circumstances, but I can assure
you that Tim harbors a great deal of remorse and
guilt over what he did. I agree with Dr. Astbury—I

think it could benefit everyone involved if you would allow Tim to become part of this group."

"I don't mean to sound crass, either," added Dr. Astbury, "but the truth of the matter is, legally, we cannot prevent Timothy from joining. It would be preferable if we agreed to welcome him, but one way or the other, he will be here next week."

"He might goddamn well be the only one here, then," said someone from the back row.

Several people voiced their agreement.

Emerson pulled a folded sheet of paper from his pocket. "Look, folks, I can understand your resentment, okay?" He held up the folded paper. "But this is a court order. I'd really rather not have to serve this to Dr. Astbury, but I will if I have to."

"Why don't you want to serve it?" asked Lucy.

"Because cooperation is preferable to coercion."

"Good answer."

"What . . . what exactly did he do to the girl, anyway?" asked another member of the group.

Detective Emerson opened his mouth to answer but was cut off when Lucy said, "Tim Beals and his buddies were having a party. It was a Friday night and someone had brought along some crank or coke or acid or something like that, and Tim was pretty stoked. His girlfriend, the mother, was visiting her parents in Pennsylvania and had left their daughter with Tim because she was too sick to travel—says a lot about Mommy, doesn't it? Selfish bitch goes off and leaves a sick little girl with a guy she knows drinks and parties and—never mind."

"No, please," said Emerson. "Continue."

Lucy met his gaze without blinking. "Fine. About one thirty in the morning, Carol—that was the little girl's name, if anyone's interested—gets out of bed because she'd gotten sick and thrown up and needed Daddy to change her sheets. Well, Daddy's busy going down on some bimbo who was willing to spread her legs for some coke or whatever it was they had there that night, and Tim gets pissed off and hits Carol really hard and knocks her down, and Carol starts crying because it hurts but Tim's too stoked and horny to want to deal with a bawling brat, so he kicks her— about a dozen times. Then he takes her back up to her room, throws her down onto her vomit-soaked sheets, then closes and locks the bedroom door. He finishes getting it on with his bimbo, then everyone— including Tim—takes off. He doesn't come back until almost two the next afternoon and finds Carol damn near comatose. He waits awhile to see if she gets better and when she doesn't he takes her to the hospital.

"He ruptured her pancreas. That little girl lay there in her own puke for the better part of twelve hours in unbearable agony. She died ten minutes after they arrived at the hospital. I remember seeing news footage of the medical examiner. The man was damn near in tears when he described how she died and how long it *took* for her to die. *That's* what he did to the girl. And the two of you stand up there with your understanding expressions and sympathetic tones and try to convince us that it'll be for the good of everyone involved if we let this piece of shit come in here and share his grief with us."

Emerson was watching her very carefully. "Do you mind, Miss Thompson, if I ask how it is you have so much information about Mr. Beals so readily available?"

"I read the paper. I listen to the news." Those weren't the real reasons, but no one in this room would understand that. Lucy wasn't sure she understood it herself.

"Did you know the Bealses or their daughter?" asked Emerson.

"Never met them. I don't think Tim and his wife were the type of people I'd've wanted to have over for Sunday dinner, if you read my meaning."

"I think I do, yes."

Lucy looked around at the faces of the group. "Look, I didn't mean to use the kind of language I did. I'm sorry. You all know me—well enough, anyway. And I understand that people like Beals need some sort of therapeutic environment when they get out. I just don't think it should be here." There—her voice was calm again, at least in contrast to the storm she felt raging inside.

"I take it then, Miss Thompson," said Emerson, "that you'll be one of the members who won't be attending next week?"

It was everything Lucy could do not to laugh. His question was so naive it was insulting, and what calm had been regained by her quickly crumbled. "It makes me sick that I have to share this *planet* with someone like that. I'll be goddamned if I'll sit in the same room with him."

Emerson waited a moment before asking: "But don't you think that you might gain some insight, hearing from a parent who—"

"A 'parent,' Detective, is a term you can apply to any of the people in this room. Something like Beals is a different species."

"Lucy," said Dr. Astbury. "I don't think you ought to—"

"Have you mentioned to the group, Doctor, that you're one of the therapists Beals is seeing on a one-on-one basis?"

Astbury seemed to shrug. "I'm not ashamed of that, Lucy. It's my job to counsel victims of grief, no matter what they—"

"*Victims?*" Lucy was surprised she didn't hurl a chair at the good doctor's skull. "You have the nerve to stand there and call *him* a victim? I suppose that you think that little bitch who strapped her kids into her car and drowned them is a victim, too? The fucking jury sure did."

Astbury glared at her. "Lucy—"

"*Don't.* Just . . . don't, okay? It may very well be that people who do that to children had something done to them when they were kids that forever ruined them, and if that's the case then my heart breaks for them *as children.* But at the same time, as adults, what they've done is irredeemable, understand? Without a thought for the fear or pain or loneliness or suffering of their children, they beat, torture, mutilate, and kill them. I'll shed tears for whatever happened to these people as children, but as adults I think we'd all be better off to expunge them from the face of the earth."

Emerson was unblinking now. "So if you had your way . . . ?"

"If I had my way, I'd kick Tim Beals until he died from internal bleeding. Hopefully his death would be long and painful."

Very calmly, Emerson said, "I have to warn you,

Miss Thompson, that you're dangerously close to making a public threat."

"That's not a threat, that's an answer to your question. *That's* how I feel as a mother who is never, *ever* going to hold her little girl's hands again! Now let me ask you one question, Detective—where the hell do we draw the line?"

Emerson blinked. "I'm not sure I understand what you mean."

"*The line,* you politicking talking head! At what point do we say to monsters like Beals, 'Our system will let you go this far but no farther. You go beyond *this point* and you automatically lose your right to walk safely upon the earth.'"

"There are rules and procedures and constitutionally guaranteed channels that a person charged with a crime is entitled to, and—"

"And no one has the balls to draw that line. I know." She rose from her seat; if anyone noticed the way she had trouble getting her balance, they showed no sign of it. "So we can log on to the Web and find sites of babies having sex, or being fucked by animals, or even tortured. And there is no punishment severe enough for people like that. And I will not be back here again, not if Beals is to be part of this group." She started toward the doorway, stopped, and turned to face Emerson and Astbury. "Earlier you accused me of coming close to making a threat. That was not a threat, Detective, but this is: If it were in my power, if I thought I could get away with it, I'd kill that worthless bastard with my bare hands. And to hell with his remorse. What good does his remorse do his daughter now? What good will his remorse do the next little kid who has to suffer at the hands of a monster?"

Before anyone could reply or even attempt to stop her, she ran out of the room.

But not in tears.

She often wondered if she had any left.

CHAPTER TWO

When Sarah Thompson was two years old, her mother and father took her to the first of many parking-lot carnivals. This particular carnival featured a freak show which consisted of a bearded lady, a goon calling himself The Strongest Man in the World, a woman who was only two-and-a-half feet tall, and Thalidomide Man.

Born with only fleshy, boneless stumps where legs should have been, Thalidomide Man walked around on his larger-than-average hands, which he protected with thick, heavy gloves. Upon his back he kept a quiver filled not with arrows but little hand-carved figures: horses, soldiers, tiny dolls, and a small batch of gourd-shaped figures that had only stumps for legs, incredibly long arms, and almost ridiculously large hands. He joked with passersby that these last figures were "cartoon versions of myself—or the way a lot of people see me." Why a *cartoon* version of himself? "Because," he'd said to Lucy, "I wanted to work for Disney once, but they never took to the idea of an animated character named Dickey Dildo. Life is so unfair."

He'd given Sarah one of each figure he carried in his quiver, but the one she loved the most was the gourd-shaped carving with the long arms and large hands that was supposed to be the Thalidomide Man.

"It's Misserhands," she said, proud to have named it.

"Take good care of him," said Thalidomide Man, "and he'll take care of you."

From that day on, whenever Lucy and Eric had taken her to a carnival, Sarah would inevitably ask where "Mr. Hands" was, thinking that they were bound to run into Thalidomide Man again.

Regardless of never having seen him again, Sarah always carried her little carved Mr. Hands with her at all times whenever she went out. "Mr. Hands is good luck," she'd say. "He won't *ever* let anything happen to me."

That figure was the thing Lucy had found the night her daughter vanished forever. It had been covered by mud a few feet from where Sarah's first shoe was found. The figure—like all the other items of Sarah's found that night—had been spattered with blood.

Lucy never reported finding it to the police or FBI, nor did she tell anyone else—even Eric, her husband of almost ten years—that she had it.

And she never washed the blood from its body. Somehow, she came to believe (with more than a little help from her ever-present friend, Crown Royal Scotch) that because the figure had part of Sarah on it, maybe Mr. Hands was watching over her, wherever she was, and doing his best to keep her safe.

She thought then of her secret room back at the house, the one where she kept all the clippings taped to the walls. Newspaper and magazine stories detailing parents who had brutally killed their children, or tortured them, or raped and mutilated them, a shrine to the monsters of this world. She had begun collecting them a few months after Sarah's disappearance, much to Eric's dismay. At first there had only been a small file filled with the stories, but as the months went on, she became obsessed by the sheer amount of stories detailing the abuse, neglect, and murder of children. She'd even gone so far as to do some math and was sickened to discover that at least five children were murdered or found murdered every month.

And that was just from the stories in the Ohio papers.

That's how she'd had the information about Tim Beals so readily available to her. She had read each story taped to her walls so many times that she had the facts in at least seventy different cases memorized; the age of the children, the parents, the method of the child's abuse and/or death, and the punishment bestowed—or, in too many cases, *not* bestowed—on the killers, abusers, torturers, and rapists.

Knowing full well that all of that didn't even take into account the number of cases that were never reported, the bodies that were never discovered, or the fates suffered by the little ones like Sarah who'd been snatched away by one of the countless filthy monsters out there.

It was a fucking miserable world. She often wondered why she bothered sticking around.

She thought of the hand-carved figure Thalidomide Man had given to Sarah.

(*"It's Misserhands!"*)

Now that figure was all she had left to remind her that she once had a family.

That, and her memories: of a family that now could never be, of a daughter gone forever, of a husband now living apart from her in another city because he could no longer stand to be around her bitterness, anger, and never-ending grief. "We have to move on, honey," he'd said a few days before moving out. "And you won't. I miss her, too, and the thought of what might have happened to her makes me sick, but we can't spend the rest of our lives cut off from the world, moaning and groaning over our loss. And drinking won't help bring her back. It only makes you ugly."

Right. Very practical, was Eric. Like losing his daughter to some monster was no different from losing money on a bad stock investment—but, of course, Eric never made any bad investments, which is why Lucy was left so well-off in the divorce settlement. If she were careful, frugal, she could afford to never work again.

Guilt money, that's what his generous settlement amounted to.

She never touched it unless she had to.

After leaving the meeting, Lucy stopped off for a few drinks at some dive between Heath and Cedar Hill, and those few drinks turned into a few more, then one more, then one for the road.

She was quite drunk by the time she got behind the wheel of her car.

And didn't give a tinker's damn about it.

It was a little after nine P.M. The late September weather had taken one of its many unexpected turns ("If you don't like the weather in Ohio, come back in twenty minutes," as the saying went) and what had been a balmy, pleasant evening was now gearing up for a strong storm. The rain was already getting fairly heavy and flashes of lightning could be seen in the distance. The low rumbles of thunder, like the growl of a starved beast creeping stealthily up behind you, were getting louder and more threatening.

She had maybe fifteen minutes before things really ripped loose.

Since early afternoon, a front of cold air nearly five hundred miles long had been pushing its way down from Canada and crawling its way across several regions of the Midwest that had, until this evening, been dry for this time of year. As the front moved into Ohio, rising air began picking up particles of dirt and sections of small, fallen branches, eventually creating a spiraling vortex of debris that rose churning into the night air. As the front moved closer to central Ohio, it grew in intensity, picking up yet more of nature's debris and feeding on itself until it formed a massive, whistling, rolling wall that mounted to a height of four thousand feet. On the ground, visibility was decreased to less than half a mile.

This was what greeted Lucy as she left the bar and ran, stumbling and cursing, to her car.

As it bulldozed forward, the cold front drove itself like a spike into the remaining dry air. As they collided, the air masses of differing densities struggled to overpower one another. This disturbance caused a massive low-pressure system to form, wheeling counterclockwise past most of the center of the state. Ultimately, the warmer air rising from the ground penetrated the colder mass above, boiling into towering cumulonimbus clouds that rose taller and wider until they appeared to be dark angry mountains against the sky, as large as Everest but not quite as friendly looking. The great mountain chain of clouds flattened against the tropopause, spreading out and breaking up into a series of massive, anvil-shaped thunderheads.

As the storm matured and gathered strength, it separated into several furious cells that moved together as a disorganized and unfocused yet single unit: mature cells forming at the storm's center, with newer ones developing on the periphery. In the cells that approached Licking County, the anvil-shaped top of one of the cells began to bulge upward, creating what meteorologists would, the following morning, refer to as an "overshoot"—an augury of sorts, an indication that the rising torrents of air at the storm's center had become so powerful so quickly that they had broken through the tropopause and moved into the stratosphere. On the underside of the storm, ugly, bulging, pulsating pouches appeared, bellwethers for massive, heavy rainfall and damaging hail, possibly even windbursts or tornadoes.

Massive cells of rain were hovering over the county, evaporating as quickly as they fell, blasting the area with localized microbursts that uprooted small trees and peeled shingles from roofs still sporting them. Hailstones spilled from the sky, shattering windows and pounding dents into the hoods of automobiles. Drivers on their way home from work had to pull over because visibility was reduced to damn near nothing, and some had to throw themselves prone across the car seats when their windshields shattered.

As the world exploded in bursts of lightning and screaming wind and flying debris, Lucy drove on, taking almost no notice. The weather seemed to have kept everyone but her inside; she hadn't passed another car since pulling out of the bar's parking lot, which was a blessing because she crossed the center line three times in her first five minutes on the road. *Probably should have eaten something earlier,* she thought. No matter. If she ran off the road and wrapped her car around a tree, she might cheer in the moments before death.

The world was too full of monsters for her taste.

By the time she pulled up to the stoplight by the entrance to Moundbuilders Park, the booze buzz had kicked into full gear, and the storm was practically right on top of her. Even sober, Lucy hated driving through rainstorms. You could never tell what might jump out into the middle of the road.

So she sat at the stoplight, hoping a police car didn't happen by and trying not to nod off while waiting for the green.

She rubbed her eyes as she at last took full notice of the monstrous storm falling down like a curse from heaven—*Jesus,* the wind suddenly sounded like the way she imagined Sarah must have screamed at the hands of the monster who took her away.

A sputtering strobe of light from above illuminated the large sculpture just beyond the closed entrance gates to the park; it was so bright, in fact, that Lucy thought it looked something like a spotlight designed to draw her attention to it.

The piece, carved from a series of stones, was entitled *Things Left Behind* and had been commissioned from a Cincinnati artist by the Cedar Hill city council to memorialize the victims of a mass shooting some fifteen years ago. A kid named Andy Something-or-Other had gone nuts one July Fourth and mowed down over thirty people, many of them right here in

Moundbuilders Park. The artist had chosen to memorialize the victims by carving rows upon rows of faces into the gigantic circular stones, then setting the rows one on top of the other, creating a crowded stack of faces that went around and around and around. Depending on your mood, the faces looked either cherubic or shroudlike, sometimes a disturbing combination of both. The artist claimed that by walking around the piece—which stood well over twelve feet high and was hollow in the center, like a gigantic candle holder—that one would feel the lasting effects of the "cycle of suffering." Almost everyone praised it as brilliant. Lucy thought it was pretentious bullshit, but kept that opinion to herself.

But now . . .

Now, in the jagged, stroboscopic lightning, sheened in rain and covered with dead, drenched, wind-blown leaves that obscured many of the faces' features, she found something sadly compelling about it.

She pulled over to the side of the road and sat staring at it. She had no idea how long she stared, only that something about it was so mesmerizing that she couldn't turn away. It were as if something from deep inside the sculpture were reaching out to her, calling to her, *begging* her to come closer, closer, closer. . . .

CHAPTER THREE

The trucker dropped off Ronnie in Heath, on the outskirts of Cedar Hill, wishing him luck and driving off with a friendly wave. At first, stranding by the side of the road, Ronnie felt a twinge of panic, wondering if he'd be able to thumb a ride into Cedar Hill or if he'd have to walk over to the Southgate Shopping Center and call for a cab.

The years on the run had taught Ronnie many important lessons in survival, one of the most important being that when you're not sure whether to stay put or move, the best thing is to move.

So he turned, found the silver thread only he could sense, and began walking toward Cedar Hill.

The walk didn't take nearly as long as he'd feared—just under forty-five minutes—and he found himself in Cedar Hill proper when he realized he was on Eleventh Street and White's Field was to his left. But instead of continuing uphill on Eleventh, he backtracked half a block to the intersection of Union Street and West Main, turned left, and started toward downtown. He didn't know why he was going this way, only that the thrumming in the silver thread became stronger as he did so.

He tried not to look too closely at the cheerless houses that sat along the street; tried not to count how many of them were in need of new paint, or roof repair, or repairs to windows, front porches, doors, and—in one case—all the wood surrounding the front window. Rolls of insulation were piled up next to the exposed area, and something—a dog or cat, or so Ronnie hoped—had torn through the protective plastic covering and yanked large pink chunks of the material out into the yard. Recent rains had turned it into soggy cotton candy. He hoped none of the children in the neighborhood had actually *thought* it was cotton candy and eaten the material.

A few houses farther down the street, an old, decrepit-looking dog raised its head from where it had been resting on the arm of a discarded sofa on the curb. It blinked a pair of nearly white eyes in Ronnie's direction and growled, then went back to its nap.

Children in dirty clothes playing in dirtier front yards with broken toys stopped their activity to watch in silence as Ronnie walked by.

He was *really* starting to wish he'd gone another direction.

In every city in every state, there are always one or two particular sections of town that never change, regardless of how fast or deliberate the march of progress affects everything around them. In Cedar Hill those two sections were this strip of houses along West Main Street, and the area known as "Coffin County" just over the East Main Street Bridge. Oh, the faces might have changed, the cars parked in front of the houses or in the yards might be different, but one thing remained constant: the hopelessness that hung over every house like a shroud.

As a child it had made no sense to Ronnie. The few people he'd known who'd lived on West Main or in Coffin County weren't lazy or ignorant; they were hardworking people who did their best to take care of their families and maybe get ahead a little . . . but somehow the "getting ahead" part never seemed to become a reality. Sometimes people were laid off and had to apply for food stamps; sometimes they were hurt on the job—nothing crippling, but enough to keep them off work longer than the unemployment would pay for—and they'd have to apply for further government assistance; and sometimes people simply lost their jobs and their luck ran out faster than the money. Oh, sure, there were people who were just irresponsible drunks who somehow could muster enough brains to find a way to take advantage of the system, but most weren't. But it didn't stop this area from garnering the nickname "Welfare Row."

It made Ronnie sad, and he didn't want to feel sad right now. He had to stay focused on the thread and the lady who would be waiting at the end of it and the (*pleaseGod, pleasepleasePLEASE*) little girl who would be with her.

He left Welfare Row and continued on, passing the library, a flower shop, a pool hall, a bar called the Wagon Wheel, the big faded blue building that housed the offices of the *Cedar Hill Ally*, and the Sparta Restaurant (he thought about going in for a cheeseburger—the Sparta made the best cheeseburgers in the world—but knew he couldn't, despite being hungry).

He slowed down as he passed a sign taped to the inside window of a card store: LAST WEEKEND! THE LAND OF LEGEND FESTIVAL AND CARNIVAL! BRING THE FAMILY! RIDES! GAMES! LIVE MUSIC! AND GREAT FOOD!

As he stood staring at the sign, he felt the silver thread pull taut once again, and vibrate so violently he could feel it all the way to the center of his bones.

—Suzanne?

Right here, Ronnie.

—Do you think that's it? I think that must be it.

I wouldn't be surprised in the least. Look—you're not that far from it. North Cedar Street. Do you know where on North Cedar?

—It ain't really *on* North Cedar. There's a big field where they set it up every year.

The more he thought about it, the more it felt right; and the more it felt right, the less pressure he felt around his center from the silver thread.

—I'm right, Suzanne. I know I am.

Well, then, what are we waiting for?

—I want to hear it from him.

Really?

—Yeah, I do.

Silence for several moments, and Ronnie began to wonder if Suzanne had gone away, but then she said, *I'll go get him.*

This time Ronnie *felt* as well as heard the silence, and knew that Suzanne was gone for the moment, and while he could have used the time to get a head start on his walk to North Cedar Street, he instead found a nearby bench and sat down for a few moments, not really admitting to himself until this moment how *tired* he was.

Looking around to make sure there were no police

cars cruising the downtown square, he sat forward, propped his elbows on his knees, and held his head in his hands. He just needed a minute or two to rest, to calm down, to settle himself, then everything would be okay.

He hoped.

He closed his eyes for a moment, and no sooner than he did so he found himself back in the motel room in Kentucky, a minute or so before he came awake with the sick realization that he'd made a terrible, awful, *horrible* mistake.

Suzanne and the other children were singing lullabies to him, telling him stories, telling him how happy they were, and Ronnie was enjoying the sound their voices made (he always enjoyed this sound, all of their voices merging into one), when he became aware that there was something *different* about their voices, something new, some discordance in the collective sound that hadn't been there before. He asked all of them to please *Shhh,* just for a few seconds, and one by one they began to fall silent until there was only the sound of a single, alien voice that sounded as if it were echoing to him from a great and forgotten distance.

It wasn't me you felt.

Like the others, this was child's voice, but there was something about it that sounded . . . *incomplete;* the voice of a being who hadn't yet lived long enough to discover it had a voice to use.

It wasn't me you felt.

Ronnie had reached forward with his dream hands (that's how he thought of them) and sorted through the various silver threads (every child had one that connected them to him) until he found the one belonging to this alien, incomplete voice.

The incomplete child placed a warm, loving hand on Ronnie's shoulder, a touch so sensual in its silent softness that its physical pleasure transcended the merely sexual. This incomplete child leaned forward and kissed Ronnie on the lips, long and lovingly, a kiss of gratitude from all the children Ronnie had saved from further hurting; then, with great tenderness, he cupped Ronnie's face in magical yet unformed hands and squeezed until Ronnie had no choice but to part his lips. When he did this, this nameless child breathed into his mouth an age-old breath filled with the breath of all children before and yet to come. It seeped down into Ronnie's core and spread through him like the first cool drink on a hot summer's day; an ice-bird spreading chill wings that pressed against his lungs and bones until Ronnie was flung wide open, dizzy and disoriented, seized by a whirling vortex and spun around, around, around, spiraling higher, thrust into the heart of all creation's whirling invisibilities, a creature whose puny carbon atoms and other transient substances were suddenly freed, unbound, scattered amidst the universe—yet each particle still held strong to the immeasurable, unseen thread that linked it inexorably to his soul and his consciousness; twirling fibers of light wound themselves around impossibly fragile, molecule-thin membranes of memory and moments that swam toward him like proud children coming back to shore after their very first time in the water alone, and when they reached him, when this memory of a very specific moment emerged from the sea and reached out for his hands, all of the children merged into one, giving momentary shadow and shape to the incomplete child, and Ronnie ran toward it, arms open wide, meeting the

incomplete child on windswept beaches of thought,
embracing it, accepting it, absorbing it, becoming
Many, becoming Few, becoming One, knowing, learning, feeling; his blood mingled with the incomplete
child's blood, his thoughts with its thoughts, dreams
with dreams, hopes with hopes, frustrations with frustrations, and in this mingling, in this unity, in this actu-
alization, he became lost and lonely, Ronnie feeling
himself being wrenched backward, down through the
ages, through the infinite allness of want and desire
and isolation and dreams and shames and moments of
pride and self-worth and meaning that all his actions
had been leading to, and Ronnie felt himself being
crushed under the weight of this terrible knowing, his
eyes staring toward the truth that was his soul, his whole
body becoming involved in drawing it back into him in
one breath, and in the moment before he came away
knowing what had gone wrong, in the millisecond before he found himself once again lying in a shabby bed
in an even shabbier room in a motel in Lexington, Kentucky, in that brief instant of eternity that revealed itself
to him just this once before his final metamorphosis
took place, he broke into a clammy sweat as the incomplete child made him understand: what he had sensed
so many years ago when he touched the pregnant
woman's belly was *not* the pain that would be suffered
by the incomplete child she was carrying *then,* no; what
he felt was the suffering that would be waiting for the
woman's *next* child, her daughter, the one with whom
the incomplete child had already forged a connection.

The boy who was being carried by Lucy Thompson
that day had been trying to tell Ronnie—so young
and still trying to understand his power—that he

needed to walk away, he needed to let Lucy have her boy, because that boy would grow up to be a great and watchful big brother who would be there to protect his little sister when the hurting came to try and claim her.

The incomplete child had been trying to warn Ronnie, to stop him from doing what he had done, after all.

And Ronnie came awake knowing that he'd made a horrible, unforgivable mistake.

And there was no time to waste.

Ronnie?

He jerked his head up from his hands and blinked against the daylight.

—Sorry. I'm real tired.

It's okay. He doesn't want to talk to you, Ronnie. I'm sorry.

—Did he tell you? Am I right? Is this it?

Yes, Ronnie. It is.

He heard something, felt something, in Suzanne's voice that made him anxious.

—What's wrong, Suzanne?

I don't want to tell you.

—Please.

No.

—I'll love you. That won't be any different. I'll always love you.

I'll love you, too.

Ronnie waited until, finally, Suzanne said, *He said that if anything happens to his little sister, it'll be because he wasn't there to stop it, and it'll all be your fault, Ronnie. I'm sorry, but that's what he said.*

—He said something else, didn't he?

Yes.

—Tell me, Suzanne. Please tell me.

He said that if that happens, you'll be no different from the monsters who hurt all the others. But don't you listen, Ronnie. He's upset, he's scared, and he's just looking for someone to be angry with.

Ronnie shook his head.

—Uh-uh, Suzanne. He's right.

It was a mistake, *Ronnie. Anyone can make a mistake. You were only a* little boy! *You didn't understand what was going on, what you were capable of.*

—Don't matter, Suzanne. I gotta go now. You go tell him that I'm real sorry, and that I'm gonna get to his little sister in time.

He did not even wait for Suzanne to say good-bye; he just closed off the sound of her voice and took off running. There was no room in his thoughts for anything other than finding that lady and her daughter.

The thread was choking him.

The carnival at twilight:

Wood shavings and sawdust that cling to the bottoms of shoes, neon signs that cast ghosts of random light from each booth, the colors blending to give the midway the mysterious glow of a dawn sky in another world, clusters of people moving by, some of them couples holding hands and kissing, some of them families looking harried but content, nonetheless, all of them looking in the same direction when they hear the cry of a *"We have a winner!"* from one of the game booths, followed by the ringing of a bell, then there are the children with their clown-painted faces and wide eyes glittering against the lights, smiling as they've never smiled before, the epitome of joy and innocence and wonder, as a child's face at a carnival should be, excited voices underscored by squeals of laughter in the distance and the thrumming music from a carousel. Take a deep breath, and there's the cotton candy, the popcorn, the scents of cigarettes and beer and taffy, damp earth, hot dogs, and countless exotic manures from the animals in the petting zoo. Look up, and you can see the giant Ferris wheel that stands in the center of it all, the lights decorating its spokes streaking round and round in the night like a whirling ribbon of stars come down to earth for just this night.

The air is warm, just slightly humid but not uncomfortably so.

The night is newly arrived, dark enough for the carny to rise from its depths like a phoenix.

One last hurrah before August bows to September, and summer fades away.

Carnival night.

Roll up, roll up, plunk down a quarter and try for a prize, take your sweetheart on a ride to the stars, lotsa room for the kiddies, yessir, no need to push, plenty of room, plenty of time, plenty of fun for everyone.

Roll up, roll up.

It's carny time.

And then a woman screams, and a young man who's been searching for her all day feels the silver thread around his throat tighten even more, and staggers toward the sound. . . .

For the first hour of the search, Ronnie couldn't get anywhere near Lucy, so he joined in with the dozens of other people who'd volunteered to help the police

distribute photocopied photos of Sarah and search
the immediate grounds.

Ronnie nearly wept at the sight of Sarah's face.
Whatever was happening to her right now—or whatever *might* happen to her—she did not deserve it, no
child ever did . . . but Sarah . . . Sarah was his fault, so
she was his responsibility.

"I love you, little Sarah," he whispered to the picture, folding one of the photocopies and slipping it
into his pocket.

By the time he was able to get near Lucy, he was so
scared he couldn't think straight. He ran up to her
through the people milling around her, grabbed her
by the shoulders, and—fighting back tears—asked if
there'd been any word, if Sarah had been found yet,
and when he was told by a nearby police officer to
move it along and help with the search, he squeezed
her shoulders, hoping she'd recognize him, but she
didn't, but that was all right, so he let go of her and
ran toward the next group who was getting ready to
search the areas immediately outside the festival
grounds.

It was getting dark. So dark.

Ronnie helped them search until around midnight, and then word started spreading that the police and FBI had found something; no on was sure
what, exactly, only that Mrs. Thompson was being escorted there by authorities.

The various groups of volunteers moved toward an
area at the far end of the festival grounds where trees
and other thick foliage were alive with dancing
lights—flashlights.

Ronnie felt his stomach shrink to the size of a pebble when he saw Lucy Thompson stagger out of the trees, held upright by two police officers (both women), one supporting each of Lucy's arms.

Lucy looked up at the group of volunteers once, just long enough to try to say "Thank you" to all of them, but she couldn't speak, the grief was too much, and Ronnie's chest sort of imploded on him and everything went numb.

. . . if anything happens to his little sister, it'll be because he wasn't there to stop it, and it'll all be your fault, Ronnie. . . . He said that if that happens, you'll be no different from the monsters who hurt all the others. . . .

Not saying a word to anyone, shaking his head at an offer for free coffee and sandwiches at one of the tents, not feeling the hands that pressed briefly on his shoulders ("We tried, folks, we did our best . . ."), Ronnie, now on autopilot, walked the length of the festival grounds, soon found himself back on North Cedar Street, and continued on toward downtown.

Adjusting his backpack, he tried to find some sense of Sarah around him, but the silver thread was still and slack.

. . . you'll be no different from the monsters who hurt all the others. . . .

For a few hours, he just walked, oblivious to the night, his surroundings, even to the voices of Suzanne and the others calling to him, trying to get his attention.

Eventually, realizing that he was once again walking toward the same road he'd used before, he smiled to himself as something occurred to him. But first, he had to make sure.

He found a dark stretch of road and retreated into the bushes, kneeling down and opening his backpack, rummaging around until he found the thing he hoped he still had.

He did.

Putting everything back in its place, Ronnie zipped up his backpack, slung it over his shoulder, and walked back out into the night, following the road back toward Heath just as he'd followed it coming to Cedar Hill.

He reached the place where Union Street connected to Twenty-first Street via a small side street whose name he didn't know, had never known, *would* never know, turned right, and followed it along the log fence–lined border of this end of Moundbuilders Park.

He knew exactly where he was going.

It took him less than five minutes to reach the Twenty-first Street entrance of the park using this side street, and once there, he saw what he'd come for.

The sculpture, carved from a series of stones, had been commissioned by the Cedar Hill city council to memorialize the victims of a mass shooting many years ago. A kid named Andy Something-or-Other had gone nuts one July Fourth and mowed down over thirty people, many of them right here in Moundbuilders Park. The artist had chosen to memorialize the victims by carving rows upon rows of faces into the gigantic circular stones, then setting the rows on top of each other, creating a crowded stack of faces that went around and around and around, getting a little thinner as it rose toward the top, like a stone volcano made out of stone faces.

Ronnie took a moment to study the faces.

At least none of them seemed to be in pain. That was nice.

He walked around the sculpture to see if the gaps

were as he remembered them being, and they were. A careful person could climb all the way to the top—which is exactly what he began to do.

The piece rose to nearly twelve feet from the ground, and by the time Ronnie reached the top, the cumulative effect of the past twenty or so hours hit him hard, and it was all he could do to pull himself over the rim and look down to where the small, rotting (and in some cases, desiccated) corpses of rabbits, squirrels, and something that once might have been a dog lay in the mud.

He reached over, grabbed two gaps on the inside of the piece, and—with the very last of his strength—flipped himself over the edge.

It didn't even hurt when he landed in the mud and muck and corpses. Not one little bit. *Stank,* though; stank something awful . . . but you couldn't smell it from outside. That was good.

He opened his backpack and dumped everything out, found the flashlight, turned it on, and then carefully removed the photocopied photo of Sarah Thompson from his pocket, unfolded it, and lay it atop the rest of the contents of his pack, using a couple of small rocks and the skulls from a squirrel and a rabbit to hold down the corners.

He wanted to make certain that Sarah's face would be the last thing he ever saw.

  . . . you'll be no different from the monsters who hurt all the others. . . .

After a few minutes—or it might have been a few hours, he couldn't tell and didn't care—Ronnie reached into the pile of items from his pack and dug out the knife. It wasn't a particularly *dangerous* knife, just an old pocketknife . . . but it was sharp. He always made sure of that. Three-inch blade, nice and sharp.

He unfolded it and ran it along his thumb. He didn't feel any sharp pain—in fact, he didn't feel any pain at all—but he saw the cut, and he saw the blood, and that was all he needed.

"I'm so sorry, Sarah," he said to the picture, tracing his thumb over her smile and leaving a smear of blood to mark its route. "I really tried. I love you, okay? I wouldn'ta tried if I didn't love you."

Some water began dripping down onto the photo, and at first Ronnie was afraid that he'd started to cry, but then looked up and saw that it was sprinkling; he took his jacket from the pile and threw it over his head and shoulders and leaned over the photo like a human tent. He would keep her dry and safe and warm. He could do that.

After.

So he took a deep breath, rolled up his sleeves, inserted the tip of the knife at the base of his left wrist, and drew it as far up the length of his arm as he could before the pain registered. Biting down on his lip to keep from screaming, he waited until the pain began to ebb, then repeated the process on his right arm—albeit not quite as deep (but deep enough, as it turned out).

Only then did he lie on his side—taking care to keep the jacket tent in place so Sarah wouldn't get wet—and allow himself to smile.

"It's okay now," he whispered to her. "I'm not no monster, Sarah. I love you, okay?"

Ronnie? It was Suzanne's voice.

—Hey'ya . . .

Why did you do it?

—Because I failed.

Oh, Ronnie. . . .

—Because he's right. I'm no different.

But you are. *You always have been. There's still time, you can still—*

—Nah. Time's up, Suzanne. I think maybe it always was. Still love me?

Of course. She sounded sad.

—Don't be sad. I'll see you soon.

That's just it, Ronnie . . . you won't. And we were all hoping that you'd tell us some stories and we could sing songs together and—

—What?

But there was no reply at all.

So there, in the rain, in the silence from within and without, with only the photocopied picture of a little girl he'd failed to save, Ronald James Williamson died, thinking himself a monster and wishing there had been some way he could have taken the other monsters with him. . . .

CHAPTER FOUR

Sometime in there—the buzz getting so strong it nearly drowned out the thunder—Lucy Thompson reached into her purse and pulled out Mr. Hands, tightly holding him in her grip, aware of the caked blood and mud, now flaking away, that fell into her palms or attached itself to her fingers.

Sometime in there she started weeping for Sarah, both surprised and relieved that she could still find it in her to mourn the loss of what might have been.

And sometime in there her fury awoke from its dark hiding place in the center of her mind, threw back the covers with a snarl, turned on the lights, and decided it was time to *do something*.

And somewhere in there the spirit of Ronald James Williamson, having been left, abandoned, in the place where his body died, felt the silver thread of long-ago pull taut once again.

Lucy threw open the car door and stumbled out into the incredible storm, falling twice before she reached the gate. The rain instantly turned her hair to dead weight, heavy ice hanging in her eyes, and the merciless wind turned each drenched strand into a painful whip against her face.

She didn't care.

She climbed over the fence and walked toward the sculpture.

Let the dead rest with the dead, she thought.

Then she stood before the sculpture. She'd forgotten about the empty spaces the artist had incorporated into the piece, small, gaping holes between some of the faces— *"Lost fragments of time they never lived to see,"* he'd explained, further asserting his pretentiousness. She realized, looking at the way the holes formed patterns all the way to the top, that a person could climb twelve feet to the opening, it if they so desired.

And she did. Drunk, crying, angry, and unsteady as hell, she was going to climb the damned thing and give Mr. Hands to the dead.

To her surprise, she only slipped a couple of times on the way up.

She looked down into the pit that was the center of the piece. Already it was filling with water and mud and dead leaves . . . she could even spot the remains of small, dead animals—birds, rats, squirrels, it seemed, pieces of tiny skeletons . . . It was a testament to death, this thing was.

She got a good grip on the rim of the piece with her left hand, then held out her right hand but did not yet open it.

Jesus Christ, what was she doing? Why couldn't she get past this? Why was it so impossible to get past the grief and go on with her life? Why couldn't she just pay the fine and go home?

Because, said a voice somewhere within and without her. *Because she had to have suffered horribly at the hands of the monster. And as much as you try, you can't keep yourself from imagining the depravities the monster must have inflicted upon her. You can't not imagine her screams, her crying "Mommy, Mommy, help," or "Please, mister, stop, it hurts, it hurts, ithurtsithurtsithurts!"*

Because monsters like that must be punished, and without fury, there can be no proper punishment.

Another burst of lightning and ear-splitting thunder, and the wind blew her hair straight back as the rain cleansed the mud from her face.

"You dirty, filthy fuck!" she screamed against the roar of the storm. "Goddamn you to hell for what you did to her! *Goddamn you!* I'd kill you myself if I could . . . *I'd kill you myself if I could!"*

She opened her fist and let Mr. Hands enjoy the storm.

"I wish you could have protected her," said Lucy. "I wish you could have bitten the head off the fucker who took her from me."

She brought the figure to her lips and kissed it, then dropped it into the pit.

"I wish you could avenge them all. Good-bye, Mr. Hands."

Then a powerful gust of wind caught her by surprise and she slipped, tried to regain her footing, hit a slick patch of stone, and fell to the ground. She landed in a puddle of mud that was deep enough to prevent any serious injury but not so deep as to prevent her back and legs from screaming in pain.

She tried to stand but couldn't.

Able to see only by the flashes of lightning, she half stumbled, half crawled toward the gate.

Somewhere in there she was able to stand again, and staggered the rest of the way to her car.

She got inside, slammed the door closed, and immediately lay down across the front seat.

A few seconds later, she passed out.

But not before muttering to herself, as if in prayer, "Kill them all if I could. Filthy fucking monsters. All of them . . ."

Lucy Thompson lay in her car, unconscious, shuddering and jerking in the grip of a nightmare.

Outside, hidden by the darkness and baptized by the storm, a confluence began in a damned place where grief and rage meet and say *No more*.

Within the pit of the sculpture, something began to form around the carved figure of Mr. Hands. A soupy, shapeless pool at first, with no discernable hint of structure—bits of dead leaves, pieces of tree bark, pebbles and exposed bones of dead birds and squirrels mixing with the mud and water—but there was life there, pulsating like a spurting heart suddenly torn from a chest, and it continued to grow as the ground drank in the essence of Sarah, hidden in her blood, which still clung to Mr. Hands's body, as he slowly came into awareness, developing senses left for him by others who had suffered the fate of Sarah, the blood of children long dead and forgotten whose bodies might never be found, or whose place of torture and death was never known; their blood and tears and fear finding its way into the earth, and Mr. Hands drank it all in, drawing his energy from the death all around him, beneath him in the ground, trapped in the bits of consciousness that drifted through the air around him.

In her car, Lucy's thrashing began to subside. . . .

And the mortal remains of Ronald James Williamson, now over a decade under the mud and rot and wetness of the seasons, buried so far down that not even the small animals could dig far enough to get to his meat, these remains gave themselves over to the figure above, offering bones and remaining flesh and tissue and sinew and cartilage and what veins remained as Mr. Hands drank in the blood that Ronnie had allowed to soak the ground around him. . . .

And in her car, Lucy shuddered once more, for an instant remembering the face of a young man who'd grabbed her shoulders and asked nearly in tears if Sarah had been found yet. . . .

And Mr. Hands felt his limbs growing, unfurling into life, accepting all that Ronnie had to offer him, all the strength, all the power, all the *sight* of the hurting, and Mr. Hands took in his first sentient breath, sucking in the pain and anger and grief like a vacuum taking in dust; moving, yes, he was moving now, growing, he could feel the sensations of existence as he began to move his body, intermingling his being with the essence and blood of what the dead once carried with them, tasting the pain still so strong in those who were left behind, and he turned his head and opened his cold, black eyes to gaze upon the beauty of his form, the glory of his hideousness, and something more fluttered to life in his center as he absorbed the remains of every once-living thing that shared the wet pit with him. . . .

Lucy's body began to relax, the shudders growing less constant, the jerking gone. . . .

And in the orgy of his terrible birth Mr. Hands let forth a scream that was the cry of a million babies doused in gasoline and set aflame, and then, as the storm was reaching its peak, he thrust up one of his huge hands, its tree limb–sized fingers grabbing the upper edge of the rim around the pit. . . .

And in a series of rain-soaked, exploding-light flashes, Mr. Hands pulled himself upward and out of the pit. One hand shot upward, covered in vines and dripping weeds that looked more like veins; then the next hand, pulling upward toward the strobing light, its fingers unfurling in glory like the wings of a butterfly emerging from its cocoon, followed by his massive, skull-like head, wreathed in worms and dead spiders; and finally his wide, rounded torso arose and he burst fully from his place of birth and stood upon his hands, towering nearly three feet over the sculpture, and sloughed the water and soaked earth from his leg stumps like a snake shedding its skin.

His long, lethal fingers rhythmically clawed the wet ground as they gained strength.

He smelled the storm and the sky; it was pure ether to his awakening senses, filling him with life, making him sick with pleasure.

His limbs pumped with blood, juicing with exhilaration.

And he laughed.

It was a wet sound, loud, choked, filled with dirt and bile. . . .

Lucy lay very still now, peaceful in her car, and no longer heard the screams of her daughter; instead there was a voice, strong and soothing, that made her feel safe, and this voice said to her: *Shall there be mercy, then?*

And, in peaceful sleep, she answered: *Not for the likes of monsters like them, no.*

Under no circumstances?

Absolutely not. Anyone who would do such a thing doesn't deserve it.

So, then . . . under no circumstances? asked the part of Mr. Hands where Ronnie and his children were settling in, happy at last to be together, but wanting to make absolutely sure.

Goddamn right, under no circumstances, replied Lucy.

So be it, said Mr. Hands.

There was an unbelievably powerful rumbling in the night that many people who lived near the park believed to be merely another strong burst of thunder.

Mr. Hands ran off into the storm and darkness, knocking down a few of the smaller park trees on his way.

Joyous; wrathful.

Enraged; exultant.

The bittersweet taste of human terror on his tongue.

It was time to begin what she had brought him here to do.

Fourteen-and-a-half miles away, just across the street from St. Francis De Sales Church on Granville Street, in a large but still cramped garage behind the Spencer Halfway House, Timothy Beals, occupying his time by trying to repair an old radio with one of the house supervisors, was beginning the last ninety minutes of his life.

INTERLUDE
The Hangman, 1 A.M.

Henry waited in the silence for someone to say something; when no one did, he finished off his coffee, set the cup on the bar, wiped his mouth with his napkin, and said, "*That's* the part where most of the doctors whip out the prescriptions pads, by the way."

"Yeah, I can see that," said Jackson. "By the way, the fellow you mentioned, Thalidomide Man. We know him."

Henry's mouth actually fell open a little. "You're kidding?"

The Reverend shook his head. "Nope. His name is Linus—*not* after the *Peanuts* character, mind you."

"After the character Humphrey Bogart played in *Sabrina*, with Audrey Hepburn," said Grant. "He'll lecture you for ten minutes if you don't understand that."

Henry stared at all of them for several moments. "How do you know him?"

"He's a regular at the open shelter," said the Reverend. "I've known him for . . . oh, I'd say at least ten years."

"Eight for me," said Jackson.

Grant nodded. "Same for me."

Henry's eyes grew wide. "Is he still alive?"

"I'd say 'and kicking,' but that would be in questionable taste," replied the Reverend.

"Linus'd laugh at it," said Grant.

"Yes," said the Reverend, "and then make me suffer for it. No thank you." He turned back toward Henry. "Why the interest in Linus? You actually damn near jumped off your stool when we said this."

"No . . . no reason, really. It'd . . . it'd just be nice to actually meet someone from this story," said Henry.

The Reverend nodded his head, saying nothing, only casting a quick glance at both Grant and Jackson. "Yes, I imagine that it would—but come, dear fellow. We've once again interrupted your story for no good reason. Please continue."

Henry saw Grant glance once again at the long knickknack shelf above the bar. "What is it?"

Grant turned. "Beg pardon?"

"When you guys started talking about Linus, you looked at something on that shelf. What were you looking at?"

The Reverend placed a gentle hand on Henry's forearm. "One story at a time, okay?"

Henry nodded. "Okay . . . but you guys have to tell me at least *one* of the stories behind something on that shelf or I'm gonna be mad."

The three of them looked at Henry.

"You feeling any better yet?" asked Grant.

"A little. Maybe. I don't know," said Henry.

"Well, I'll tell you what," said Grant. "You finish your story and help the rest of us clean up after last call, and you pick any item up here and ask us about the story behind it."

Jackson coughed. "What's this 'help the rest of *us* clean up' shit?"

Grant smiled. "No such thing as a free lunch, Sheriff."

Jackson sighed. "Fine, I'll help." Then, to Henry: "So, what happens next?

Henry got a refill of coffee and asked for more popcorn. "Well, Timothy Beals . . ."

PART THREE

THE MOUNT OF MERCURY

"Every thought and its resultant action should be judged by what it is able to draw from suffering. Despite my dislike of it, suffering is a fact."

—Albert Camus, *Notebook IV*,
January 1942–September 1945

"I saw the hideous phantasm . . ."

—Mary Shelley, *Frankenstein*

CHAPTER ONE

Timothy Beals was still looking for the damned Phillips head screwdriver when Steve Morse—one of three fulltime supervisors at the Spencer Halfway House—looked across the worktable and said, "Okay, that's it for me. It's starting to sound too damned nasty out there."

Tim looked over his shoulder to the only window in the garage and saw that the storm was turning into one mother of a *whompbompbaloobomp,* as Little Richard might say. He sighed, rubbed his eyes, and looked back to Morse.

"Can I just find the screwdriver and get the casing put back on this thing?"

"You know the rules, Tim."

"Yeah, yeah, *'Residents must be accompanied by a supervisor after normal curfew hours,'* cha-cha-cha. Look, you can stand right at the sink and keep an eye on me from the kitchen window. It's not like there's a second door I can sneak out of. Besides, you think I'd try taking off in *this* burg after all the flattering press I've gotten the last couple months?"

"You might. People here have tried dumber things."

Tim located the Phillips head, proudly displaying his triumph to Morse. "Steve, I'm asking . . . please? Working out here on all this busted crap is the only real enjoyment I get out of the day."

"Me and my sparkling personality will try not to take that personally."

Tim reached across the worktable and gently gripped Morse's shoulder. "Look, Steve, I'm asking you for ten minutes out here by myself, okay? I'm not gonna hang myself or drive a screwdriver through my eye into my brain or manufacture a nuclear device. It's just that . . . look, since I got out I haven't had any time to myself except upstairs at lights-out. Then I just lay there and stare at the ceiling and think about . . . a lot of different things, ya know?"

Morse shook his head. "No, I don't. You haven't exactly been the chattiest new resident we've had here since your arrival."

Tim was looking down at the newly repaired radio, waiting for its protective casing. "Mostly I think about what a . . . a puddle of *dog puke* I was. I think back on that night with Carol and . . . and I keep hoping that the years will have muddled some of the details, but they never do. I remember everything that happened as clearly as if it'd happened yesterday." He wiped something from one of his eyes. "Christ, Steve, I can't even use being stoned as an excuse. *I killed my daughter.* It's that simple. I kicked her until I ruptured her pancreas and then shut her in her room and went back to partying and screwing while she was laying up there in . . . in pain I can't even begin to imagine. I mean, when the Joy-Boy Brigade gang-banged my ass in prison—to this day, I'm not sure why they didn't just kill me—anyway, I thought that was the worst pain anyone could ever endure . . . but from everything I've read about what happens to a person with a ruptured pancreas, what I felt when they were buttbuddying me a wider asshole was *nothing* compared to what Carol went through.

"Ah, *hell*, Steve, I think about the look on her face when she came in asking me to help—'I sick, Daddy, I made a mess, I sorry'—and the way I was too . . ." He shook his head. "I look back on the miserable piece of shit I was back then and *I* want to kill him! She had the greatest little laugh. You should've heard her. And I killed her—call it involuntary or not, I did it, and I'm more sorry than I can ever make anyone understand and I miss her and it hurts and makes me sick and every day I have to go *out there* and see the disgust and hatred on peoples' faces when they realize who I am and . . . and the thing I look most forward to is sitting out here for two or three hours every evening and fixing broken things. Can you understand that, Steve? At least here, with these tools in my hands, I can *fix*, I can repair, make right again. It helps me to face the next day, ya know? I can't tell you if I'm a good person or one of the bad guys, but, man, I *need* this, okay?"

Morse stared at him for a moment, silent and unmoving until a deafening crack of thunder and a jagged flash of lightning broke the spell.

"Ten minutes?"

Tim nodded his head. "I promise I won't rat you out to the rest of the staff."

"Or construct a nuclear device?"

"The plutonium I ordered hasn't arrived yet."

Morse rose from his metal stool and grinned. "Okay, ten minutes—but I'll be clocking your ass, so no more, understand?"

"I really appreciate it."

"I know." He stared at Tim a moment, then said, "Would it kill you to say any of that stuff at one of the nightly meetings?"

A shrug. "I don't know. I guess I'm still worried about being judged." He looked Morse straight in the eye and said, "What about you, Steve? What's your opinion of me?"

"I don't have one."

"Don't lie to me. I've seen that picture of your two little girls that's on your desk. As a parent you have to have an opinion about what I did."

"If I answer it, there's no way you're not gonna take it personally."

"Try me. I might surprise you."

Morse thought about it for another second, then said, "Do I have an opinion about what you did? Sure, I've got an opinion about that. It was a hideous, violent, monstrous act of brutality against a defenseless child, and it makes me sick, too, thinking about what she went through during those twelve hours she was left locked in her room. What you *did* makes me depressed right down to the bottom of my spirit . . . but we're talking about the *act* here. You're not the same man now that you were then. As a person, I don't judge you for what you did. It's taken me a lot of years to get that point, and I never wander too far off that particular highway. So I have no opinion about you as a person one way or the other. But what does that matter? You've already condemned yourself, pal. What can any of the other residents do to you?"

"Take away my oatmeal privileges for a week. Then I would truly have no reason to go on."

Morse laughed as he opened the door and steadied himself against the wind and rain. "You are so full of it."

"Yeah, I get a lot of complaints about that."

Then Morse closed the door and Tim was alone.

It was bliss.

And so Timothy Beals—gently, with great concentration and even greater skill—made a last check of the repairs to the radio and replaced it in its protective casing.

Then he sat there and looked at his handiwork.

After a few moments he unwound the radio's electrical cord and plugged it in to an outlet under the table, switched on the power, then turned the radio's knob as various layers of static entered the room. It took almost a full trip around the dial before he picked up an oldies station: the 5 Stairsteps singing, "Ooh, Child."

The sad irony of the first verse was not lost on him; nonetheless, he was surprised to feel a swelling in his throat and a soft, persistent burning behind his eyes.

Carol had loved this song. He remembered the way she used to sing herself to sleep with it most nights. Seemed she used to do everything for herself or by herself. Four years old going on thirty-six.

He reached over and snapped off the radio, then jerked the plug from the outlet.

For some ooh-children, things never did get easier.

People like him made sure of that.

Take it easy, bud, he thought. *Just think about what you've accomplished today.*

He stared at the repaired radio, then slowly, almost reverently, laid his hands on it, feeling its solidness, its worth, and knowing that it was *he* who had given it back its purpose.

Maybe, in a way, this was what redemption was all about: not condemning yourself for past sins but learning to live with them, with the guilt and shame and hurt and pitiless bouts of self-loathing, while trying to get on with the business of living, contributing what little you could to make things easier for those who shared the planet with you; maybe, in some obscure way that only heaven fully comprehended, these little things, these tiny kindnesses and acts of reparation, maybe they, bit by bit, one dark spot at a time, balanced out the shadow of your sin, whatever it might be.

At times like this, Timothy could almost believe in the love of God, could almost believe in mercy and forgiveness.

Almost.

His reverie was broken by another thunderclap and the loud, persistent scritching noise made by the branches of the cedar tree outside as the high winds bent them down against the metal roof of the garage.

Tim looked out the window and saw the silhouette of Morse at the kitchen sink. Doubting the supervisor would see it, he waved.

The silhouette did not wave back but instead moved away from the window, in the direction of the downstairs bathroom.

Told you that second can of Pepsi'd make your bladder madder, thought Tim.

He busied himself with straightening up his work area in preparation for tomorrow night when he was going to tackle a troublesome portable color television set. If prison had left him with nothing else, it had at least taught him some useful skills.

Like how to bleed rectally, he thought, not without a touch a bitterness.

Then again, you don't really deserve anything better, do you?

I sick, Daddy. . . .

The sound of the branches against the roof was getting a lot louder now, nagging and rhythmic.

Daddy, Daddy, I sick, Daddy. . . . Daddy, Daddy, I sick. . . .

Time to pack it up and go beddy-bye.

He looked once more upon the repaired radio (which belonged to his parole officer, for whom Timothy was fixing it as a favor) and felt a sense of pride and accomplishment.

A good day's work. Yessir.

And with a heart as close to peaceful as anything he'd known for the last thirteen years, Timothy Beals climbed down off his stool, stretched his back, groaned, and was reaching for the light switch when half the roof was torn off the garage.

At first he couldn't get his head wrapped around what he was seeing—it looked too much like something from a Saturday morning cartoon, the metal just *peeling* back like the lid on a can of tuna—but after a second or two, after the coldness and violence of the rain drenched his face and torso with all the gentility of shattered glass, he rallied himself to get the hell out of there and back to the house because any wind strong enough to rip half the roof from a garage could sure as hell lift a man off his feet and make him do a Dorothy-into-Oz, so he grabbed his coat and started for the door. . . .

And the roof peeled back a little farther, seeming to follow his retreating steps. . . .

And then the moon, so cold and gray, dropped from its place in the storm-shrouded sky and landed right outside.

The *suddenness* with which the thing appeared, coupled with its size, caused Tim to stumble, but not fall. *Christ on the cross,* but it looked like those old storybook drawings of the Man in the Moon, only in those drawings he was smiling and friendly, his face so kind and gentle, not like this. *This* looked more like a skull unearthed from a concentration camp graveyard than any storybook illustration—cold, deep, dark sockets that might have been eyes but the blackness was too total to tell, and its mouth was twisted into a grimace, not a grin, and it was covered in dirt and rot and dead leaves and wriggling worms and now it was reaching . . .

A section of wall splintered outward, pulled down as easily and quickly as you might knock down a house of cards; a moment later, when the dust had been drowned by the rain or scattered by the fierce winds, Timothy Beals saw the thing in its totality.

He was aware neither of wetting himself nor of dropping to his knees like a celebrant before the image of a divine god; he was conscious only of the rain, the coldness, and the impossible thing that towered over him.

This is it, pal, right out of that damned nightmare you used to have in prison. Here it is, found you at last, your punishment; retribution in the flesh.

He stared up at the thing in wonder and awe.

There was no fear in his heart; fear was for someone who actually had a chance of survival, and Timothy Beals knew he had none.

So, drenched in freezing rain and his own fluids, Timothy spread his arms apart in awe, throwing back his head and crying out.

He might have screamed, "I'm sorry," but he couldn't hear himself.

The thing reached down for him with one of its huge hands and wrapped his torso within its quadruple-jointed fingers, slowly crushing him.

The pain brought with it a sad form of glee to Timothy's heart, for of all the punishments he'd imagined for himself, of all the tortures and degradations and countless cruelties of which he felt he was so deserving, none could compare with the exquisite agony of what gripped him now. With every stab of pain there was, in his mind, a choir of angels singing the "Hallelujah Chorus" from Handel's *Messiah*; with the snarling, power-drill sensation of every breaking rib puncturing a new organ there were celebratory candles lighted as children approached for their First Communion; and with the first trickles of blood that spluttered from his mouth, soon to become a fountain, there was the priest, covered in colorful robes, lifting the chalice skyward and intoning, "Take this, all of you, and drink from it, for this is the cup of my blood that was shed for you and all men so that you might live. . . ."

He was going to die the kind of magnificently horrible, gloriously painful death he'd often wished for himself, a death to rival that of his daughter's, filled with a suffering that dwarfed—and maybe, if there was a Divine God, canceled—her own.

For you, honey. This is for you, he thought as his body, independent from his mind, began to thrash in the thing's powerful grip.

His bowels emptied themselves of their contents, releasing liquid shit down the backs of his legs, fouling him as he wished to be fouled, a final humiliation in this life to prepare him for those awaiting him in the next.

The creature eased Timothy closer to its face.

He saw himself reflected in the obsidian pits of its eyes.

He looked so pathetic.

And that made him happy.

Then the creature, the miracle, the impossible thing, stretched out its arms, holding Timothy at a distance, and as he looked down at his executioner's body, Carol Beals's father saw retribution's torso begin to move, to ripple, its crypt-gray pallor seeming to be lit brightly from within, the blue veins underneath becoming fragments of a broken rainbow as its center became alive with shapes that appeared in bas-relief: faces, all of them, dozens, hundreds, thousands of faces, all belonging to children, all of them screaming in agony.

No! Timothy thought with what little consciousness remained him. *They shouldn't be screaming, they should rejoice! Another monster is dead and can't hurt them anymore!*

And indeed, the childrens' expressions changed from the pain of the abused to the ecstasy of the avenged as he heard, clearly, beautifully, their cries and shrieks become Handel's majestic, angelic chorus.

The creature began to pull Timothy back, closer, closer—almost there, yes, that's right, *shh,* be patient, I'll make it last—and Timothy once again, with his last burst of energy, opened his arms wide to embrace this most splendid of deaths as the creature opened the gaping maw of its mouth and the lightning crackled above and the thunder roared with the sound of cheering multitudes and then, at the moment before the creature's rot-scented mouth closed around Timothy's neck, all the sounds coalesced into one; simple, pure, untainted:

"I sick, Daddy."

Daddy's coming, thought Timothy in the last five seconds of his life. Daddy's coming. He'll make things right again, he'll repair the damage done. . . .

Daddy'll fix it.

No one was there at the park to see Mr. Hands's triumphant return.

He didn't mind.

Within him, children sang happy tunes filled with love and devotion.

He was more than happy to let them sing their praises.

The storm was beginning to die down. Soon there would be light and people and too many eyes that could see him.

So Mr. Hands gripped the sides of the sculpture at the entrance to Moundbuilders Park, gracefully swung his mighty body upward in a smooth arc, and slid back down inside the pit, making himself smaller—but not too much smaller—so as to fit inside and not be seen.

A few minutes later, the storm ceased.

Wrapped in the warmth of the childrens' cumulative essence, Mr. Hands closed his eyes and slept the sleep of the just.

CHAPTER TWO

Lucy did not so much wake up the following morning (a task that, though simple enough on the surface, proved far too complicated for someone in her condition) as she did *lurch* into consciousness.

Most mornings now there was no greeting the day for her, only a knee-jerk response to its threat: *Don't make me come in there.*

And so she sat up, rubbed her eyes, and took stock of her surroundings.

Eric's old desk. The computer monitor and keyboard. The office chair. The lamp attached to the cubby above the desk's surface, turned on, its circle of light illuminating a section of the Walls of Madness.

She was on the couch in the study.

She unsteadily rose to her feet—marveling once again how she never had a classic hangover but instead just a case of cotton-mouth compounded by the dreadful dizzies—and made her way to the light switch, flipped it, and flooded the room with brightness.

That's when she got a good look at the state of her clothes.

Torn hose, caked mud and vomit over nearly every inch of her skirt and blouse, dried leaves stuck here and there for aesthetic effect, small cuts and abrasions on her hands, arms, legs . . .

Jesus, what had happened last night?

It wasn't until she was pouring a small shot of Bailey's Irish Creme into her coffee that she remembered the police officer shaking her awake and asking what was wrong. She remembered that he didn't seem to notice the smell of liquor on her, and so she told him that she was driving home when she suddenly got sick, pulled over to get out of her car and throw up, then slipped in the mud while getting back inside. The officer bought it, then asked if she was okay to drive herself home. It took some Academy Award–worthy acting on her part, but she at last convinced him that she was sound enough in mind and body to operate an automobile. The officer and his partner followed her anyway, their cruiser idling right outside as she slipped the key into the front door, waved her thanks to them, then stumbled inside and to the couch in Eric's study.

She stood in the doorway now—freshly showered with wounds cleanly dressed—in her terry cloth bathrobe, sipping her Irish coffee and getting her bearings.

Staring at the Walls of Madness—Eric's moniker, that.

Nearly every available inch of space on three of the four walls was covered with newspaper clippings, each one detailing the disappearance, rape, murder, torture, exploitation, or mutilation of a child. Many had pictures of the crime scene. Some of them in color.

There were at least forty grainy black-and-white photographs of small, sheet-covered bodies.

Lucy knew the name and age of each pictured body, as well as those for which there were no photographs.

She scanned the various rows of stories, saying good morning to the ghosts of Heather Wilson, Daniel McKellan, Rosie and Thad Simpkins, Billy Lawrence (who'd been only eleven months old when his mother decided the best way to stop him from crying was to hold a hot iron over his mouth until he stopped), Crystal and Emily Ransom, and dozens and dozens more.

She made it a point to say good morning to each of them every day.

Just to let them know that someone remembered, someone still mourned.

Then she saw the gaping, empty space halfway down the second wall—where all the clippings about Timothy Beals and his daughter Carol had been.

She walked slowly toward the empty space, staring at the torn and wadded clippings on the floor near the base of the wall.

The warmth of the coffee in her suddenly turned to ice as she remembered climbing up the side of the sculpture, holding Mr. Hands.

A seed of fear began to sprout within her, but not any form of adult fear, mortgage, the bills, rising crime and cost of living, no; what was inside her now was akin to childhood's fear of the bogeyman lurking out there in the dark or waiting in the closet for when Mommy and Daddy shut the door and turned out the light because you just knew that's when he was going to come creeping out of the closet and get you.

This feeling, this silly childhood fear, passed after a moment. Half laughing, half snarling at herself, she wiped her forehead and whispered, "Get a grip, kiddo."

A loud knocking at the front door startled her, and she nearly dropped her coffee; as it was she managed to spill some, leaving a lovely little blotch right at the area that covered her crotch.

"Dammit!" she snapped, then made her way to the door.

Staring through the peephole, she found herself looking at the shrunken, fish-eye lens image of Detective Bill Emerson.

The childhood fear wafted through her yet again, whispering, *You're in trouble now.*

She straightened her wet hair, adjusted her robe to make sure she was fully covered, then disengaged the locks and opened the door.

"Detective Emerson."

"Miss Thompson," he replied somewhat curtly. "I'm sorry to bother you at this hour, but I need to ask you a few questions."

Saying nothing, she stepped back and gestured for Emerson to come inside. Declining her offer of coffee (she could tell he smelled the Irish Creme on her breath and must have thought, *It's not even ten in the morning yet, for chrissakes!*), the detective took a seat in the middle room and opened his notebook, then glanced up and saw the open door of the study. Trying to be as casual about it as possible, Lucy pulled the study door closed, hiding the Walls of Madness.

By now Emerson's seemingly wandering attention had spotted the gun case and the impressive variety of firepower contained within.

"Yours?" he asked.

"All of that belonged to my ex-husband's late father. He was a member of a search-and-destroy unit in Vietnam. Two tours. My ex inherited that when his father died, and when we divorced, Eric gave them to me—I guess he thought they didn't convey the proper image for a new partner in a prominent financial consultancy firm. Stare all you want—none of those are loaded and I've all the legal paperwork and permits to own them."

"Did I say anything after 'Yours'?"

"No."

"Green Beret?"

"Beg pardon?"

"Your ex's father?"

"Yes."

Emerson gave a low, long whistle. "Boys're crazier than the Marines. Being an ex-Marine, I feel qualified to make the judgment call."

She almost decided to freak him out and tell him about the flamethrower of his father's that Eric had stored in the basement, but she was still too anxious about Emerson's presence to test his sense of humor. "What can I do for you, Detective?"

Emerson stared at the closed study door a couple of seconds more, then turned his gaze toward her. "First of all, Miss Thompson, I need to tell you that while my questioning you is part of an official investigation, you are not a suspect."

Lucy nearly choked on her coffee. "A—A wh-what?"

"Suspect." A beat, then: "Timothy Beals was murdered last night."

Lucy said nothing, nor did her face betray the shock, terror and—maybe worst or best of all—the elation she was feeling inside.

"What did you want to ask me?"

"Where were you around ten fifteen last night?"

She had to think, be sure, be absolutely certain of the time she thought she saw on the dashboard clock.

"I think I was being woken up by one of your patrolman. I, uh . . . I got sick while driving home, then I sort of . . . passed out, I guess. This was right around Moundbuilders Park. A patrolman woke me up, then he and his partner followed me home. I think that was right around ten fifteen—I think. I wasn't in the best of shape."

Emerson searched back a few pages in his notebook. "It was ten twenty. According to Officer Banks, you were in a pretty sorry state."

"Charming."

Emerson flipped the notebook closed. "I just needed to check."

"Do you think I did it?"

"After your exit from the meeting last night, yours was the first name that sprang to mind when the call came in."

"That doesn't answer my question."

"No, I don't think you did it. You couldn't have done to him what . . ." Emerson let the sentence remain incomplete.

Lucy had to know. "How did he die?"

A beat, then, "He was decapitated and his torso crushed. To be more specific, his head was bitten off, most of his bones were crushed damn near into powder, and all of his internal organs were pulped. You'd have to run over someone with a steamroller to do that to a body."

"You said his head was . . . was—"

"Bitten off, yes—and, no, I can't come up with any animal that could do that, save for a lion or tiger or gator, and Cedar Hill isn't exactly a haven for that sort of wildlife. Least, not the last time I checked." He slipped the notebook back into his jacket pocket, stood, and started toward the front door but stopped at the study. "You mind some advice, Miss Thompson?"

"Why not?"

Emerson gave her a look she couldn't read, then said, "Be careful what kinds of things you say in public when you're drunk and upset."

That caught her by surprise. "You could tell I'd been drinking?"

Something like a smile ghosted across his face. "You been a cop as long as I have—always wanted to say that in real life, so rarely get the chance—anyway, you learn how to spot a drunk, even one as outwardly steady as you were."

Lucy stared down into her coffee cup, embarrassed.

She snapped her head up again when she heard the sound of the study door being opened. "What are you . . . ?"

"Jeezus-H . . ." whispered Emerson. He looked back at her and said, "Mind if I take a closer look?"

"You got a warrant?"

"No, but like I told the group last night, cooperation is preferable—"

"To coercion. Yes, I remember. I wasn't quite that drunk."

"I repeat, Miss Thompson, you are not a suspect."

Lucy sighed, set down her coffee, and escorted Emerson into the study, explaining the Walls of Madness to him.

She found his fascination with the Walls amusing in

a sad sort of way, right up until he bent over and picked up one of the wadded newspaper clippings and unfolded it.

"All about Beals's release last month," he said matter-of-factly. He seemed to consider something for a moment, then turned and handed the clipping to Lucy. "Under any other circumstances, Miss Thompson, I'd be reading you your rights about now. How come you tore down only the Beals stories?"

"I don't know. To be honest, I don't even remember going into the study after I came inside."

"Still drunk, were you?"

"Falling-down fractured, yes."

"Ah, an honest one."

"Going to charge me with DUI?"

Emerson shook his head. "Not much point now. Banks saw no reason to suspect you were intoxicated, and for all I know you might have taken some kind of medication that exacerbated the effect of the alcohol. Doesn't matter. You didn't hit anything or run over anyone." He looked down at the clippings on the floor, halfheartedly kicking at a few of them. "Besides, I know there's no way you could have gotten over to Beals's side of town in less than twenty minutes, not in that god-awful storm."

"You're sure he was killed at ten fifteen?"

"We have something of an eyewitness. A supervisor at Spencer named Morse. He'd been working with Beals in the garage. Came inside to take a leak and heard what sounded like the wind blowing the roof off the garage. By the time he gets his fly zipped up and can run outside, there's what's left of Beals lying outside the wreckage of the garage." He looked at her again. "You're also not suspected of any complicity in

his death, Miss Thompson. Besides, even if that were
the case, if you know someone or something that can
do to Beals and that garage what was done to
them . . ." He shook his head. "I don't want you sicc-
ing them on me." He paused. "That's a joke. My humor sometimes leans toward the macabre."

"You must have them rolling in the aisles down at
the morgue."

"Packed house every night."

She opened the front door and he stepped out
onto the porch, then turned to her and said, "Look, I
know it's none of my business, okay, but have you ever
thought about getting involved in volunteer work? I
mean, I think you should continue going to counsel-
ing, but why the hell not focus your anger and grief?
I could give you names of people at a couple of different child welfare organizations who'd be more
than happy to bring you aboard, train you. It's a way
to make a difference."

"You're right," said Lucy. "It's none of your business."

She was closing the door when he pressed his hand
against it and said, "Listen to me. Fifteen years ago a
kid named Andy Leonard went on a shooting spree
and killed a bunch of people, a lot of them in
Moundbuilders Park, where they were watching the
fireworks that Fourth of July. My sister was there with
my niece and nephew. My wife and me, we don't have
any kids ourselves, so my sister's kids sort of adopted
us as their second parents. We loved them dearly. My
nephew was seven and my niece was three. Andy
Leonard killed them both. My sister got a bullet in
her leg—that was all. It damn near killed all of us, the
kids getting shot to death like that. My sister didn't
handle it very well—hell, who could? There was more

than one night I had to leave work early to go talk her out of a drunken, suicidal rage. But she got through it. You know why? It finally dawned on her that being bitter like she was, thinking about killing herself and hating the whole goddamn world, well . . . it was an offense to the memory of her children, to all the love and happiness they'd brought into her life. For a while there, I didn't think any of us were going to be able to move beyond what happened, but we did. I'm not saying that I don't find myself just crying like a baby sometimes when I think about all the things I'm never going to be able to do with my niece and nephew . . . but I remember all the hugs and kisses they gave me; I remember their sweet childhood secrets they told me with these serious looks on their little faces . . . and I'm grateful for being blessed with what little time I *did* have them in my life. You can move beyond that kind of pain. I also think you can move beyond your Walls of Madness and use your anger and grief to do something positive."

"Why do you even care?"

"Because I loathe *waste,* Miss Thompson, and that's all you're doing with the drinking and those newspaper clippings. You're wasting life that you'll never get back. Never."

"I'll be sure to impart your wisdom to my daughter, if I ever see her again."

With that, she slammed closed the door, locked it, then ran into the bathroom and threw up.

After she finished expelling her stomach's scant contents, she leaned her head against the cool porcelain and closed her eyes.

At the exact same moment, hidden within the pit

of the sculpture in Moundbuilders Park, Mr. Hands opened his eyes.

Shall there be mercy, then? he asked.

The words sliced into Lucy's brain as easily as if they were a scalpel in a skilled surgeon's hands. She snapped up her head, gasping aloud as the memory of what she'd believed to be a dream played itself out.

Running through the park yet looking down at the treetops, filled with *purpose*, with power, the rain and lightning, the roaring thunder urging on the mission; then the structure, so easily was it torn open, and the monster offering itself for sacrifice . . .

Lucy cowered against the bathtub, burying her face in her hands: No, no, no, *no, no!*

Within his hiding place, Mr. Hands smiled, children singing joyous songs within him. *No mercy. So be it.*

Lucy cried out as the memory of Timothy Beals's death replayed itself.

Then she saw it again.

And again.

And one more time.

And with this last repeat of the memory, she knew with profound certainty that she had, after all, handed down Beals's death sentence.

I wish you could've bitten the head off the fucker. . . .

Her wish, her order; but she'd been thinking of the monster who'd stolen Sarah, not Beals. . . .

But a dead monster is still a dead one, whispered the voice of Mr. Hands inside her brain.

Lucy sat very still, letting those words sink in.

A dead monster is still a dead one.

A dead monster is still dead.

Dead.

Shall there be mercy, then?

"Not for monsters like them, no."

Under no circumstances?

"Absolutely not."

So be it.

"So be it."

It's probably wrong to assume that madness is something born on a note of epiphany; sanity rarely ends amidst a glorious, cataclysmic, earth-shattering moment of Götterdämmerung. No: when a human mind can no longer maintain a wakeful, staring, unrelenting grasp on reason, when it begins to buckle, when it's been confronted with too much horror, or grief, or confusion, or pressure, or fear, or a quietly crystallized combination of all five, sanity slowly grinds to a halt in a series of sputtering little agonies, flaking away in bits and pieces, flotsam of a refugee column casting off sad little remnants—a hope here, a fond memory there—on a road of defeat as a deeper and deeper darkness falls. And perhaps this is why so many madmen are found laughing in locked cells; at some point the only thing left them is their sense of humor, and it all becomes rather funny.

A dead monster is still a dead one.

Sitting there with closed eyes, almost—not quite, but *almost*—unaware of it, Lucy Thompson laughed.

Very softly.

Just for a moment.

Because something in her mind had just sputtered, broken free, and deserted her.

"So be it," she whispered again, the last word rising slightly in pitch as her voice cracked.

She rose from the floor with renewed energy, empowered, and strode toward the study and the Walls of Madness.

She could make a difference; she and Mr. Hands.

A difference the likes of which Detective Bill Emerson and everyone else couldn't begin to comprehend.

She scanned the clippings on the wall, promising Heather Wilson, Daniel McKellan, Rosie and Thad Simpkins, Billy Lawrence, Crystal and Emily Ransom, and the dozens upon dozens of other children whose sad and pained final hours were detailed before her, that their deaths would not go unavenged.

Not as long as they had her.

And Mr. Hands.

For a dead monster is still a dead one.

She walked slowly, almost reverently, toward the Walls of Madness.

And there shall be no mercy for the likes of them.

She reached out and plucked a clipping off the same wall from which the Beals stories had come.

She read the details over, though she already knew the facts in the case by heart.

"Oh, yes," she whispered. "You'll do nicely."

CHAPTER THREE

"She's here again."

"Who?"

"Who do you *think*?"

The young couple were walking the mounds in the park, something they made it a point to do every week. It was late October, a crisp autumn afternoon on the breeze of which you could smell winter's approach—perfect for a romantic stroll. On their last five visits, every time they reached the end of their hike, there was the Sculpture Lady (as they'd come to think of her) standing before *Things Left Behind* and chattering on as if she thought the thing were somehow alive and could understand what she said.

"It's so sad," said the young woman.

"I think it's kinda creepy," replied her fiancé.

"Maybe because neither one of us has ever been that lonely?" The young woman stared. "She must be awfully empty to do something like this every week."

"What makes you think it's just every week? For all we know, she might come here every *day*."

The young woman—whose friends often accused her of being too empathetic for her own good—wiped the beginnings of a tear from one of her eyes. "That'd just be too terrible. Poor woman."

The young man kissed her among the swirling, dry, colorful leaves, then said, "I promise you that you'll never be that sad."

"I hope not." She cast one last glance at the Sculpture Lady and thought, *I hope it gets better for you, somehow.*

And then they were off for one more stroll around the mounds, the Sculpture Lady soon forgotten as the romantic spell of autumn consumed them.

In her high school days, Three Dog Night's "One" had been Lucy's favorite song, and remained so (though she'd never admit it) well into her adulthood.

Later she would think, albeit briefly, that there must have been some kind of irony at work, though she was hard-pressed to fathom its subtleties by the time this occurred to her.

For, in the end, it was the number one that undid her.

Somewhere between the death of Timothy Beals and the October afternoon when the young lovers had their brief discussion about her, Lucy Thompson came to the conclusion that God's affection for humankind could best be measured by the joy He/She/They/It seemed to take in the suffering of the innocent. If ever she had doubts on that score, there were always the occupants of the Walls of Madness to remind her, to reinforce her belief that God was a sadist and probably didn't even know it, and it seemed to her that a being of that sort deserved a more fitting title than the one given it by those ancient scribes who'd invented purple prose and decided to celebrate by authoring the Bible. She then took it upon herself to bestow this being with a more appropriate moniker, and when at last it came to her, it was so *simple*. . . .

Lucy had always thought of God not as He, but in terms of He/She/They/It. She wrote those four words down one night while, on the outskirts of Ross County, some ninety-plus miles away, Mr. Hands was slowly, gleefully peeling the face off Karen Lawrence, who'd killed her infant son Billy with a hot iron because he wouldn't stop crying, and who was later acquitted by a jury of her peers because several reputable doctors had testified that she was suffering from a severe case of post-partum depression and was not responsible for her actions.

As Karen Lawrence was releasing the last horrified, ragged, gore-clogged scream of her life, God's new title came to Lucy.

Rearrange the words He, She, They, and It so they read: She, He, It, and They, then take the first letter of each word and—presto!—you have the perfect acronym for a being who seemingly created the innocent so It could rejoice in their suffering.

Ergo, God became SHIT.

Lucy liked that right down to the ground.

Vengeance is Mine, sayeth SHIT; Let us pray to SHIT and rejoice in SHIT's love for us; I believe in one SHIT, the Feces Almighty, maker of monsters and death; SHIT is great, SHIT is good, let us thank SHIT for this food. . . .

Yes. To the glory of SHIT, who rejoiceth in the tortured screams of the innocent.

It restored certain grace notes to her soul, and made the rest so easy. There was never any guilt over the deaths of the monsters; in fact, she hadn't slept so well in years as she had in the last fifty days—and she had Detective Emerson to thank, in part, for that.

For almost two months now, three times a week, Lucy had been volunteering at the local offices of Licking County Children's Services. Most of it was grunt work—filing, typing, routing phone calls, making coffee—but it was the type of grunt work that, while very much appreciated, went for the most part unsupervised.

Which meant access to files. Two of the dispatched monsters had been chosen from those files. Lucy had been very careful to choose monsters who lived outside of Cedar Hill, and had made doubly sure that Mr. Hands dispatched them while she was at the office, in full view of witnesses.

It felt good to be giving a little something back to the community.

Today she was at the park to add to the scrapbook she kept for herself and Mr. Hands; after all, they were partners, on a mission from SHIT, and should document their good deeds for posterity. So each time Mr. Hands dispatched a monster and Lucy could remove the case from the Walls of Madness, she added those clippings to the scrapbook along with the stories about the odd, horrible, and usually painfully slow manner in which they were banished from this world.

When they were found, that is.

On this late October day, Lucy Thompson and Mr. Hands had rid the world of exactly eleven of the very worst monsters, and they would rid it of many, many more—Lucy had vowed as much to the memory of her daughter.

"Did you know that there are two kinds of time, Mr. Hands? I read about it in a book once. *Chronos* and *kairos. Kairos* is not measurable. In *kairos,* you simply *are,* from the moment of your birth on. You *are,* wholly and positively. In *chronos* you're nothing more than a set of records, fingerprints, your Social Security number; you're always watching the clock, aware of time passing and of being vulnerable to outside forces that are creeping up on you, pushing you closer to the moment of your death . . . but in *kairos,* you simply *are. Kairos* is especially strong in children, because they haven't learned to understand, let alone accept, concepts such as time and age and torture and starvation and death. In children, *kairos* can break through *chronos:* when they're playing safely, drawing a picture for Mommy or Daddy, taking the first taste of the first ice cream cone of summer, when they sing along to songs in a Disney cartoon or talk to an imaginary friend or invent secret places in this world only they can see, there is only *kairos.* As long as a child thinks it's immortal, it is."

She applied glue to the back of a newspaper article about the torturous death of Karen Lawrence, then carefully smoothed it in place next to a color photograph the *Cedar Hill Ally* had run while covering the woman's story—a reproduction of Billy Lawrence's only photograph taken outside the hospital. He was dressed in an infant's baseball player uniform, holding a small plastic bat and smiling the widest, most radiant baby-boy smile you ever saw.

Lucy could look at it now and feel her heart grow warm at how happy and loveable he was, instead of thinking, *He was dead six days after this was taken.*

It might have just been a trick of the light, but she could *swear* his tiny smile actually grew wider when the article detailing his mother's death was pasted next to his picture.

"It's important that we continue this, Mr. Hands. Think of every living child as being the burning bush that Moses saw: surrounded by the flames of *chronos,* but untouched by the fire."

An image in her mind: *children sitting around a birthday-party table, singing to Sarah, who was smiling and embarrassed and happy, and next to her, safe and secure in a baby seat, was Billy Lawrence, cute as a button in his baseball outfit, giggling as Carol Beals played nosey-nose with him. . . .*

"Children don't know about *chronos,* Mr. H., and as long as we continue SHIT's work, that's how it remains."

"Blow out the candles! See if you can get 'em all in one breath!"

"I've been wrong in thinking that Sarah was my only child, Mr. H. Heather Wilson, Daniel McKellan, Rosie and Thad Simpkins, Billy Lawrence . . . all of them are mine—are *ours*—because no one else wants the responsibility. And there're hundreds more just like them, too many of whom died at the hands of a parent who was supposed to love them, care for them, protect them from harm, or who died at the hands of family friends, or suffered unspeakable deaths inflicted on them by people who stole them away for their own twisted pleasures. We have *babies,* Mr. H., some who lived less than a month because they were starved or beaten or dumped in trash cans or left out in the cold to freeze to death or locked in cars on summer days to slowly suffocate. . . . But that can't touch them now, because when we dispatch those who snuffed out their lives, they come into our care, and in our care they live only in *kairos*. *Chronos* isn't part of them any longer."

She turned the scrapbook around so as to give Mr. Hands a glimpse of the Lawrence section. She suspected that he peeked out from between the rows of stone faces and was pleased with what he saw.

"The world will not be this way within reach of my arm, Mr. H. We will continue to punish the monsters who have already killed, but from now on we will also save as many *living* children as we can from having to die at abusive, neglectful, violent hands. And there shall be no mercy. Under any circumstances."

A cool autumn breeze kissed her cheek as she gently closed the scrapbook and filled herself with the scent of the dried leaves whispering around her.

Somewhere between the breeze and the sound of the leaves brushing against the ground, she heard Sarah's voice saying, *What a great birthday party! I'm so glad you're my mommy. . . .*

And thus, under the all-seeing eye of SHIT, the focus of their mission expanded.

CHAPTER FOUR

Lucy spotted the couple outside the Sparta restaurant downtown two days later. Everything about them screamed welfare recipients (the despicable type who gave the truly needy a bad name—both obviously available and able to work but deciding instead to bilk the system for everything they could get, feeling that the world owed them and screw anyone else); the two of them, dressed in not-cheap winter clothing and loudly arguing over who was going to pick up the "party supplies" for that night, seemed oblivious to the infant in its stroller, who dressed in clothing far too thin for this type of weather (not to mention far too small, as if they'd chosen to spend the money on beer instead of proper seasonal attire for their baby), the child's cold-reddened face showing open misery. The woman—twenty, maybe twenty-one—kept kicking at the back of the stroller every time the baby cried too loudly, while the father flicked his cigarette ashes thoughtlessly to the side, more than a few of them, still red and hot, landing on the child's exposed hands and causing it to cry all the louder, which in turn compelled the mother to kick the back of the stroller even harder.

For a moment, the child's eyes met Lucy's as she stood staring from across the street, and in its small, pained eyes was a wordless plea: *Make it stop*.

"You got it, precious one," Lucy whispered.

She closed her eyes and summoned Mr. Hands, then followed the couple on foot until they stopped by a phone booth at the opposite end of the square.

The father went into the booth to make a call while the mother stood outside, adjusting the fluffy collar of her pricey coat because she was cold. The child looked up at her with teary eyes, trying to turn around in its seat, arms extended, wanting so very much to be in Mommy's arms.

Lucy crossed the street and walked past them just to test a theory; sure enough, as she slowed her steps to smile down at the baby, it reached out toward her, a moment of hope on its freezing face.

Simple human contact, that's what it wanted, a warm touch from anyone.

Please.

Lucy winked at it, then went to the end of the street and turned around.

This was the part she'd grown to like the best, knowing that only she and those monsters who were about to be dispatched could see Mr. Hands. There was a crack between the walls of the finite and the infinite, and in this place, when she summoned him, Mr. Hands could freeze things—time, perception, matter, she wasn't entirely certain—but for the few moments it took for him to dispatch a monster, Mr. Hands, his targets, and herself existed only in that space where the walls of the finite and infinite didn't quite fit together as tightly as they should have.

It was their little secret, one that she was happy to keep from the *chronos*-bound world of consensual reality.

It made her laugh sometimes, the idea of consensual reality. Why did people think so small?

She called for him again.

And there he was, looming over the phone booth like a curse from heaven, a soldier of SHIT. Lucy noticed the quiverlike basket that he'd recently fashioned from tree branches and roots that was slung over his back, held in place by a strap that she suspected was constructed of equal parts sinew, sticks, and flesh.

Protruding from the rim of the basket were a couple of arms and part of a leg.

Mr. Hands did not leave the body of every monster behind; he kept a few for his own amusement. What that amusement might be, Lucy didn't care to imagine.

He looked at her and she made a small pushing gesture with her arms.

Balancing on his stumps, Mr. Hands reached out and gently, silently, without the mother even noticing, moved the child out of harm's way. Aware not only that it was being pushed, but that it was being pushed by something unseen, the child's face lit up with mystified glee.

This pleased Mr. Hands no end, and with one of his fingers he tenderly mussed the child's hair, which sent it into another fit of wondrous giggling.

That done, he turned, raised up a mighty fist, and brought it down on top of the phone booth, crushing the structure as easily as an aluminum can. The woman screamed as some of the pulped remains of her husband splattered outward and covered her face, and then she was in Mr. Hands's grip and he was looking at Lucy.

Do it somewhere very, very cold, she commanded him. *I trust you'll make it appropriate.*

He nodded his understanding, then—knocking the young woman unconscious by slamming her skull against the pavement—placed her in his basket and ran off.

Later, several witnesses who'd been driving by all reported seeing the same thing: The phone booth had simply *crumpled,* crushing the man within, and then the young woman, screaming, had seemed to leap into the air and . . . vanish.

This latter incident was chalked up to shock and panic, it being far too fantastic for anyone to believe.

The mother's naked body was discovered two days later by two teenagers who'd gone out to Buckeye Lake for some ice-skating. One of them had stopped to tie their laces and they found themselves staring into the dead, frozen face of a crushed body beneath the ice of the rink.

The child was taken into protective care by children's services. Newspaper reports over the next several days confirmed Lucy's suspicions. The couple had been investigated three times, not only for welfare fraud, but for suspected mistreatment of their baby, who was now doing very well and was happy and feeling much better and would undoubtedly be adopted soon by a more deserving and loving couple.

Lucy celebrated by buying a bottle of expensive

wine and toasting Mr. Hands in front of the sculpture a few days later.

The young mound-walking couple saw her making her toast. Lucy stopped midsentence and waited for them to leave, which they did when they saw the writhing of something unhinged behind her gaze.

They never came back there again.

CHAPTER FIVE

At six ten P.M. the following Friday night, Lucy was getting ready to turn off the television when a late-breaking story came in: A two-year-old girl had been killed in Cedar Hill, and her older brother had confessed to it.

She remained very still as the anchor read from the teleprompter.

The facts were scant but spoke volumes nonetheless.

Kylie Ann Patterson—who would have turned three in less than a week—had been burned to death by her brother, Randy, age sixteen, during a party.

"Details are sketchy at this point," intoned the anchor, "but it appears that her older brother doused her in gasoline and then set her on fire. We have a team on the way to the scene and will update you as soon as more information becomes available."

Lucy turned off the television and then sat in the still, sudden silence and wept for the horror and agony of Kylie Ann Patterson's last few minutes of life.

Then she stepped outside and closed her eyes and conferred with Mr. Hands.

What a miserable world this has become, Mr. H. We're rearing an entire generation that doesn't care about the suffering of the innocent.

He agreed with her wholeheartedly.

They decided to punish Randy next Tuesday—what would have been Kylie's third birthday.

In the age of instant communication, tragedy is often unwittingly compounded by the sheer amount of venues through which it can be recounted; a perverse, modern-day variation of Telephone.

There might have been someone to blame for what happened next, or there might have been no one at all.

One could have blamed the sheriff's deputy who was first on the scene, and the first person to see up-close the charred, still twitching remains of Kylie Ann's body. Who among us could look on such a sight and not suffer some form of revulsion, heartbreak, or shock?

It was easier still to place the blame on those at the television station whose job it was to monitor all police calls. Upon hearing the shocked and tearful voice of the deputy as he radioed in, who wouldn't get so caught up in the excitement that maybe a syllable or two of his report wouldn't get lost in the radio static?

Or point fingers at those who entered the information into the television station's system so that it came up on the teleprompter almost as quickly as the deputy spoke.

Lay blame, if you like, on the anchor himself, who

on this particular night chose to wear his new contact lenses instead of his glasses (which he thought made him look older than he cared to appear).

Take your pick: A shocked and weeping deputy who maybe slurred a word or two as he radioed in his report; communication monitors who perhaps didn't hear everything quite right through the static and so unconsciously filled in the gaps created by muffled syllables; excitement on the part of those who entered the information into the station's computer because their broadcast *had* to be the first to break the story; an anxious, middle-aged anchorman who was worried about losing his position to a younger man and so tried to take ten years off his appearance by wearing new contact lenses and who, maybe as a result, just *perhaps,* misread something in the blurry, scrolling text.

Add these elements to an already horrifying tragedy and loose them in the self-perpetuating machinations of the information age.

Where all can be undone by a single numeral.

Lucy Thompson was not watching television seventeen minutes later when the anchorman, displaying the proper amount of concern, professionalism, and gosh-we're-just-human humility, looked into the camera and said, "We need to correct something we told you about earlier in the broadcast concerning the death of two-year-old Kylie Ann Patterson. Her brother, Randy, whose age our sources initially reported as being sixteen, is actually *six* years old. We have information coming in now that the girl's death was an accident and not a homicide. For the full story, tune in tonight at ten."

CHAPTER SIX

Feeling drained and heartsick about Kylie Ann Patterson, Lucy took Saturday off from all sources of news; there was no Web surfing, no newspaper, no radio, no television.

It wasn't until she sat down with the Sunday paper that she read the full account of what had happened at the Patterson house the previous Friday night.

The family had been grilling out in their backyard, a Halloween tradition in their household regardless of how chilly it was. Randy had been trying to help his father get the fire started while Kylie and her mother were readying themselves to go trick-or-treating. They'd come out back to tell Randy and his father they were leaving. Mr. Patterson asked his wife to help him get some lawn chairs from the garage and the two of them left the grill unattended. Wanting only to help, Randy picked up the can of lighter fluid and was squeezing more onto the smoldering coals when the fire unexpectedly roared to life. The force of the fire startled him and he dropped the can of lighter fluid onto the grill and fell to the ground. The can exploded before Kylie could move from harm's way, and the little girl was immediately covered in flaming fluid. She screamed and ran and Randy went after her. She collapsed a minute later, her body and highly flammable costume engulfed in flames. Randy, screaming and crying, tried to save her, to drag her down to the creek and throw her in the water, but a neighbor stopped him from getting too near the conflagration.

There was nothing anyone could do to save her.

Later, Randy, still hysterical, was heard by other witnesses screaming, *"I did it! I did it! It's all my fault!"*

No criminal charges were being filed against any member of the Patterson family.

Stunned, Lucy slumped back in her chair and pressed her hand against her mouth.

Six years old. The same age Sarah would be now if . . .

If.

Six years old.

Dear God, Dear SHIT, what am I going to do now?

Thirty minutes later, she stood before the sculpture in Moundbuilders Park, pressing her face against one of the openings between those faces chiseled into the rounded stones, whispering, "I was wrong, Mr. H. Do you hear? I was wrong about Randy Patterson. We're not to punish him, understand?"

There was only silence for a response.

"Say something!" she hissed into the opening.

No mercy.

"But this is different, Mr. H. I was wrong and it was an accident and—"

No mercy. Under no circumstances.

"Goddammit, no!" she shouted, beating a fist against the stone. "No, we—*you* can't!"

But his reply remained unchanged.

Under. No. Circumstances.

Lucy could only stand there, bloodied fist held against her chest, and stare at the ground.

Sometime later, she stumbled back to her car and drove home, where she cleaned and bandaged her wounded hand, poured herself a generous drink, then stood before the Walls of Madness. The faces and words of the articles seemed to shift the longer she stared at them, becoming liquid and flowing, reshaping themselves into a small newspaper figure, and that figure shimmered in *kairos* until it was paper-flesh, and that flesh seemed so alive, so close, so near.

So familiar.

"Mommy," said Paper-Flesh Sarah. "Mommy, whatcha gonna do?"

"I don't know, honey," replied Lucy from her prison of *chronos*.

"He didn't mean to. It was a accident. Did ya tell Misserhands?"

"Yes. He doesn't care."

"Can I help?"

Lucy sadly smiled. "I don't know how, babe."

"I gotta do *something*, Mommy."

"I know how you feel."

"Mommy?"

"What is it, honey?"

"Are *you* a monster now?"

Lucy had no answer. She downed the rest of her drink and when she looked again, Paper-Flesh Sarah was gone, and in her place were the usual occupants of the Walls of Madness.

"Please don't hate me for this, honey," Lucy whispered.

Then: "You don't hate me, do you?"

No reply.

"I'll make this right, somehow," Lucy swore to her daughter. "I promise."

Then, very quietly: "Please forgive me."

Silence.

CHAPTER SEVEN

At the same moment Lucy stood before the Walls of Madness asking her daughter to forgive her, Randy Patterson—sleeping off one of the mild sedatives prescribed for him—came violently awake in his bed, crying loudly and calling for his parents. When they came rushing into the room he threw himself into their arms, shuddering and coughing. "I had a dream 'bout this little girl. She s-s-said that a monster was coming to get me b-b-because of what I d-d-did to Kylie. . . ."

"Shhh, honey," whispered his mother, refusing to cry in front of him, wanting to be strong for her remaining child. "It wasn't your fault."

"I d-didn't mean it," he cried.

"We know, hon, we know. . . ."

"I'm scared." His voice was loud and raw and ragged with fear. "Don't let Mr. Hands get me. Please?"

His parents looked into one another's eyes, both their gazes asking the same question: *Mr. Hands?*

* * *

Lucy stopped by the children's services offices Monday morning under the pretense that she'd left something there last week. The director and three case workers were there, all of them busy.

She made a show of looking around for her lost something-or-other until everyone else filed into the conference room for the morning meeting. Moving quickly and quietly, Lucy went into the director's office and took the woman's purse from under her desk, opened it, and removed the small wallet that contained her CS identification and badge. Slipping the wallet into her pocket and replacing the purse where she'd found it, she stopped by the conference room to say good-bye, telling everyone she'd be back on Wednesday.

She would never see any of them again.

The rest of her busy day: A stop at the bank to close one of her three accounts, this one to the tune of five thousand dollars, one-third of which was spent over the next several hours—two hardware stores, an electronics "warehouse," a sporting goods clearance center, Toys "Я" Us, and the grocery store.

Back at the house, she packed all the food into the coolers she'd bought. That done, she picked up a medium-sized duffel bag (another new purchase), went into the middle room, and unlocked the gun cabinet.

She chose a Mossberg handle-grip pump-action shotgun, an M19-11A Colt .45 pistol, a 9mm Python, a snub-nose .22, and—after much debate with herself—her late father-in-law's M-16 and two hunting knives, one with a five-inch blade, the other a ten-inch with a serrated edge. She slid the knives into their leather sheaths, then loaded chambers and clips, set safeties, and carefully placed all but two of the weapons into the duffel bag along with boxes containing extra rounds.

The .45 went into its shoulder holster (which had taken her longer to get on than she'd thought), and the five-inch knife, after some fidgeting, was strapped to the back of her belt, where it would be easily concealed under her coat.

She loaded the duffel bag into the trunk of the car along with the other supplies.

She checked her watch. Almost seven thirty. Visiting hours were over at nine.

She spent ten minutes tidying up the house and rinsing her breakfast dishes.

The last thing she did before leaving the house was blow a good-bye kiss to those faces that were still part of the Walls of Madness.

"Don't forget me," she whispered.

A photograph of Kylie Ann Patterson, taken at her second birthday party, had been enlarged and set on an easel near the head of the closed casket. Even from the back of the crowded room, you could see her sweet, grinning face and know how much had been lost.

There must have been at least seventy-five people there, possibly more.

Lucy looked upon the scene and released a small sigh of relief; she'd been hoping it would be just like this.

She spotted the Pattersons near the center of the room, surrounded by mourning friends and family. Randy was not with them.

Lucy spotted him sitting by himself in a chair along one of the walls. He held a Styrofoam cup of juice that he did not drink from but rather stared into. He was far too pale and thin and looked as if he didn't want to stand because he was afraid the earth might fall away beneath his feet.

After a moment, he lifted his head and saw her looking at him. She smiled and waved.

"Do you know Randy?" said a voice beside her. She turned around and found herself facing both Pattersons.

"No, I've never met him."

"Do we know you?" asked Mr. Patterson.

Lucy removed the director's wallet and flipped it open, careful to make sure her thumb covered the face on the ID, but she knew at once she needn't have worried; all they saw was the badge.

"I'm Rachel Wagner, director of children's services." She slipped the wallet back into her pocket. "I wanted to offer my condolences. I . . . I lost my own daughter about eighteen months ago and . . ."—surprisingly, she found there were tears forming in her eyes—"and I just wanted to let you know that you're not alone in your sadness." Her voice cracked on the word *alone*. "My heart goes out to both of you . . . and to Randy."

The Pattersons were both visibly touched by her words. After a moment, Mr. Patterson wiped one of his eyes and said, "He's not been doing too well, poor little guy."

"That's the other reason I'm here," said Lucy. "If you think I'm being presumptuous or tactless, please say so and I promise you I won't be offended—nor do I mean to offend. It's just that . . . look, I'm a licenced grief counselor for children. I thought perhaps the two of you might . . . well, might have thought about getting some help for Randy, but might not have any idea how to go about it."

"We've talked about it some," said Mrs. Patterson. "He's been having these dreams—hell, nightmares, really, about some little girl named Sarah who tells him that a monster is coming to get him."

Lucy hoped the shock didn't show on her face.

(*I gotta do* something, *Mommy.*)

Mr. Patterson put his arm around his wife. "He even has a name for the thing. He calls it Mr. Hands."

Lucy was astonished that she was able to hold her composure. "Even though what happened was a horrible, tragic accident," she said, "he still feels guilty. This monster, this Mr. Hands, is it? It's just a subconscious manifestation of his guilt." It was oversimplified pop-psychology bullshit, but it must have sounded good to the Pattersons because both of them smiled relieved smiles.

"Could you maybe talk with him a little tonight?" asked Mrs. Patterson.

Lucy smiled, took hold of the other woman's hand, and squeezed it with genuine affection. "I was hoping you'd let me. There's a small coffee lounge at the end of the hall. It was empty when I came in. I could take him there for a little while."

Their faces filled with so much gratitude that Lucy had to fight her own feelings of guilt over what she was about to put them through.

Mrs. Patterson moved forward and gave Lucy a short but warm embrace. "That would be so kind of you, Miss Wagner."

"Rachel, please."

So much gratitude in Mrs. Patterson's eyes. "*Rachel.* Like in the Bible."

They took her over and introduced her to Randy and told him that she was going to take him some-place for a little bit and talk about Kylie Ann and how he was feeling.

"I want you to tell me all about Mr. Hands," Lucy said to him as they walked into the hallway. She turned and smiled at the Pattersons, who smiled their grateful smiles in return before returning their attention to the room where Kylie Ann's face grinned at the world over her closed casket.

Taking hold of Randy's hand, Lucy led him toward the lounge, then—with a last sad, apologetic look over her shoulder—veered right and went out the nearest exit.

Randy offered no resistance.

Through the parking lot and into her car; she secured Randy's seat belt, then her own, and a minute later they drove into the welcoming night.

CHAPTER EIGHT

Randy Patterson said nothing for the longest time, only sat staring down at his hands or looking out the window. They had been on the freeway for the better part of ninety minutes before he spoke.

"Are you taking me to Mr. Hands?" he whispered.

Lucy looked at him and wanted to cry. He looked so broken and scared and alone . . . but there was also something too-soon-dead in his eyes, infecting the rest of his face. She reached over and squeezed one of his hands. "No, honey, I'm not taking you to him. I'm trying to get you as far away from him as I can."

Randy's head snapped around, his eyes wide. "You . . . you d-don't th-think I made him up?"

"No."

His face sparked with something like hope. "You *b-believe* me?"

"Yes, Randy, I do."

He tilted his head slightly to the side. "Are you really from . . . from, uh . . ."

"Children's services?"

"Uh-huh."

"No, I'm not. I had to lie about that and I'm sorry." She fumbled in her purse and removed her wallet, keeping one hand on the steering wheel while she flipped through the photographs.

"Here," she said, holding up the wallet so he could see the picture. "Know who that is?"

His eyes grew even wider. "That's . . . th-that's *Sarah!* Sh-she's th-the one who told me that Mr. Hands was coming to get me."

Lucy dropped the wallet back into her purse. "I'm Sarah's mother, Randy. My name is Lucy Thompson."

"Oh."

She couldn't quite get a reading on that.

Randy swallowed once. Very hard. Then asked, "Is Sarah . . . is she dead?"

Lucy swallowed once. Very hard. Then replied, "I don't really know for sure, but I think she probably is."

"What happened to her?"

Some part of her wished that she'd just said yes, Sarah had died, and left it at that, but this little boy needed to hear truth and nothing but. "Someone took her."

"You mean, like, they stole her?"

The bloody underwear, the bloodied toy horse, the stains on Big Bird's wings . . .

A deep breath, hold it . . . there you go. "Yes, Randy, someone stole her."

"Awww." There was genuine sorrow in his voice, and he reached over and patted her arm. "I'm sorry."

"Me, too."

"Is she a ghost now?"

"Yes . . ."

"She wasn't scary, not really."

"Not all ghosts are scary, hon."

"You believe in *ghosts*?"

A nod. "Very much."

"Me, too." He sounded so serious and grown-up.

After a few moments of silence, he said: "Mom and Dad are gonna be mad at me."

"Why?"

" 'Cause I ain't there. Kylie's funeral is tomorrow."

"I know."

"I d-didn't mean to do it. It was a accident."

Lucy squeezed his hand again. "*Of course* it was. Everyone knows that. You were only trying to help."

"Uh-huh, I was. The grill wouldn't start and I was hungry, so . . . so . . . so I wanted t-to—you know what? I wanted to cook for Dad 'cause he always does the cooking. I wanted to make the hamburgers for everybody. And Kylie, sh-she was standin' there and giggling at me and I said, 'What're you laughing at?' and she pointed at the grill and she said, 'Cold!' on account there was only some smoke and everybody knows you can't cook a hamburger with just smoke, so I got the can of lighter fluid an' . . . I was *real careful*. Really, I was!" His face was getting red. Tears glistened in his eyes. "Dad always told me that y-you had to be real careful when you squirted the lighter fluid, and *I was!* But all of a sudden it just made this big . . . this big *whoosh!* and there was all this fire and it scared me and I didn't mean to drop the can but I was *scared* and . . . and you know what? I fell down, and then there was another big 'splosion and then I saw Kylie, sh-she was on fire *all over* and she . . . she was *screaming*, I heard her, she even said my name, she s-said, 'Wandee!'—she always said it like that, 'Wandee,' and I tried to help but she ran away and when I caught up sh-she was too h-h-hot to touch and . . . and . . ." His face collapsed in on itself and he reached out to her. "I'm *sorry!* I'm *so sorry!*" The words came out in thick, wet splutters. "Kylie's d-d-dead and . . . I *killed her!* I didn't mean to, it was a accident and I m-m-miss her so much and I'm . . . I'm . . . so . . . *s-s-sorry* . . . ."

He began to weep so violently that he had trouble breathing.

Despite her not wanting to stop, Lucy pulled over to the side, unfastened her seat belt, and slid across the seat, taking him in her arms, stroking his hair, kissing the top of his head while he wept and shuddered against her. "Shhh. There, there, hon, it's all right, it's okay, it wasn't your fault, it was an accident, nobody blames you, he won't get you. Mr. Hands won't get you, I promise, nothing's gonna hurt you, I swear it. . . ."

She held on tighter. It felt good to be holding a child in her arms again, to be *needed* by a child, to feel a child's fragility and know that she could protect it, could make things better, could take away the fear— and she *would* protect him, at all costs.

You will not harm him, she thought to the night, hoping Mr. Hands heard her.

You won't. Under. No. Circumstances.

When his sobs finally subsided, she gave him a few Kleenex to wipe his nose and eyes, kissed his head, then touched his cheek and said, "Hey, I've got some ice cream sandwiches in one of the coolers in the backseat. You want one?"

"Yes, please."

She dug one out and gave it to him, then put her seat belt back on and drove back onto the freeway.

"Thank you very much, Mrs. Thompson."

"You're quite welcome, Randy. And you can call me Lucy."

He almost laughed.

"What?" said Lucy. "What is it? C'mon, you—what's so funny?"

"You're the first grown-up who ever told me I could do that."

"Call them by their first name?"

"Uh-huh."

"That's because I'm your friend."

"Really?" It was a prayer.

"Really. You can count on that—but you have to trust me, Randy, all right?"

" 'Kay," he said around a mouthful of the sandwich. "You gonna take me back home later?"

"Yes, of course."

"Good. I like it there." He paused. "You're a nice lady."

Lucy smiled. "I like you, too."

For a while, Randy played with the handheld *Star Wars* video game Lucy had bought earlier that day, but every time it seemed that he was enjoying himself, the ghost of his little sister crossed his face and he looked away, sniffling, the game lying bright and blinking on his lap.

Eventually, around eleven forty-five P.M., he fell into a deep, exhausted sleep. Stopping for gas a few minutes later, Lucy covered him with a blanket and managed to raise his head enough to slip a small pillow underneath it.

Illuminated only by the glow of the dashboard's lights, he looked even smaller and more vulnerable.

Watching him now, Lucy thought of a passage from Shakespeare that she'd come across in her college days, one that returned to her time and again in the weeks and months after Sarah's disappearance:

> *Grief fills up the room of my absent child,*
> *Lies in his bed, walks up and down with me,*
> *Puts on his pretty looks, repeats his words,*
> *Remembers me all of his gracious parts,*
> *Stuffs out his vacant garment with his form . . .*

Try as she did, she couldn't recall the last few lines of the passage.

Then, looking at the child sleeping next to her, decided that maybe that was for the best.

A little while later, too exhausted to go on, she pulled into a rest stop and parked among the trucks and campers and slept a little.

She did not feel the presence of Mr. Hands anywhere near them.

Maybe, just maybe, he hadn't tracked them down yet.

CHAPTER NINE

She spotted the parking-lot carnival around six thirty P.M. as they drove through one of the many small, nameless towns that lay between Cedar Hill and the cabin.

Randy spotted it a second later and his face lit up; no longer a grief-stricken, heartbroken, soul-sick shell of the child he once was, but a kid again, eyes filled with wonder and excitement.

"Do you want to stop for a little bit?" Lucy asked, hoping that the cold terror she was feeling in her gut wasn't evident to him.

"*Could* we?"

"Of course."

"It'll be fun."

It was a prayer.

Lucy took Randy on the Ferris wheel—not so much because either of them wanted to ride the damned thing; both of them were scared of heights—but because, from up there, Lucy could look about for some sign of Mr. Hands approaching from the distance.

He might be able to slip between the cracks in the walls of the finite and the infinite, but he could not hide from her gaze.

She neither saw nor sensed any sign of him.

Back on the ground, she reluctantly agreed to let Randy ride on the kiddie train. She remained outside the partitions and watched as the train went round and round its circular track, all the time following it on foot, her eyes wide and unblinking, her gaze never once, not once, not even for a *second,* leaving Randy Patterson's face.

The other parents standing around the train ride were more than a little wary of her intensity.

After he disembarked the ride and she'd taken hold of his hand—a little too tightly, but of that she was unaware—Randy asked her if they could get a couple of hot dogs and root beers. They did, and sat down at one of the many picnic tables set up under a canopy just off the midway. Randy devoured his hot dog, then, seeing that she was not eating hers, asked, "Can I have your hot dog?"

"Of course," she said, pushing it toward him.

He took a bite out of it, then stared at her while he chewed.

"What is it?" she asked. "Is something wrong?"

"How come you followed the train like you did?"

"I wanted to make sure you were okay."

"But you could see me okay just standing there. You didn't have to follow me like that."

She smiled, trying to lighten his suddenly serious mood. "Did I embarrass you?"

"Uh-uh. But I was . . . you know what? I was wondering why you ain't having no fun."

She was surprised by his statement. "I'm having fun. I am. I like to watch you have a good time."

"But you didn't play any of the games."

"I'm not much of a game person."

He took another bite from the hot dog, chewed slowly, and swallowed.

Not once did he look away from her face.

"Lucy?"

"Yes, hon?"

"How come you don't like carnivals?"

If a few of the things he'd said up to this point had surprised her, *this* left her stunned. "H-How do you know I don't like carnivals?"

He shrugged. "Just seems like you don't, that's all. How come?"

She looked into his child's eyes and decided to tell him the truth—trying not to laugh at how pathetic she'd become; of all the relationships she'd ever had in her life, this one, with this child, was the only one in which she'd spoken nothing but the truth.

She reached across the table and took one of his hands in hers. "I lost Sarah at a carnival just like this one. Just a little carnival, in a parking lot. There weren't a lot of people there, either, but I lost her anyway. I let go of her hand and looked away for a few seconds, and wh-when I turned back, she w-was gone." She lowered her head and tried to pull the tears back in.

Randy, careful to not let go of her hand, came around to her side of the picnic table and gave her a hug.

"It's okay," he said, squeezing her tight. "It's okay. I didn't mean to make you cry. I'm sorry about Sarah."

"Me, too." She slipped a hand around his waist. "I'm sorry, Randy. I didn't mean to spoil this for you."

"You didn't spoil anything. This's been *fun!*"

She looked into his bright face and smiled. "You mean that, don't you?"

"Uh-huh!"

She kissed his cheek and rose from the table, still holding his hand (only now it was Randy who held on tighter than was necessary), and headed for one of the food carts.

"Where we goin'?"

Lucy grinned. "To get some funnel cake for the road. You ever had funnel cake?"

"Uh-uh."

"Oh, you'll love it. It's warm and crispy and has all this sugar on top of it. It's yummy."

Randy laughed. "Yummy. That's a funny word."

She found the funnel cake stand, placed her order, and was waiting for the vendor to create his culinary magic when Randy tugged on her hand and said, "Look-it that man over there."

"What man, hon?"

"*That* one," he replied, pointing.

Lucy followed the direction of his pointing finger and saw—*sweetjeezusno!*—him bobbing along, walking on his white-gloved, too-large hands while the stumps of his legs, hidden by pinned-up pants legs, dangled above the ground.

"Souvenirs!" barked Thalidomide Man, his quiver full of hand-carved treasures bouncing on his back. "Get your official and *guar-on-teed* authentic souvenirs right here. Hand-crafted! One of a kind!"

Some children waved at him, he made a few sales to some parents, and then seated himself on one of the crates outside one of the game booths.

Lucy stared at him.

Thalidomide Man looked around to make sure no one was paying any attention to him, then carefully but forcefully rubbed the stumps of his legs as if they pained him.

He stopped when he saw Lucy staring at him.

And Lucy was staring because she had just realized something.

She paid for the funnel cake, handed it to Randy, then took hold of the child's hand and walked over to where Thalidomide Man was sitting.

"Ah, a new customer! Ma'am, young sir. May I interest you in—"

"You weren't born this way, were you?" asked Lucy.

Thalidomide Man's face suddenly became granite, his manner cautious. "You with the police or the sheriff's department? 'Cause if you are, we already took care of—"

"I'm not with the authorities," she said, removing a one-hundred-dollar bill from her pocket and offering it to him. "This is yours if you'll answer my question."

Thalidomide Man looked at the money, then at her face. "How do I know you're not a reporter, then, come here to do one of those exposés on carny life— you know, where you 'reveal' all the cons and corruption and all that?"

"I am not a reporter."

Thalidomide Man looked at Randy. "This woman your mother, son?"

"No, sir. She's a friend of me and my parents."

"That a fact, is it?"

"Uh-huh. And she ain't no reporter."

Thalidomide Man nodded. "Well, then, handsome sir, I'll take your word for it." He looked at the bill in Lucy's hand. "You produce a twin for that Benji in your hand and I'll answer your question."

Lucy found another hundred, then gave them to him.

"Son," he said to Randy, "do me a favor, will you?" He removed the quiver from his back and offered it to Randy. "Take this here and go sit on that other crate right over there and count how many little rocking horses I got left, would you?"

"I don't want him out of my sight," whispered Lucy.

"He won't be. He'll just be right over there." Then Thalidomide Man produced a small device that looked like a fountain pen and gave it to Randy. "Keep hold of this, son. Anyone bothers you or tries anything, you click on the top of this pen like you were gonna write something, okay?"

"How come?"

"You click on that, and it lets fly with a noise so loud it'd scare the hair off a dog's ass. Ain't no one gonna bother you after that." He looked at Lucy. "That help relieve your anxiety any?"

She exhaled, then looked at Randy. "Go on. Go count the rocking horses for him."

"Okay," he said with a smile.

Randy seated himself on a crate less than six feet away from them and set about his duties, stopping occasionally to take a bite of yummy funnel cake.

Thalidomide Man grinned at Randy, then faced Lucy once again. "To answer your question, ma'am, no, I wasn't born like this, not exactly. I had problems with my legs as a kid—don't really remember what the disease was called, but my legs didn't grow at the same rate as the rest of me. I had to use leg braces and crutches. My daddy hated me 'cause I was damaged goods, a cripple. Said something about his manliness, I guess—that he sired a crippled son. My daddy was a rotten, mean drunk. One night he went on a real toot and killed my mother with a hammer right in front of me because she was always defending me to him, and then he started in on me—my legs, to be specific. Hammered my kneecaps into pulp and then mashed holy hell out of the rest of the bones below the knees. He was getting ready to work on my skull when the police broke in and shot him dead on top of me. I was seven. Doctors couldn't save my legs, so they amputated them from just above the knees."

Lucy stared at him.

"I leave something out?" asked Thalidomide Man. "My story. I think I hit all the high points."

"How long have been with this carnival?"

"*This* one?" A shrug. "Couple of years, I guess." Then, "How did you know I wasn't born like this?"

"I honestly don't know. The way you rubbed your stumps, I guess. I don't remember much about it from school, but thalidomide babies whose limbs are . . . malformed . . . there's not supposed to be any feeling in those limbs, I think."

Thalidomide Man considered this, then nodded his head. "Huh. I gotta remember that. Don't think I'd much like gettin' arrested for fraud. The lines of work I'm qualified for are a bit . . . limited, as you might guess. Can I ask you something?"

"Of course."

"Have we met before?"

Lucy nodded. "You sold my daughter a couple of your carved figures."

"I did, huh?" He stared at her face a few moments longer, then shook his head. "Wish I could say that I remembered you and your daughter, but the fact is, I see so many people in the course of any given year, all I remember's the money in their hands and the way the kids giggle."

"There are programs you can get into—training programs. You could—"

He held up one of his gloved hands and shook his head. "You wanna know why I do this?"

"I guess so, yes."

He watched the families wander by. The mothers. The fathers. The teens.

The children, most of all.

Finally, he looked at Lucy and said, "Look at them, will you?" He gestured toward a group of children who were being led along by two harried-looking mothers. "Everything's still *new* to them. Even if something bad's happened to them recently, they still laugh and giggle and, I don't know, *hope*, I guess. Remember when we were that young? How nothing bad ever followed us to the next morning? Maybe something bad happened *before*, but *now* it's fun, you've got a ball to bounce or a model plane to fly or a doll to pretend with, and the day's full of mystery and wonder and things to look forward to and—" He stopped himself with a shake of his head. "And there's that funny-looking man over there selling his little carved figures. Let's go see him."

"I don't understand," said Lucy, casting a quick glance at Randy, who sat busy with his task, not bothered by anyone.

"I like to think I give 'em something to remember, right? They might forget everything else about the carnival where they saw me, but I don't think many of 'em will ever forget me. I look like a human wind-up toy, right? Sure, some of 'em might laugh at me, but believe it or not, most of them don't. Most of them are little ladies and gentlemen. I also give their parents a little something, as well. They can remind the kids how damn lucky they are to be whole and healthy and not 'like that man at the carnival.'" Another shrug. "Don't mind it a damn bit."

Randy came back over, handing the "pen" and quiver back to Thalidomide Man.

"You got fifteen rocking horses," Randy said proudly.

"That a fact? Well, this's a good day for me—I thought I only had eleven left. Thank you, son. I think your work ought to be rewarded, don't you?"

Randy shyly looked from him to Lucy, who nodded her head.

"I guess so," Randy said.

Thalidomide Man reached into his quiver and came out with a carved figure very much like the one Sarah had named Misserhands, but something in Lucy's face told him this was not a good choice, so he dug around until he came up with a figure of an astronaut. "How's this?"

"Aw, that's so *cool!* A spaceman!" Randy gave a radiant smile and accepted it, but Thalidomide Man insisted that Randy take one of each figure—including that of Misserhands.

Lucy took Randy's hand and thanked Thalidomide Man and began to leave.

"Hey, ma'am?" called Thalidomide Man.

Lucy turned. "Yes?"

"I assume that our discussion will remain private?"

"Yes."

They started away again, and again Thalidomide Man called after her.

"Ma'am?"

"Yes?"

A pause, then: "How's your little girl?"

Lucy couldn't say anything, so Randy said it for her: "She died."

A few minutes later they were back in the car and moving again.

CHAPTER TEN

The cabin was located in the Waretown woods of New Jersey. Lucy was never really sure if this area was considered part of the Pine Barrens or not, but judging from the overwhelming stands of Atlantic white cedar, sour gum, and red maple that began to swallow the car as she drove along, she supposed the point was moot.

It was a little after six thirty in the morning. The first official snow of the season had begun falling last night, and the area surrounding the cabin looked like something torn from one of those "Winter Wonderland" calendars come to life.

She and Eric used to come up to this cabin at least twice a year while they were married; those visits increased after Sarah turned two. She'd loved the short canoe trips they'd take in the river nearby, and those quick, one-day excursions to Wells Mills County Park to the south. In the winter when they came here, Sarah loved to build as many snowmen as possible; the bigger, the better.

Eric had given her the cabin in the divorce settlement, and he still insisted on paying the property taxes and for all maintenance, his codicil being that if he ever needed to get away for a little while, he could use the place—providing he gave her notice.

They'd had a lot of good times here—especially those nights when Eric would tell them stories of the so-called "Jersey Devil" said to roam the area. Sarah was always a little frightened by the stories, but loved them just the same. "Spoooookeeeeee," she'd intone, then collapse into a fit of giggling.

Staring at the cabin now, Lucy shook her head, thinking that even a legendary beast like the Jersey Devil would probably shit his britches at the sight of Mr. Hands.

She remembered the way Sarah had started creating "legends" of her own (Thank you, *kairos*), her favorite being the "secret-secret mountain" only she could see. It was made of gold, this mountain, and it had places in it where treasures were hidden, and dinosaur fossils, and caves full of magic. Lucy tried to pretend that she could see the secret-secret mountain, but Sarah always called her on it.

"Only kids like me can see it," she'd said, looking out the cabin window. "Grown-ups aren't allowed, unless I say so."

Lucy decided to let Randy sleep while she unloaded the car, carrying the supplies only as far as the porch so as not to let him out of her sight.

She woke him later, and he helped her carry everything inside.

"This place is so *cool!*" he said, grinning, looking a little bit more like a child should.

Once inside, Lucy activated the security system (a

paranoid carryover from city dwelling) and for the first time was glad that Eric had gone slightly over-board with it; aside from the usual alarms for windows and doors, this system came equipped with floodlights on the roof outside that were tied into a quartet of motion sensors installed on the grounds surrounding the cabin; when activated, the sensors created an invisible fence. Nothing bigger than a deer could get within fifty yards of the cabin from any direction without setting off all the fireworks.

That done, she and Randy set about putting away the groceries, removing the covers from all the furniture, getting a fire started in the fireplace (Randy only flinched once at the crackling flames, and Lucy hugged him; to her surprise and delight, he returned the hug, then kissed her cheek as if she were his own mother); then she let him open the new DVD player she'd bought and they hooked it up to the television set. She gave him a box full of DVDs and told him they were all his and they could watch whatever he wanted.

He was so excited he actually shook. "Oh, *cool!* Look-it all these! *Mighty Joe Young* and *Godzilla* and . . ." He looked up at her, puzzled. "*Barney* and *Rugrats?*"

"I wasn't sure what you'd like, so I bought pretty much everything I could find."

He shrugged. "These're okay, I guess." He paused. "Kylie liked Barney and the Rugrats. Tommy was her favorite."

"We don't have to watch those."

He shook his head. "I wanna make popcorn and watch these *first*, okay? Kylie can watch 'em with us from up in heaven. It's her birthday today. This'll be a good present for her."

Something caught in Lucy's throat and she swallowed it down. "Sounds like fun."

She eyed the duffel bag. *Later,* she thought. *After he's asleep.*

She took off her coat and Randy saw the .45 in its shoulder holster.

"Is that real?"

"Yes. And it's loaded."

He looked at her with something like awe. "You really *ain't* gonna let him get me, are you?"

"Absolutely not. While I'm thinking of it, come here."

She opened another bag from the electronics store and gave him his own cellular phone, fully charged, along with a portable two-way radio, and explained how to use both.

"A walkie-talkie!" he shouted.

"Okay, sure, but this one's already set, see here? It's tuned into the emergency assistance channel they have around these parts, so don't mess with it, please." She pointed to the cell phone. "You know about nine-one-one, right?"

"Uh-huh."

"Good." She pulled him close, held his shoulders, and looked directly into his eyes. "Listen to me, Randy, okay? If for any reason you and I get separated, you use the walkie-talkie to call the emergency assistance people, then call nine-one-one on the cell phone and *don't hang up.* Don't disconnect the call. If you stay on the phone, they'll find you. It's got a battery that runs for an extra long time, so you don't have to worry about losing power, okay?"

"Okay."

"Promise me?"

"I promise." He was starting to sound scared again.

She took his hand and led him back to the kitchen, lifting him onto the counter and pointing out the window over the sink. "See that trail way back there, that starts by that old well?"

"Uh-huh."

"If you need to get to the main road, you just follow that trail, okay? It's almost a straight line, so you don't have to worry about getting lost. I'm only telling you this *just in case* something happens."

"A backup plan!"

"What?"

"That's what Dad calls things like this. I been on trips before, and Dad says you should always have a backup plan."

"That's right, and this is our backup plan. Later tonight, I'm going to fix up a backpack for you—food, water, pop, comic books, a blanket; there's a compass and a pair of binoculars, things you can use while you're waiting for emergency assistance people to come get you.

"But don't worry about anything, hon, I'm not gonna let you out of my sight, okay? We just have to be real careful until I . . . until I get rid of Mr. Hands, understand? So promise me that you'll keep the radio and the phone on you *all the time,* even when you're sleeping or have to go to the bathroom. The phone folds up and you can keep it in your pocket, and the radio, see, it can hang off your belt. Promise me you'll always have these with you?"

"Promise."

"Good." She planted a big wet one right on his face, making silly slurping noises that made him laugh.

"Okay, then," she said. "Let's make popcorn and watch movies!"

"Yay!"

He fell asleep on the double-wide sofa around nine fifteen that night, and Lucy set about placing the weapons at what she hoped were strategic locations.

The .45 she kept on her person, along with the knife (she decided to switch the five-inch for the ten-inch with the serrated edge), which she strapped to her boot.

Double-checking the security system, she took the Mossberg shotgun and placed it on the floor in front of the sofa, then snuggled down next to Randy, covering them with a heavy quilt.

Kylie's birthday was now nearly over and they were still safe.

She tried to take comfort in that.

Staring into the dying embers of the fire, she tried to remember the rest of the Shakespeare passage, couldn't, and so tried to sleep.

Somewhere around five ten A.M. she nodded off, a part of her still very much aware of every sound, every movement, every vibration made by the wind outside as a second dusting of snow covered the world with a fresh layer of crystalline white.

Next morning, it was buttermilk pancakes and sausage for breakfast, then building another fire. Then they built a fort from boxes and pillows, then more movies and a *Star Wars* spaceship-racing game on the Super Nintendo system she surprised him with.

It was a great day.

As Randy fell asleep next to her on the couch that

night, a Gordon Lightfoot CD softly playing on the portable boom box, Lucy looked out into the snowy night. If Sarah had been here, she'd have been raising holy hell to get out there and build a snowman, and Lucy thought: *Where are you?*

Kylie's birthday was over. Maybe Mr. Hands had given up trying to find them.

Is that it? Will there be mercy, then?

Silence.

She didn't think that could be good, no matter how you looked at it. The two of them were connected in a way few people could understand. She had created him and he, in return, had sustained her.

I know you can hear me, sense me. So why won't you answer?

She drifted off to the refrain of "If You Could Read My Mind."

She came awake around five thirty when her bladder announced to her in no uncertain terms that she'd had too much Pepsi with the pizza they made for dinner. She pulled herself up—careful not to jostle Randy—and sat on the edge of the sofa. Her side hurt like hell from where the gun and holster had been pressing into it while she slept, and her head was screaming for codeine.

She slowly rose and shuffled toward the bathroom— leaving the door open so she could lean forward to see Randy—then she pulled a bottle of water from one of the bags and found the codeine tablets.

She wandered over to the front window and stood there, staring out into the night. The moon was full and made the snow shimmer. Light moved like glissandos over the treetops in the distance as the wind caused them to sway side to side, sometimes forward, then backward, and—

And then she saw him.

He was so still among the trees and swirling snow that he looked like part of the scenery.

Mr. Hands just stood there, motionless, staring with his black pit eyes.

Lucy moved quickly and quietly; she picked up the Mossberg, grabbed her coat, disabled the alarm, and stepped out onto the porch, pumping a round into the shotgun's chamber.

Mr. Hands did not move, only continued staring coldly, an entomologist observing the behavior of an insect under glass.

Lucy looked behind her once—*I won't let him harm you*—then stepped off the porch, down the steps, and crossed the distance between herself and the thing she'd brought into the world.

She raised the shotgun and thought about firing, but that would wake Randy and the last thing she wanted right now was for him to awaken and find himself alone in the dark in a strange place.

Still, she kept her finger near the trigger.

"Leave him alone," she said. "I'm begging you, please leave him alone."

Mr. Hands still did not move or give her any indication that he cared.

The wind came up again, blowing snow against her face. She blinked, stopped moving, and brushed her eyes clear.

Mr. Hands began to bend down toward her. For a crazy second, she thought he was falling, the movement was that stiff, but then she didn't think about it any longer because she knew what it meant when he started to bend down toward a person. She had no choice, so she pumped off three shots from the Mossberg in rapid succession, straight into his gut, and that must have done something because he seemed to explode from the center as he fell toward her and . . . a moment before he hit the ground, one of his eyes dropped from his head.

Or, rather, a large black stone dug up from the shore of the river.

She snapped her head back up just as the rest of the giant snowman Mr. Hands had fashioned after himself crumpled into a white heap.

"*Oh God—*"

The sound of logs and wood being smashed reached her even before she was fully turned around, then the sight of Mr. Hands—pummeling the top of the cabin like some rabies-mad animal, turning the roof into kindling—and the sound of Randy's horrified screaming grabbed hold of her and pulled her forward, running, screaming in terror and rage, firing to no avail because she was too far away and couldn't get a decent aim while she was moving.

Mr. Hands threw away a section of the roof, then shoved his arm down inside and began ripping out the heavy ceiling beams. . . .

Lucy forced herself to stop about fifteen yards from the porch, knelt on one knee, took aim with the Mossberg . . . screamed "*Leave him be!*" once and once only. . . .

And when Mr. Hands didn't heed her warning, she fired once, twice, the recoil knocking her backward, but not before she saw both shots hit him squarely in the neck.

But when he screamed it wasn't the scream of a

monster, it was the agonized wails of tortured children, and Lucy thought she'd rather be rendered deaf than endure another moment of that hideous sound.

But he wasn't stopping, didn't seem to be hurt at all, and with a hard yank he ripped out the section of ceiling beams he'd been working on.

Lucy scrambled to her feet, slipped in the slick snow and twisted her ankle and went down again, crying out from the pain.

This time Mr. Hands screamed his own sound, a dark, furious sound full of death and dirt, as he dropped the ceiling beams and teetered on the verge of falling. Lucy wondered if Randy had found one of the guns and fired it at the monster that had come to punish him for Kylie.

But as she struggled onto her feet again and the pain of her ankle shot up her leg, Lucy saw Mr. Hands shudder.

She stood still for a moment, as did he.

And then, slowly, with as much pressure as she could stand, Lucy pressed the business end of the shotgun down against her injured ankle.

The pain registered with Mr. Hands at the same time Lucy forced back a shriek.

And then she knew.

Dropping the shotgun, she pulled out the .45 and aimed at the ground, placing the palm of her left hand alongside the front of the weapon.

Mr. Hands stared down at her.

Lucy fired, and the muzzle-flash from the gun seared a second-degree burn onto the palm of her left hand.

Mr. Hands screamed again as he threw his left hand into the air.

Lucy shoved her injured hand into the snow and felt immediate relief as the cold, wet snow sucked away the pain.

Mr. Hands's screams began to fade.

Lucy rose to her feet and walked toward the cabin. When it looked as if Mr. Hands were going to start after Randy again, Lucy didn't fire another shot but instead shoved the business end of the gun directly under her chin.

Mr. Hands stood very, very still.

Lucy said, "Try anything and I'll kill us both, Mr. H. I'm serious."

He moved slowly away from the cabin.

"Farther!" shouted Lucy.

He did as she said.

"Remember what I said." And with that she went into the cabin.

After climbing over several mounds of debris, she found Randy in the kitchen, huddled between the pantry door and the refrigerator. He was shaking and crying, but he'd been composed enough to remember his backpack, winter coat (another present from Lucy), new boots, and the two-way radio.

"I . . . I g-g-got my phone in m-my pocket," he said.

"Good boy."

"Is he gone?"

"No, but he's not going to try to hurt you now."

"Promise?"

"Promise." She slipped the .45 back into its holster, then grabbed a battery-operated lantern from the kitchen table, checked to make sure it worked, and handed it to Randy. "Okay, hon, here's what we're gonna have to do. You take your backpack and this lantern, go out the back door, and get on the trail like we talked about, okay? You keep walking and . . . here"—she pulled off her watch, a birthday gift from Eric and Sarah, and stuffed it in Randy's pocket— "you keep track of the time. It's almost a quarter of six in the morning, right? You keep walking until it's six thirty. If I haven't caught up with you by then, you'll—"

"I use the radio, call the emergency people, then call nine-one-one and don't hang up."

She cupped his face in her hands and kissed him. "That's exactly right." She turned him around and started pushing him toward the door. "Now scoot."

She opened the back door and shoved him out onto the steps.

"I don't want to leave you alone," he said, his voice cracking.

"I'll be fine, honey. Remember, if I haven't caught up with you by six thirty—"

He spun around and threw his arms around her waist. She touched the top of his head.

"You're a good boy, Randy," she said, kneeling down and taking hold of his shoulder so she could look him in the eyes. "Always remember that. What happened with Kylie was an accident, a terrible accident, but those things happen and it's *nobody's fault*. Cry if you want. But it won't do you any good. It never does. So don't bother trying to blame yourself. Promise me?"

"I promise."

"Good. Now get going."

He pulled away from her and ran toward the trail. Lucy was proud of him; he never once looked back at her.

"Good boy."

Then she reached down and pulled out the serrated knife.

She knew that she should be frightened out of her mind, but an odd, almost empowering calm was taking hold of her. She limped outside and down the front steps and made her way toward Mr. Hands.

He stood there, shaking his head back and forth like a child pleading *No, no, NO!*

Lucy smiled at him, then closed her eyes, remembering, at last, the rest of the passage from Shakespeare:

Then I have reason to be fond of grief.
Fare you well. Had you such a loss as I,
I could give better comfort than you do.

Mr. Hands made a deep, soul-sick sound from somewhere deep in his core.

Lucy opened her eyes. "I know, and I'm sorry, but . . . but thank you."

She plunged the knife deep into her stomach, then collapsed on the ground, watching the snow turn red around her.

"This is the only way now," she croaked as Mr. Hands, doubled over with pain, dragged himself beside her.

Lucy stared into his face and tried to smile but only coughed up a spattering of blood and mucus. "I hope it doesn't take us too long to die."

Mr. Hands gently took her into his grip and lifted her from the ground. He was in tremendous pain, but they weren't dead yet.

Before closing her eyes for the last time, Lucy saw a winter carnival on the ground beneath her, and there she saw Heather Wilson, Daniel McKellan, Rosie and

Thad Simpkins, Billy Lawrence, Crystal and Emily Ransom, and the dozens upon dozens of other children whose sad and pained faces had decorated the Walls of Madness, only now they were smiling, laughing, playing happily, and among them was a little girl holding a small wooden doll as if it were the greatest treasure in the world. *"It's Misserhands!"* shouted the child, dancing in *kairos*. *"He's good luck! Misserhands won't* ever *let anything happen to me!"*

Kylie Ann Patterson clapped her hands and giggled, asking Sarah if she could hold Misserhands.

A toy rocking horse was there, its snout unstained.

Blood no longer bound Big Bird's wings.

Randy stopped running at six fifteen, when he came upon a large rock. He climbed to the top of it (it seemed like a good place to be) and dug into the backpack for some water and some bread and cheese. He cried for a while, then cried some more, and then, for a while, there were no more tears.

He wasn't as scared, though, and that was good.

He pulled the watch from his pocket. At six thirty he radioed for emergency assistance just like he promised, then called 911 and told them he was lost in the woods. They told him to stay where he was and not to hang up and they would find him.

Then he waited.

Later, when the sun was bright and the sky was clear, he took out the binoculars and stood up, looking around at the trees and hills in the distance.

Until he saw something glint.

Something that looked almost gold.

He steadied his hands until he again found the mountain in the distance.

Even with the snow, it looked gold in the sunlight.

He saw Mr. Hands, climbing up the side. He looked like he was hurt. There was some kind of big basket on his back.

Randy fiddled with the focus until the image was clearer.

Then he wished he hadn't.

Lucy, her blouse covered with blood, her head hanging limply to one side, had been stuffed into the basket on Mr. Hands's back.

Randy dropped the binoculars and threw up, then started crying again.

When he was able to move again several minutes later, he grabbed the binoculars and tried to find Mr. Hands and Lucy again.

He saw only the mountain and nothing more.

He was still looking for them three hours later when the first of the rescuers found him, but they were gone forever, somewhere up on the mountain of gold. . . .

The same mountain of gold that he returned to many years later, that he'd been fighting for the last seven hours, and whose summit was now in sight.

He gripped the ledge and pulled himself over. This ledge was a wide one, wide enough for a man to roll out his sleeping bag and rest upon for a while.

The sunlight cast golden light onto the surface of the mountain wall behind him. Blinking, he turned around and saw—*Oh, sweet Jesus, ohGod*—the skeletal remains of Mr. Hands embedded in the mountain.

His chest hitched and his vision blurred but he refused to weep.

"You were *real*," he said, the last word shining, full

of glory, and in his mind Randy Patterson, now almost thirty years old, wiped away all the stares and questions and "Are-you-sure's" that had blended together into a lifelong mantra of doubt.

"I'm not crazy," he whispered toward the fossil hands. *"I'm not crazy."*

And then he saw her.

There were other human skeletons and parts of skeletons embedded into the mountain, but he saw the one that was looking down at him, that seemed to be trying to free itself from the fossilized remains of Mr. Hands so it could come down and embrace him, and he knew without question or doubt that it was Lucy.

He had no strength left to climb or he would have tried to get to her, to touch her; instead he pressed himself against the mountain's wall and looked up toward her remains, his left hand reaching up as far as it could so she'd know he *wanted* to touch her, and called out: "I never thanked you, Lucy! I just . . . I just needed to do this, to know that it was all real—that *you* were real and I . . ." He released a long breath and cast a glance downward to the world he would return to in a little while, where, finally, he could shake away the ruins of the past and start his life.

He saw something lying at his feet, and carefully reached down for the hand-carved figure that the odd little man at the carnival had given him so many years ago.

Something had been carved into the back of Mr. Hand's body: *Sarah says hi.*

Randy looked back up at the magically fossilized remains of Lucy Thompson. "I'm fine now, really, and . . . and I just . . . I just wanted to thank you," he whispered.

And he was freed.
Later, he began the climb back down.
It seemed a lot easier, somehow.
He suspected a lot of things would from now on.

EPILOGUE
The Hangman, 3:20 A.M.

Grant McCullers finished drying off the last of the glasses, slid them into the overhead racks, dried his hands on the towel he'd thrown over his shoulder, and offered his hand to the guy at the bar. "Pleased to make your acquaintance, Randy."

"Likewise," said Randy Patterson, shaking Grant's hand.

"Welcome home," said the Reverend, also shaking Randy's hand.

"Thank you."

"Hope you're planning on staying with us for a while," said Jackson as he shook Randy's hand.

Randy shrugged. "I . . . I don't know. I don't really have any family or friends here anymore. I'm not even sure why I came back here, to tell you the truth."

"I am," said Grant, reaching out and taking the carved figure of Mr. Hands off the bar and placing it on the long shelf of knickknacks. "Where else would he belong, if not here?"

Randy stared at the figure for a long while, then

nodded his head and grinned. "He looks almost at home up there, you know?"

"You bet he does," said the Reverend.

Randy looked at the three faces around him. "Don't you guys have, like, a thousand questions you want to ask me about this?"

"Not a one," said Grant. "We know bullshit when we hear it."

Randy nodded. "So . . . what do I do now?"

"Well," said Jackson, "considering that you've had a bit of a trip, all things considered, I think maybe you ought to go back to the shelter with the Reverend here and—hey, wait a second. Where'd you get all that money you're carrying?"

Randy reached into his pocket and pulled out the wad of fifties that Grant had seen earlier. "This? This is a little over six hundred dollars, and it's every penny that I've managed to save from working odd jobs over the past several years. Reverend, you're welcome to some of it if you'll let me sleep over at your place tonight. I'm suddenly so . . . so *tired*."

Before the Reverend could respond, Grant said, "I won't hear of it, Randy. Look, I've got a spare room upstairs—it's not much, but it's pretty homey. We can maybe fix it up for you over the next few weeks. I can offer you room and board plus a hundred bucks a week to help me out here in the bar and kitchen. What do you say?"

Randy looked at all three of them again. "But you . . . you hardly know me."

"We know you just fine," said Jackson.

"And now we've got enough people for a decent game of Monopoly," said the Reverend.

"Plus," said Grant, picking up the broken guitar

neck from the shelf, "if you want to hear one of the stories behind one of these things, well . . . you've got to be a regular. Only regulars get to hear."

"And you now have friends," said the Reverend.

"Count on it," said Jackson.

Grant leaned on the bar and waved the broken guitar neck in front of Randy. "So, what do you say, my friend? You got a new home, if you want it—and besides, I'm sure that Linus would get a kick out of seeing you again. I'll bet he'd like to hear your story."

"C'mon," said Jackson. "We don't beg well. What do you say?"

Randy looked around the bar, then at the three men—his three new friends—and then, finally, at the broken guitar neck. "I guess if I want to hear the story behind that damn thing, I'm staying."

And then he looked up at the carved figure of Mr. Hands and, just for a moment, thought he heard Lucy and Ronnie and Sarah and Kylie and all of the others laughing as they said, *Well, now we can all be together. Welcome home, Randy. Be happy.*

"Whoever fights monsters, should see to it that in the process he does not become a monster."

—Nietzsche

AND NOW, A BONUS:

GARY A. BRAUNBECK'S
INTERNATIONAL HORROR GUILD
AWARD—WINNING NOVELLA,

KISS OF THE MUDMAN

"Music's exclusive function is to structure the flow of time and keep order in it."

—Igor Stravinsky

"Without music, life would be a mistake."

—Friedrich Nietzsche

1

Of all the things I have lost in this life, it is music that I miss the most.

I read once that humankind was never supposed to have had music, that it was stolen by the fallen angels from something called *The Book of Forbidden Knowledge* and given to us before God could do anything about it. The article (I think it was in an old issue of *Fate* I found lying around the open shelter) said this book contained all information about science, writing, music, poetry and storytelling, art, everything like that, and that humanity wasn't supposed to possess this knowledge because we wouldn't know what to do with it, that we'd take these things that were supposed to be holy and ruin them.

I remember thinking, *How could God believe we'd ruin music?* I mean, c'mon. Say you're having a rotten day, right? It seems like everything in your life is coming apart at the seams and you feel as if you're going under for the third time. Then you hear a favorite song coming from the radio of a passing car, and maybe it's been twenty years since you even thought about this song, but hearing just those few seconds of it brings the whole thing back—verse, chorus, instrumental passages . . . and for a frozen instant you're *back there* when you heard it for the first time, and back there you're thinking: *I am going to remember this song and this moment for the rest of my life because the day will come that I'm going to need this memory,* and so you-back-there taps you-right-here on the shoulder and says, "I can name that tune in four notes. How about you?"

You can not only name it in *three,* but can replay it in your mind from beginning to end, not missing a single chord change, and—*voila!*—your rotten day is instantly sweetened because of that tune. How could any self-respecting divine being say that we might ruin music when a simple song has that kind of power? I'll bet many a sad soul has been cheered by listening to Gordon Lightfoot's "Old Dan's Records," or broken hearts soothed by something goofy like Re-union's "Life Is A Rock (But the Radio Rolled Me)"; how many people in the grips of loneliness or depression have been pulled back from the edge of suicide by a songs like "Drift Away," "I'm Your Captain," "(Get Your Kicks On) Route 66," or even something as lame as "Billy Don't Be A Hero"? You can't really say for certain, but you can't discount the thought, either, because you *know* that music has that kind of power. It's worked on me, on you, on everyone.

(It never occurred to me before, but Byron Knight—yes, the Byron Knight—said to me the evening it happened, how frighteningly easy it is to reshape a single note or scale into its own ghost. For example, E-major, C, G, to D will all fit in one scale—the Aeolian minor, or natural minor of a G-major scale. Now, if you add an A-major chord, all you have to do

is change the C natural of your scale to a C sharp for the time you're on the A-major. Music is phrases and feeling, so learning the scales doesn't get you "Limehouse Blues" any more than buying tubes of oil paints gets you a Starry Night, *but you have to respect the craft enough to realize, no matter how good you are, you'll never master it. Music will always have the final word.)*

Of all the things I have lost in this life, it is music that I miss the most.

I can't listen to it now, and it's not just because I'm deaf in my left ear; I can't listen to music anymore because I have been made aware of the sequence of notes that, if heard, recognized, and acknowledged, will bring something terrible into the world.

(The progression seemed so logical; leave the G string alone—tuned to G, of course—so the high and low E strings go down a half step to E flat respectively. The B string goes down a half step to B flat, the A and D go up a half step, to B flat and E flat respectively. The result was an open E flat major chord, which made easy work of the central riff. For the intro, I started on the twelfth fret, pressing the first and third strings down, dropped down to the seventh and eighth fret on those same strings for the next chord, and continued down the neck . . . as the progression moved to the fourth string, more and more notes were left out and it became a disguised version of a typical blues riff. The idea was to have a rush of notes to sort of clear the palette, not open the back door to hell . . . but that's a road paved with good intentions, isn't it?)

Some days I'm tempted to grab an ice pick or a coat hanger or even a fine-point pen and puncture my good eardrum; total deafness would be a blessing because then I wouldn't have to worry about hearing *that melody* . . . but the tune would still be out there, and I'm not sure anyone else would recognize it, so who'd warn people if (. . . *B string goes down a half step to B flat, the A and D go up a half step, to B flat and E flat* . . .) the Mudman hears his special song and shambles in to sing along?

2

The Reverend and I were out on our second Popsicle Patrol of the night when Jim Morrison climbed into our van.

That Friday evening was one of the crappiest nights in recent memory. It was November, and it was cold, and it was raining—the kind of rain that creates a gray night chiseled from gray stone, shadowed by gray mist, filled with gray people and their gray dreams; a dismal night following a string of dateless, nameless, empty dismal days. The forecast had called for snow, but instead we got rain. At least snow would have been a fresh coat of paint, something to cover the candy wrappers, empty cigarette packs, broken liquor bottles, losing lottery tickets, beer cans, and used condoms that decorated the sidewalks of the neighborhood; a whitewash to hide the ugliness and despair of the tainted world underneath.

Can you tell I was not in the best of moods? But then, I don't think anyone was feeling particularly chipper that night, despite the soft and cheerful classical music coming through the speakers, one in each of the four corners of the main floor. (I think it was something by Aaron Copland because listening to it made me feel like I was standing in the middle of a wheat field on a sunny day, and that only made me feel depressed.) The shelter was about a third full—there were twenty-five, maybe thirty people, not counting the staff—and the evening had already seen its first "episode": a young guy named Joe (I didn't know his last name; people who come here rarely have them) had kind of flipped out earlier and took off into the dreary night, upsetting everyone who'd been eating at the table with him. The Reverend (the man who runs this shelter) spent a little while getting everyone settled down, then sent one of the regulars, Martha, out to find Mr. Joe Something-or-Other. Neither one of them had come back yet, and I suspected the Reverend was getting worried.

The Cedar Hill Open Shelter is located just the other side of the East Main Street Bridge, in an area known locally as "Coffin County." It's called that because there used to be a casket factory in the area that burned down in the late sixties and took a good portion of the surrounding businesses with it, and ever since then the whole area has gone down the tubes. Most of the serious crime you read about in the *Ally* happens in Coffin County. It's not pretty, it's not popular, and it's definitely not safe, especially if you're homeless.

As hard as it may be to believe, there are not all that many homeless people in Cedar Hill. If pressed to come up with a number, the Reverend would probably tell you that our good town has about fifty homeless folks (give or take; not bad for a community of fifty-odd thousand), most of whom you'll find here on any given night, which explains how he knows all of them by name.

The shelter is in the remains of what used to be a hotel that was hastily and badly reconstructed after the fire. The lobby and basement were left practically unscathed, but the upper floors were a complete loss, so down they came, and up went a makeshift roof (mostly plywood, corrugated tin, and sealant) that on nights like this amplified the sound of the rain until you thought every pebble in the known universe was dropping down on it. Luckily, the lobby's high ceiling and insulation had remained intact after the fire, so that it, combined with the soft classical music the Reverend always has playing, turned what might have been a deafening noise into only an annoying one. When it became evident that "Olde Town East" (as Coffin County used to be called) was not going to recover from the disaster, the city decided its efforts at a face-lift were better employed elsewhere. As a result of the Reverend's good timing in getting the city to donate this building, the Cedar Hill Open Shelter was the only one in the state (maybe even the whole country) to have Italian marble tile on its floors and a ballroom ceiling with a chandelier hanging from it. Makes for some interesting expressions on peoples' faces when they come through that door for the first time.

The shelter has one hundred beds on the main floor, with thirty more in the basement adjacent to the men's and women's showers and locker rooms. (Aside from storage, the basement was used by the hotel's employees, many of whom worked two jobs and came to work at the hotel after finishing their shifts at one of the steel mills or canneries. Those too are now long gone.) A third of the main floor is covered with folding tables and chairs—the dining area; the Reverend's office, which is a pretty decent size and doubles as his bedroom, is past the swinging doors on the right—go straight through the kitchen, turn left, you're there.

During the holidays you'll see more unfamiliar faces and crowded conditions because of transients on their way to Zanesville or Dayton or Columbus, bigger places where there might be actual jobs or more sympathetic welfare workers. The shelter turns no one away, but you'd damned well better behave yourself while you're here—the Reverend might look harmless enough at first, but when you get close to him it's easy to see that this is a guy who, if he didn't actually *invent* the whup-ass can opener, can handily produce one at a moment's notice. (Opinions are divided as to who the Reverend more resembles: Jesus Christ, Rasputin, or Charles Manson. Trust me when I tell you that he can be *very* scary when he wants to.)

Almost no one does anything to piss off the Reverend. The business earlier that night with Joe was a rarity—even those folks who come in here so upset you think they'll crumble to pieces right in front of you and take anyone in the vicinity with them know that you don't ruin things for the rest of the "guests." That's what the Reverend calls everyone, and treats them with all the courtesy and respect you'd expect from someone who uses that word. Still, the business with Joe was enough to set everyone's nerves on edge a bit. It wasn't even ten thirty yet, so the regular guests who weren't already here would be wandering in by midnight. Of the two dozen or so guests who were here, I only recognized a few.

We had four new faces tonight: a young mother (who couldn't have been older than twenty-three), her two children (a boy, five or six; a girl, three years old, tops), and their dog (a sad-ass beagle with an even sadder face who was so still and quiet I almost forgot he was there a few times until I nearly tripped over him). It breaks my heart to see a mother and her kids in a place like this. The Thanksgiving and Christmas periods are always the worst, and the most depressing. At least for me.

"That's about all the excitement *I* can stand for one night," said Ethel, the old black woman who mans the front door. She's a volunteer from one of the churches—St. Francis—and sits here every weeknight from seven P.M. until eleven, greeting folks as they come in, handing out all manner of pamphlets, answering questions, and you-betcha happy to take any donations; she's got a shiny tin can at the edge of her folding card table marked in black letters for just such a purpose.

I smiled at her as I cleared away some more of the empty plastic plates left on the various tables. "But you gotta admit, there aren't many places like this that offer a free floor show with dinner."

"Mind your humor there; it's not very Christian to make light of others' woes."

"Then how come you grinned when I said that?"

"That was not a grin. I . . . had me some gas."

"Uh-huh."

"That's my story and I'm sticking to it." She winked at me, then looked out at the guests. "I don't mind doin' the Lord's work, not at all, and heaven knows these poor people need all the help they can get, but I swear, sometimes . . ." She squinted her eyes at nothing, trying to find the right way to express what she was thinking without sounding uncharitable.

"*Sometimes,*" I said, then winked back at her. "We can leave it at that and it'll be our little secret."

She laughed as she dumped the contents of the donations can onto the table and began counting up the coins. "Oh, bless me, will wonders never cease? It looks like we might've took in a small fortune tonight. Why, there must be all of"—she counted out a row of dimes, then a few nickels and pennies—"three dollars and sixteen cents here! Might put us in a higher tax bracket."

"I'm sorry it isn't more," I said, digging into my pocket and coming up with thirty-three cents, which I promptly handed over. If you've got spare change, it goes into Ethel's till or she *will* get you.

"Always remember, Sam," she said to me as she took the change, "what the good book says: 'What we give to the poor is what we take with us when we die.' "

"Then I'm screwed to the wall."

Her eyes grew wide at my language.

I looked down at my feet. "I'm sorry."

"I'm going to chalk that up to your being tired and let it go, Samuel."

"Yes, ma'am." Both Ethel and the Reverend (who've looked out for my own good as long as I've been here) call me Samuel when they're irked at me about something. I prefer Sam. Samuel always sounded to me like the noise someone makes trying to clear their sinuses.

Ethel picked up her purse and took out a five-dollar bill and some change, adding it to the till. "I have one rule for myself, Sam—I will not, absolutely *not* hand the Reverend less than twenty dollars at the end of each week."

"How often do you have to make up the difference?"

She shrugged. "That's my and the good Lord's business. You needn't bother yourself worryin' over it." Then she gave me a conspiratorial wink. "Maybe we'll soon have enough saved up to get the basement wall fixed."

"Be still my heart," I said.

Ethel was referring to the east wall in the men's shower room. For the last several weeks, more and more of the tile and grouting had fallen out, and the cement foundation on that side was starting to crumble. Because of an unusually damp autumn, and with the almost nonstop rain of the past week or so, the soil behind the weakening cement started oozing through the gaps, slowly transforming everything into a muddy wall that was pushing out what tile still held its ground (it didn't help matters that there was a leak in one of the pipes running into the showers). I'd been down there with the Reverend earlier that day, piling bags of sand, wooden crates filled with canned food, and even a couple of pieces of old furniture against it. It was a fight we were going to lose unless one of the contractors the Reverend had been guilt-tripping since spring threw up their hands in surrender and donated the time, manpower, and materials to repair it. I didn't think Ethel's twenty dollars a week was going to help much, regardless of how often she'd been making up the difference—something I suspected she really couldn't afford to do.

I was thinking out loud as I watched Ethel slide the money into a brown envelope with the rest of the week's donations. "I worry that if something isn't done soon, that whole side's going to cave in and we'll have a helluva mess down there."

Ethel shook her head. "My, my—the *mouth* on you this evening!"

"I'm sorry—again." I rubbed my eyes. "I haven't been sleeping too well the past couple of nights."

"Which means most of the week, unless I miss my guess—don't bother denying it, either. I could pack for a month's vacation in the Caribbean with those bags under your eyes. Still taking your medication like the doctor prescribed?" Meaning my antidepressants.

"Yes."

"Still going to your weekly appointments?" Meaning Dr. Ellis, the psychiatrist who prescribes my antidepressants.

"They're *twice* a week—and, yes, I'm still going."

She tilted her head to the side. "Hmm. How about your diet? Your appetite been okay, Sam? Been eating regular?"

I nodded. "Yes, ma'am. I'm not particularly worried about anything, I haven't been drinking too much caffeine or anything like that . . . I have no idea why I can't sleep."

"Bad dreams, maybe?"

Before I could answer, a voice behind me said, "Terrible, just terrible," loudly enough to make me jump, nearly dropping the stack of plates I'd gathered.

"Hello, Timmy," said Ethel.

"Terrible, just terrible."

I did a spin-dip-balance-and-catch routine with the plates that Buster Keaton would have been proud of, then set everything on Ethel's table in case Timmy or someone else decided to test my reflexes again. "You shouldn't sneak up on me like that," I said to him, and was immediately sorry for the way I said it because Timmy got this look in his eyes like he was going to start crying. "Oh, hey, I'm sorry, Timmy. I'm not mad or anything. I didn't mean to snap at you like that." I put my hand on his shoulder and gave it a little squeeze. "Forgive me?"

Timmy is one of the more-or-less permanent residents here. The Reverend never makes anyone leave if they don't want to or have no place else to go. The city council gives him no end of grief about this come the yearly budget meetings, but like every other city body in Cedar Hill, they don't push it too far; it's all for show, to save face. I don't know what it is about the Reverend that makes them always back down, but I'm grateful for it, as are the permanent residents like Timmy.

Timmy is something of a walking, talking question mark to all of us. Nobody but the Reverend knows his last name, his story, or even if he's from Cedar Hill. He never says anything more than "Terrible, just terrible," to anyone else. But he's courteous, and quiet, and clean.

He also sees things.

I found out from the Reverend that Timmy suffers from gradual and irreversible macular degeneration. The result is, you see things that aren't there. In Timmy's case, these visual hallucinations are pretty harmless: waiters, dancing animals, buildings that have been gone for thirty years, stuff like that. Timmy talks to the Reverend and *only* to the Reverend. The rest of us make do with *Terrible, just terrible*—but you'd be surprised how much he can convey with just those three words.

"We still friends?" I asked him. I didn't want to make him cry; he was the closest thing I had to an older brother.

Timmy wiped his eyes, then pulled in a deep breath and patted my arm, smiling. "Terrible, just terrible." Said in the same tone as, *Don't ask me dumb questions.*

I pressed one of my hands over his and nodded my head.

Ethel finished getting all her things together, and was just about to head back to the Reverend's office when he came barreling through the swinging doors like a man with a pissed-off pit bull snapping at his butt. The Reverend is not known for displays of panic, but one look at the expression on his face and all three of us knew something bad had happened.

As if he knew what we were thinking (which wouldn't surprise me), the Reverend came to a sudden stop, looked up, and tried to smile like nothing was wrong.

"That man couldn't lie if his life depended on it," said Ethel.

"What do you suppose it is?" I asked.

Timmy said, "Terrible, just . . . *terrible.*"

It was the way he said that last "terrible" that made me and Ethel look at him. Timmy sounded genuinely scared. I patted his shoulder and told him everything would be all right.

The Reverend took a deep breath, held it, then let it out in a quick puff before starting toward us again, slower this time, smiling like someone had just stuck a gun in his back and told him to act natural.

"Some night, eh?" he said.

"Oh, will you *can it* with the easygoing routine?" said Ethel. "Ain't none of us blind; we saw you do that Jesse Owens through the doors. What's wrong?"

"I . . ." The Reverend looked into Ethel's eyes and shrugged. "I honestly can't say—and, no, I *don't* mean that I *won't* say. I honestly don't know what's wrong." He ran a hand through his hair. "Martha come back yet?"

"No," said Ethel. "And neither has Joe. What was troubling him, anyway?"

The Reverend walked closer to the front door and stood there a moment, staring out at the freezing rain. "It's a bad night, Ethel. Nights like this, they make some people think too much. If you think too much, you start remembering things, and some of those things are best left forgotten."

"You get that from a fortune cookie?"

The Reverend turned to face her. "Beg pardon?"

Ethel sighed. "I asked you what I thought was a fairly direct question, and what do I get for an answer? Gobbledygook that sounds like something from an Igmar Bergman movie."

"You know Bergman?"

Ethel stood up a little straighter, as if trying to decide whether or not she should be offended. "*Yes*, I know Bergman movies. I also like Kurosawa and Fellini and think the Three Stooges are *very* funny. And you're changing the subject. I asked you what was wrong with Joe?"

"He's dealing with some bad memories."

Ethel finished getting ready to leave, handing the Reverend the money envelope. "You can't save the world, Reverend. Only that part of it that comes through these doors and chooses to stay."

He took the money from her and grinned. "When I grow up, I want to be just like you."

"You'd look terrible in my wardrobe—you're an autumn."

He shook the envelope. "Ah . . . sounds like . . . let me guess . . . twenty dollars?"

"Learn to juggle while blindfolded and you could take that act on the road."

The Reverend laughed. "Oh, Ethel . . . what would I do without you?"

"*Don't* you be sweet-talking me, mister. I'm immune to your charms."

"No, you're not."

Ethel smiled. Her smile is a wonderful thing to behold. "No, I'm not, but we can't have you thinking you're special or anything like that, now, can we?" She kissed his cheek, smiled at me and Timmy, and was just going out the door at the same time Sheriff Ted Jackson was coming in. The sheriff stood aside and held the door open for her.

"Evenin', Sheriff," said Ethel. "There some kind of trouble?"

"Only my troubled heart. *Why* won't you run off with me, Ethel, why?"

She laughed and smacked his arm. "Ted, one of these days I'm gonna take you up on that, and *then* what'll you do?"

"Rejoice. Sing. Dance in the street."

Ethel shook her head. "You *men*. What goes on in those heads of yours?"

"Sweet dreams of holding you in my arms, Ethel," said Jackson. As Ethel walked away toward her car, Jackson called out, "Don't leave me! I'll crumble. I *love* you. Come back!"

I looked at Timmy. "Wow. *Two* floor shows tonight."

Timmy snorted a mischievous laugh and said in a conspiratorial tone, "Terrible, *just terrible.*"

Jackson came inside, closing the door behind him. "You know, some night that woman is going to haul off and knock my teeth down my throat. And I'll probably deserve it."

"I keep a camera at the ready for that very day,"

replied the Reverend. He shook Jackson's hand. "Thanks for coming, Ted."

Jackson shrugged. "My social calendar suddenly cleared up."

We all knew that Jackson's wife had left him after she miscarried. She's living down in Oregon with her sister now. Jackson was elected sheriff last year, after having served as a deputy for something like six years. The new title and new uniform and new power haven't changed him at all; he still looks like he is waiting for someone to come out of the shadows and take it all away from him. He and the Reverend both have a tense, lonely way about them, which is I guess what drew them together as friends. I can't for the life of me figure out what they have in common, but I guess that doesn't really matter when there's someone you can always depend on for company and small talk over a cup of coffee or a sandwich or a smoke.

They stood there chatting about Jackson's new responsibilities, the upcoming city council budget meetings, the weather, and just when I was about to interrupt and ask what was going on, Jackson said, "So how long you need me here?"

The Reverend checked his watch. "An hour, two at the most."

"What's going on?" I asked.

"Popsicle Patrol," said the Reverend. "You need to go warm up the van."

I looked out at the freezing rain—which was coming down even harder than before—and nodded my head. "I was wondering if we were going to do that tonight." And I had been. I said good-bye to Timmy and was making my way toward the back when a little voice behind me said, "Mister, the tape won't play."

She stood there in all her three-year-old radiance, mussed hair, a smudge on one of her cheeks, hands on hips, one foot impatiently tapping, lower lip sticking out in what I'd bet was a well-practiced pout. I wanted to wrap her up and take her home with me.

"Is the tape broken?" I said, kneeling down so we could see eye to eye.

She tsked, rolled her eyes, and sighed. "*Noooooo*, it's not broken. It just won't *play*. They're *not* the same thing, ya know."

I looked toward the "lounge"—an area near one of the corners with three chairs, a sofa, a coffee table, and a television set—and saw the girl's mother, brother, and dog staring at us. The dog in particular seemed irritated that the tape wasn't doing its part to share in the duties of entertaining the kids. I told the little girl I'd see what I could do, and she grabbed my hand, dragging me toward the TV.

As soon as I knelt down in front of it I saw the problem. "It's not the tape, honey—the VCR has to be set on Channel Three or it doesn't come through the TV."

"Well, did you set it?"

"Missy!" said her mother. Then, to me, "Sorry. She really wants to watch the tape and she gets . . . a little impatient."

"That's okay." I set the VCR and cued up the tape. This was a good one: *A Charlie Brown Christmas, How the Grinch Stole Christmas, Frosty the Snowman,* and *Rudolph the Red-Nosed Reindeer.* The Reverend had taped a bunch of holiday specials and movies for folks to watch, to make their holidays here less depressing.

"My name's Beth," said the woman. "This is Melissa—"

"Missy," said the little girl.

"Missy . . . excuse me. This is Kyle, and that bundle of fur on the floor is Lump"

Lump's face was buried between his paws, but he managed to raise up one ear in greeting.

Missy walked over toward me, pointing. "What happened to your ear, mister?"

"Melissa!" snapped Beth.

"It's okay," I said, touching the knot of scar tissue that clung to the side of my skull. I looked at Missy, trying to decide just how much of the truth to tell her. "Well, you see, Missy, I don't have much of an ear left, so I can only hear out of the other one."

Once again, she tsked at me, shaking her head. "I *know* you only got one ear, I *see* that. I mean, *what happened to your ear?"*

"You mean why isn't it there anymore?"

"Uh-huh."

"I got hit in the head."

"Huh? You mean you can get . . . not-hearing and lose your ear from being *hit in the head?"*

I nodded. "If you get knocked out and land in the snow like I did."

"Wow . . . you musta got hit real hard."

"Yep. I was out for about five hours." I hoped she wouldn't quiz me further; I don't lie well.

Beth saved me by mussing Kyle's hair and making him groan. She told Missy that was enough, stop bothering the nice man, then looked at me. "We're on our way to Indiana. We're going to . . . stay with my folks for a while."

"Gramma and Grampa told us we could come stay

with them because our daddy's dead," said Kyle matter-of-factly, as if he understood all about death and had accepted it and was wise beyond his years; which, in a way, I guess he was. Bad wisdom is still wisdom.

As soon as he said "dead," Beth shot me a look that was equal parts fear and pleading, and that's all it took for me to know the rest of the story: Daddy wasn't dead, Daddy was some white-trash asshole who'd decided he'd had enough responsibility for one lifetime, and so took the car (or, more likely, the truck), all the money, and however much beer he could fit in the cooler and abandoned his family— odds are in an apartment from which they were about to be evicted anyway, leaving her to fend not only for herself but for two kids and a dog. I wondered how Daddy had "died," and if Beth had taken care to cover her tracks so he couldn't suddenly resurrect himself from the dead once they were Indiana.

I saw all of this in her eyes for that brief moment; I nodded my head in understanding, and was rewarded with one of the most luminous smiles of gratitude I'd ever seen. These kids had nothing to worry about, not with this woman as their mother. I felt sorry for anyone stupid enough to try and pull anything on them. If Daddy *did* suddenly come back from the dead and show up in Indiana, my guess was he wouldn't be out of that grave for long.

I pointed to the VCR, triumphant. Missy and Kyle applauded my efforts. I took a bow, then said, "Would you guys like some popcorn and sodas to snack on?"

I expected both of them to shout yes, but instead they looked at their mother, who shrugged and looked at me. "Can I have some, too?"

"You were here in time for dinner, right?"

"Oh, uh . . . *yes,* we were. I just . . . the kids don't get treats too often and . . ."

"I'll make extra," I said. "And don't worry—we keep plenty on hand." Which we did, at the Reverend's insistence. Don't ask me why, but somehow eating popcorn and sipping a soda while watching a good movie or a cartoon seems to make everyone happy, at least for a while. A mouthful of popcorn and you're a kid again, at the movies with all the other kids, having a good time and enjoying the hell out of life, not at the end of your rope in a homeless shelter right before Thanksgiving and wondering where'd you'd be come Christmas morning. I guess for a lot of the people who come through here, the smell of popcorn is the smell of childhood, and that can make things easier, if only for a little while.

I made two bags (one butter, one plain), popped open three Pepsis, and put a couple of ham-and-cheese sandwiches on the tray, as well. (I didn't remember seeing them at any of the tables during dinner.) I even found a can of dog food, which I put in a bowl for Lump, who seemed to have a higher opinion of me after I set it in front of him.

Everyone thanked me, then snuggled together under a blanket on the couch, watching Charlie Brown and munching away.

"Ahem?"

I turned to see the Reverend standing right behind me. He looked at Beth and her children, then at Lump, then at me, raising his left eyebrow like that actor who used to play Mr. Spock on *Star Trek.*

"I know, I know," I said, moving past him toward

the rear doors. "What was I supposed to do, ignore them?"

He fell into step beside me. "No, you were supposed to do exactly what you did. It just seemed to me that you were basking in the moment a little too long . . . you knight in shining overalls, you."

"They *weren't* here for dinner, were they?"

"They were, but they were sleeping and I wasn't about to wake them. You did good, Sam."

"Your praise is everything to me."

The Reverend grinned. "Could you maybe be a little *less* sincere?"

"I could give it a whirl, but it costs extra." We smiled at each other; then the Reverend moved toward the kitchen to stock up on hot coffee and sandwiches while I made my way out back to get the van started for Popsicle Patrol.

As I was closing the door behind me, I took one last look inside; Timmy was sitting down in one of the chairs in the lounge, Lump's face seemed permanently fused to the bowl, Beth and her kids were happily munching away (on both the popcorn and the sandwiches, which they shared with Timmy), and the other guests were either settling into their cots, playing cards, or quietly chatting. Sheriff Jackson was sitting at Ethel's table, reading a paperback novel. Everything was quiet, warm, pleasant enough, and safe. It made me feel good, knowing that I'd helped make this a good, clean, decent place for folks who weren't as fortunate as me. I wanted to freeze this moment in my mind so I could take it out again sometime and look at it when I was feeling blue.

They were all fine; they were all safe.

I try very hard to remember that now: how safe it all seemed.

3

It wasn't just the freezing rain that kept my mood more on the downside that night; I'd felt like something was . . . *off* all day. Ever since I'd arrived at the shelter—well before four that afternoon—it seemed like the whole world was moving at a slow, liquid crawl. People looked out their windows at the dark skies as if they sensed there might be something looking back down at them but taking care to keep itself hidden from their gazes.

I guess that sounds a little on the melodramatic side, and I'm sorry I can't make it any clearer than that, but there was just this *feeling* in the atmosphere. The closest thing I can think of to compare it to is the day the World Trade Center buildings went down. Remember how when you went outside, even if there were no radios or television sets to be heard, even if you were alone, you could *feel* the weight of it in the air? As if the wind itself had been stopped dead in its tracks, stunned by the horror of it, and everything around you was holding its breath, wondering, *What happens now?*

That's what this day had felt like to me.

Like I'd told Ethel, I hadn't been sleeping too well the past few days, and I figured that had a lot to do with the way I was seeing things. It wasn't like some slimy, big-ass tentacled monster was going to come dropping down on Cedar Hill like a curse from heaven once the clouds parted and the rain stopped. I was just tired. That had to be it.

Once the van's engine was all warmed up, I turned the heater on and in a few minutes had the inside all toasty. I pulled around in front and waited for the Reverend, who came out almost right away, carrying a cooler that I knew was full of sandwiches, as well as three thermoses—two of hot coffee, one of hot chocolate. He slid open the side door, shoved the cooler inside, then closed the door and climbed into the front passenger seat.

"Me, too," he said.

"What?"

He shook off the rain, ran his hand through his hair to push it back from his face, then looked right at me. "I've been feeling it, too."

I blinked. "Feeling . . . wh-what? What're you—?"

He shook his head. "Don't play dumb with me, Sam. All day you've felt like something's been off, haven't you? Like something's about to happen?"

I shrugged. "Yeah, maybe. Yes."

"Hence my saying, 'Me, too.' Try to keep up." He leaned forward and looked out the windshield, his eyes turning up toward the rain. "Makes you crazy, doesn't it? That sense that something's going to happen and you don't know if it'll be something good or something . . . not."

"Either way," I said, putting the van into gear, "we got the perfect night for it."

The Reverend turned to me and smiled. "That's just like you, Sam. 'The perfect night.' Saying something like that."

"Oh, it'll be all right, Mr. Frodo, you'll see."

I pulled away from the curb and the Popsicle Patrol officially began.

Believe it or not it was the Reverend, not me, who

started calling it that. It strikes some people as offensive—Ethel, in particular, thinks it's pretty tasteless—but the Reverend defends it by saying: "Would it be in better taste if I called it the 'Corpsesicle Patrol'? Because that's what they'll be if we don't get to them in time. If you wish for us to change the name, then you have to make at least *two* runs with us. Otherwise you get no say."

Ethel declined the offer and never complained about it again after that.

There are five pickup points on Popsicle Patrol, and on nights like this, when the rain and the wind and the cold conspire to freeze you in place, the homeless folks all know where these pickup points are and know which routes to take in order to get there; that way, if we pass each other while they or we are heading in that direction, we just stop and pick them up. Cedar Hill isn't that big of a place when compared with a city like Columbus or Cincinnati, but it still takes a while to drive through it in bad weather. The Reverend established the pickup points however many years ago, when he first showed up in Cedar Hill, and since then not one homeless person has frozen to death here. Let's see Columbus or Cincinnati try and claim that.

The first pickup point is on the downtown square on the east side of the courthouse. Like all pickup points, we pull up and wait fifteen minutes, then drive on to the next if no one shows. As soon as we have a full van, we go back to the shelter, drop them off, then head to the next pickup point, and so on. The Reverend took a lot of time figuring out the route, making sure that the trips to and from each pickup point take us past the previous ones again in case anyone new has shown up in the meantime. All in all, we pass each pickup point a minimum of five times during Popsicle Patrol, which is why it usually takes us a couple of hours.

We pulled up to the courthouse and I automatically killed the headlights.

"Sam," said the Reverend.

"Sorry, force of habit." I keep forgetting that the out-of-towners are wary of approaching a dark van. I turned the headlights back on just in time to see a man with no legs rolling himself toward us on a makeshift cart built from two skateboards and a wooden crate, using two canes to propel himself forward.

The Reverend looked at his watch. "He's late."

"Probably didn't want to get stopped for speeding."

The Reverend started to laugh, stopped himself, said, "Sam, that's not funny," and then burst out laughing. The man in the cart heard the laughter, pulled back his canes, adjusted the gloves on his hands, then folded his arms across his chest and stared at us. With the canes forming a giant X across his body, he looked like some ancient Egyptian mummy, only crabbier.

The Reverend reached back and slid open the side doors, calling, "Come on, Linus, your security blanket hath arrived."

"Oh, jeez—I've never heard *that* one before." Linus—I don't know his real name, he calls himself that after that character Humphrey Bogart played in *Sabrina*, not the *Peanuts* character—pulled down his canes and pushed himself over to the van. "You were laughing at me."

"No," said the Reverend. "I was laughing *near* you. There's a difference."

"Especially when you ain't the one who's wet and cold."

"Now, now, Linus; don't get short with me."

"Oh, that's a stump-slapper, all right." He tossed his canes into the back, then pulled himself up into the van while I got out and went around to retrieve his cart, watching as he maneuvered himself around and up into one of the backseats. Most people would take one look at Linus and feel revulsion or pity; me, I marvel at the strength of the man. His arms are the most muscular I've ever seen in person. You had to feel bad for anyone who might be on the receiving end of one of his punches.

"You got any more carny work lined up?" I asked him.

"Starting in early June," he replied. "I will once again be touring the tristate area as Thalidomide Man."

"You gonna carve out any more of those little wood figures you used to sell?"

"Always."

Linus makes a seasonal living with whatever touring carnival will hire him. He calls himself Thalidomide Man because of his legs—tells people it was because his mother took the drug during her pregnancy. Every season he whittles a couple of hundred little wood figures of himself—long arms, hands, no legs—and sells them for a couple of dollars each. I have a few, and have noticed that he tends to change the look of the figure every year, usually making himself much more handsome than he really is . . . and I tell him that every year. One of these days he's going to carry through on his threat to bite off my kneecaps.

I put the cart on top of the van, covering it with the

tarpaulin we keep there, then secured it in place with a length of clothesline. The Reverend reached back and slid the side door closed as I was climbing back in just in time for their traditional Godzilla trivia game.

"All right," Linus was saying. "I got a toughie for you tonight."

"I doubt that." The Reverend knows his Godzilla trivia.

Linus made a *hmph* sound, then cracked his knuckles like some card dealer ready to toss out a losing hand to an opponent. "Okay, Mr. Chuckles, try this one: Name the first movie where Godzilla was the *good* guy *and* tell me the other monsters who were in the movie *and* how long into the movie it is before good-guy Godzilla makes his first appearance."

The Reverend looked at Linus and grinned. "Is that it?"

Linus looked at me. " 'Is that it?' he asks me. A lesser man would feel insulted."

"A lesser man would have no arms and be hanging on a wall and be named Art," I replied.

Linus made the *hmph* sound again and shook his head. "You know what you two are? You're *limb*-ists."

"That's not a word," I said.

"Then how can I *say* something that isn't a word? Huh? Answer me *that* one, Kato."

"*Godzilla Versus Monster Zero*," said the Reverend. "Godzilla, Rodan, and Ghidra. And it's thirty-seven minutes into the movie before *both* Godzilla and Rodan first show themselves."

Linus was visibly crushed. "I thought for sure you'd miss it. A *three-parter*. I'd've bet money you'd miss at least one of them."

"Try another one."

Linus shook his head. "No, thank you; one disgrace a night is my limit."

"I got one," I said. Both the Reverend and Linus looked at me in surprise. I shrugged, then said, "What was the name of the giant rosebush that Godzilla fought with?"

"Biollante," they both said simultaneously; then Linus chimed in with, "The best special effects they save for the dumbest storyline. It's a damn shame."

"Well, I tried."

Linus reached over the seat and patted my shoulder. "It was a good question, though, Sam. Most people don't know that any new Godzilla movies were made after *Terror of Mecha-Godzilla*. And I don't count that big-budget abortion from ninety-eight . . . although Jean Reno kicked ass in it."

"Yeah, he's great," said the Reverend.

After that, the three of us fell silent for a few minutes. The rain was turning into serious sleet, and a few pebble-sized chunks of hail bounced off the windshield. I turned up the defroster and ran the wipers, turning the world outside into a liquid blur of shapeless colors.

"A fit night for neither man nor beast," said Linus.

I turned around and grinned at him. "That's a line from *Rudolph the Red-Nosed Reindeer*, right?"

Linus rolled his eyes and sighed. "We three are just a fount of useless information this evening."

"No, I fixed up the VCR back at the shelter so this woman and her kids could watch *Rudolph* before we left."

"That's some truly unnerving syntax," said the Reverend.

"I work hard at it."

The Reverend poured Linus some hot coffee and gave him a sandwich, and while he ate I checked the clock and saw it was about time to move onto the next pickup point. I put the van into gear and was just pulling away from the curb when a police cruiser rounded the corner doing about sixty, its visibar lights flashing but the siren turned off—a silent approach. It sped past us, followed by an ambulance whose lights were flashing but whose siren was also turned off.

"Okay, that's interesting," said the Reverend.

Both of the vehicles stopped at the midway point on the East Main Street Bridge. One of the police officers got out and looked over the side of the bridge.

Without being told to do it, I spun the wheel and headed in that direction. There's an old fisherman's shack on the banks of the Licking River below the bridge that some of the homeless folks in town use as a flop when the weather's bad and they can't make it to the shelter.

By the time we got to the bridge, two more squad cars had pulled up and I could see that there was already another ambulance and at least three other squad cars parked down near the river bank.

"They must've taken the access road," said the Reverend, shaking his head. "I wouldn't want to try and drive back up that thing tonight." He threw open the door and climbed out. The police officer who was looking over the railing caught sight of him and turned around, his hand automatically resting on the butt of his gun, but then he saw who it was and relaxed. The Reverend went over and spoke to him for a few moments, the officer nodded his head, asked a question, and on hearing the Reverend's answer turned his head slightly to the side and spoke into the radio communications microphone attached to his collar. The Reverend thanked him, and then came back to the van.

"What's going on?" I asked as he climbed in.

"I don't know. Looks like Joe was at the shack for a little while. He's not around and they're still looking for him. They've got Martha, though, and I guess she's in bad shape. The paramedics had to sedate her. That ambulance down there is for her."

"Then who's this other one for?"

The Reverend ran a hand through his soaked hair. "Not just yet, Sam. Drive to the other side of the bridge and pull over."

Asking no more questions, I did as he asked, and saw there was an unmarked car idling by the curb, its cherry light whirling on the dashboard. A beefy man was sitting inside, talking on the radio. When he saw the van pull over, he climbed out of the car, pulled up the collar on his coat, and ran over to the side door. It took Linus a moment to get it opened, but once he did the man climbed inside and shook the freezing rain from his hands. "I smell coffee. Why has none yet been offered to me?"

"And a good evening to you, too, Bill," said the Reverend, unscrewing the top of a thermos and pouring. Detective Bill Emerson took the cup in his thin, dainty, almost feminine hands (he gets a lot of grief from the guys on the force about them), took a few tentative sips, said, "Starbucks charges you six bucks a shot for stuff this good," then stared down into the dark, steamy liquid as if expecting to see some answer magically appear. "Okay, so Joe was at the shelter earlier and got upset and took off and you sent Martha after him, right?"

"Right."

Emerson nodded his head, took another sip of the coffee, then looked at Linus. "Linus, I don't suppose you've got any smokes on you, do you?"

"Not tonight, I'm afraid."

"That's all right. My wife'd kill me if I came home smelling of tobacco."

"How's Martha?" asked the Reverend.

"Quiet, now. They've got her in the ambulance."

"Can you tell me anything about what happened?"

Emerson shook his head. "Not officially."

"Then off the record?"

Emerson looked up; his eyes were glassy and tired and haunted-looking. "Among other things—which I can't tell you about, so don't ask—we found a body down there. I don't think it's anyone you know."

The Reverend tensed. "You don't know that for certain."

Emerson reached into his coat pocket and removed three Polaroids that he passed up front. The Reverend looked at all three of them, whispered, "Good God," and passed them to me.

What happens now? I thought as I looked at them.

There's an almost-joke that we use to settle the nerves of folks who are passing through, who maybe don't know about or haven't heard some of this city's colorful history. This is Cedar Hill. Weird shit happens here. Get used to it.

Even by the standards of our usual weird shit, what I saw in those photographs was way the hell out there.

The guy had to have been almost seven feet tall. He

was naked and pale and dead, but that wasn't what caused me to gasp. He had only one eye socket, directly in the center of his forehead, where two eyes struggled to stay in place. His face had no nose; instead, there was a proboscis-like appendage that looked like an uncircumcised penis growing from the center of his too-small forehead.

I was looking at photographs of a dead cyclops.

What happens now?

I continued staring at them until Linus reached between the seats and snatched them out of my hand. No sooner had he done that and began looking at them than Emerson snatched them from him.

"That's not fair—*they* got to see 'em."

"Have you seen Joe tonight?" asked Emerson.

"No."

"Can you offer me *any* information that might shed some light on what happened at the shelter earlier this evening?"

"No."

"And is there any chance that you're ever going to replace my wooden figure of Thalidomide Man that the arms fell off of?"

"For five bucks, sure."

"I meant for free."

"What do *you* think?"

"I think that you're not connected to this case, then, so you don't get to peek." Emerson slipped the Polaroids back into his coat pocket. "Have you *ever* seen anything like that in your life?"

Both the Reverend and I shook our heads.

"Something strange and maybe kind of terrible is going on in this city tonight," said Emerson, looking out at the rain. "I can . . . *feel* it. This is a perfect night

for monsters or ghosts and—Jesus, don't I sound por-
tentous? Sorry." He took a couple of deep swallows of
the coffee, then wordlessly requested a refill, which
the Reverend wordlessly gave.

"I've felt like something bad's been going to happen all day," I said. "For a couple of days, to tell you
the truth."

"I hear you," replied Emerson, then: "Do any of
you know any other spots Joe might go to?"

None of us did.

"Do you think he might have gone back to the
shelter?"

None of us did.

"You guys are a damned helpful bunch," said Emerson. "Is it all right if I go by and see for myself?"

"You can call. Ted Jackson's holding down the fort
until we get back."

"I'll do that, thanks." Emerson finished the coffee,
handed the cup back to the Reverend, and slid the
side door open. "I don't have to tell you not to repeat
anything, do I?"

"Repeat any of what?" said the Reverend.

"There you go." And with that, Emerson closed the
door and ran back to his car.

I stared at the Reverend for a moment before finally saying, "What the hell was that?"

"*That*, Samuel, was a deformed *human being* whose
life was probably an unbroken string of lonely mis-
eries that ended on the muddy, freezing banks of this
river with no friend near to hold his hand or mark
the moment of his passing—that's *who* that was."

I nodded my head and apologized.

"Looked like something out of *Jason and the Arg-
onauts*, you ask me," said Linus.

The Reverend shot him a look that could have frozen fire. "Nobody asked you. And I'll thank you to show a little respect for someone who wasn't lucky enough to have us find him first!"

Linus blanched at the Reverend's sudden anger. "I . . . I didn't mean anything by it. I'm sorry."

The Reverend glared at him for a moment longer, then exhaled, his shoulders slumping and the anger vanishing from his face. "I'm sorry, too, Linus." He reached out and grabbed the other man's hand. "I didn't mean to raise my voice like that. Forgive me?"

"I will if I can have another sandwich."

"Done."

Linus tore into his ham-and-cheese and I pulled out, turned the van around, and headed for the second pickup point.

None of us mentioned the photographs; not then, not later, not again.

If you live here, you accept the weird shit—even if it's with a capital W—or you try to get out.

Good luck with that second option.

4

We dropped Linus off at the shelter about an hour later. Beth's kids immediately wanted to ride on his cart, and Linus was all to happy to oblige them.

We'd picked up another half-dozen folks along the way, and as soon as they were all situated, Sheriff Jackson came up to me and the Reverend and said, "Grant McCullers just called from the Hangman. He's bringing some hot food over for everyone, and it appears that he's got another guest for you tonight."

"Who?" asked the Reverend.

Jackson shrugged. "He wouldn't say. I guess he found the guy camping out between a couple of the lumber piles."

McCullers owns and operates Hangman's Tavern, a place out by Buckeye Lake. It's called that because the KKK used to hang black folks near the spot. There's even an old makeshift T post with a noose dangling from it to mark the road to the tavern.

Grant's a good guy. We hadn't heard much from him since October, when a nasty storm did some serious damage to the Hangman. I hated to think what the repairs were costing him, but even with all his own financial troubles, Grant somehow always managed to come to the shelter a couple times every month to bring some hot food. He'd even offered to donate whatever lumber was left from the repair work so that we could do something about the wall in the basement.

The Reverend checked his watch, then the weather outside. "I wouldn't want to drive from Buckeye Lake in this weather."

"Yeah, well, Grant's funny that way," said Jackson. "He'll go out of his way for someone without a second thought. Hell, during the divorce, he and you were about the only people I had to talk to."

The Reverend nodded his head, then gave the place a quick once-over to make sure everyone was doing all right. "Sam and I are going to make another Popsicle run. Can I impose on you to hang around for another hour?"

"Everybody knows I'm here," said Jackson. "But if there's an emergency, I'll have to leave."

"You've got my cell number, right?"

"I'll call and let you know."

The Reverend squeezed Jackson's shoulder. "You're a really good friend, Ted."

"Don't spread that around. I have a non-reputation to protect."

The Reverend turned to me. "You get all the sandwiches and coffee refilled?"

"All packed up."

"Let's go, then."

Back in the van, the Reverend turned on the radio as we pulled out. Someone was playing Bob Dylan's "Knockin' on Heaven's Door."

"Oddly enough," said the Reverend, "not my favorite Dylan tune." He punched a button and switched to a different station.

This next station was also playing "Knockin' on Heaven's Door."

"That's an odd coincidence," I said.

The Reverend said nothing, only looked at the radio, then back out at the night.

"I want you to do me a favor, Sam."

"Sure thing."

He looked at me. "Pay attention to where the song is when I change the station, okay?"

"Okay . . ."

He punched another button, going to a third, different station.

Not only was this one also playing the same song, but we'd come in to it at the exact spot where it had been when the Reverend changed stations.

This time, I punched a button. Different station, same song, same spot where it had been before.

"Maybe something's wrong with the radio," I said, switching it over to AM.

Same song, same place.

The Reverend and I looked at each other.

"I told you something was going on tonight," he said to me.

For the next ten minutes, we changed stations, changed bands, reset selected stations manually, and it didn't matter a damn; AM or FM, preset station or random scroll, every station we found was playing "Knockin' on Heaven's Door," and each time the song was at the same spot where it had been before we switched. Over and over for ten minutes, same thing each time.

"Maybe something happened to Dylan and every-one's playing this," I said.

The Reverend looked at me and shook his head. "First of all, if anything *had* happened to Bob Dylan, it would have been all over the news, which it wasn't. Secondly, even if that were the case and I somehow missed out on hearing it, I sincerely doubt that"—he checked the current station setting—"the Power Wad One-oh-six would be playing this song. The Wad specializes in thrash metal. If this were the Guns N' Roses cover, I might buy your explanation, but we've got—" He cut off his words as he looked up and saw some-one standing in the light fog at the pickup point.

"We've got weird scenes inside the gold mine, is what we've got." He turned off the radio and we pulled over so that a too-skinny young man—maybe late twenties, early thirties—could get in. This guy didn't so much stroll as *slink* toward the van, moving with the easy grace of a cat across the top of a wall—head tilted slightly to the left, long dark hair caught in the wind, hips swaying from side to side.

I leaned toward the Reverend. "Is it just me, or does that guy look like—"

"There's no 'look like' about it, Sam. That's him."

Okay, there's no way to say this without sounding like a basket case, so I'm just going to say it and be done: We'd just picked up Jim Morrison, lead singer of The Doors, a man who supposedly died in Paris almost thirty years ago.

Morrison climbed into the back of the van, closed the door, and sat staring down at the floor.

"Mr. Mojo Risin'," said the Reverend.

Morrison looked up at him with heavy-lidded eyes and gave a short nod.

"I'm a big fan." The Reverend offered him a cup of coffee. Morrison took it with a half grin, then sipped it.

The Reverend watched him for a moment, and then asked, "How is it you wound up here?"

And if I'd had any doubts as to who this really was sitting in the backseat, they were erased when he looked back up and said, "I am the Lizard King; I can do anything."

It was *that voice*. "The killer awoke before dawn . . . ," "Break on through . . . ," "When the still sea conspires in armor . . ." The same timbre, the same inflections. Not the good imitation of a singer from a tribute band. The real thing.

I started shaking. Morrison saw this, then reached over and squeezed my shoulder. "Easy there, Sam. You got no reason to be afraid of me."

All I could do was nod.

"Why are you here tonight?" asked the Reverend.

Morrison shook his head. "Sorry, man. I'm not allowed to say."

"Understood. Can you tell us where we need to go next?"

"Second Popsicle pickup point." Morrison grinned. "Man, alliteration. I'd forgotten what that feels like on the tongue. Not that I ever used it much— *alliteration*, not my tongue."

We drove off into the sleeting night.

5

When I was a kid, I wanted so much to be a rock star. The music, the adulation, the fame and riches, all of it.

But mostly the music.

I tried my hand at half a dozen different instruments: harmonica, guitar, bass, drums, piano, and even—hand to God—flute (hey, if Ian Anderson could use it to make Jethro Tull one of the greatest groups of all time, why the hell not?). I was a failure at all of them, except for the guitar, and even then I had the sense to realize that if I dedicated myself to the instrument, if I practiced for ten hours a day every day for the rest of my life, I would be an at-best average guitar player . . . and the world has too many of those already.

So I contented myself with the fantasy of rock stardom, and my love of music. Classical, country, prog, blues, rock, metal—I loved it all. And my admiration for anyone who can pull a tune out of the ether and make it real has never lessened. Even if it's a crap song, it's still a song, something that didn't exist until someone heard it in the back of their head and put it out into the world.

But I never understood why so many rock stars went down in flames. I could never dredge up much sympathy for someone who made millions doing what they loved, creating something that gave so much pleasure to the rest of the world, and then pissed it all away on drugs and booze or whatever the poison of choice was at the time. But then, that's an easy judgment to make when you're not the one who has to live with the pressure of always having to be *on* for the world, of not being able to go anywhere without people following you, wanting your autograph, your picture, a lock of your hair, or whatever else is required so that they can prove to themselves that they once touched greatness . . . even if that greatness were fleeting, or only in their minds, or even manufactured.

I guess any culture needs its popular icons, something for the rest of the populace to aspire to, knowing they'll never make it. Hell, there was probably some prima donna cave-wall painter back in the Neolithic days who started to believe it when his fans told him that his shit didn't stink.

I don't know how many times during the next hour or so I wanted to turn around and ask Morrison or any of the others *why* they'd allowed themselves to fall victim to their self-indulgences when they'd died still having so much more to give to the world . . . then just as quickly realized how goddamned selfish that was. Maybe that Neil Young song hit it on the head, about it being better to burn out than fade away.

People like you and me will never know, so how can we be made to understand?

Over the next hour, we picked up Keith Moon and John Entwistle (both from The Who), Gary Thain and David Byron (of Uriah Heep), Tommy Bolin (The James Gang and Deep Purple), Paul Kossoff (Free), the great blues guitarist Roy Buchanan, as well as Janis Joplin, Jimi Hendrix, Kurt Cobain, and

Billie Holiday—to whom *everyone* paid the greatest respect and courtesy.

The Reverend gave them each welcome and coffee, and asked each of them the same questions: How did you get here? Why are you here? Where are we taking you?

"Honey," said Billie Holiday, laying a thin and elegant hand against the Reverend's cheek, "what we got to do, we *got* to do. 'Taint nobody's business but ours, and that's just how it's gotta be. You got that look in your eyes, you know that?"

"What look is that?"

"Like you already know whatever it is you're tryin' to get one of us to say."

"Can we get out of this fuckin' cold already?" said Cobain.

I put the van in gear and drove back to the shelter.

"Sam doesn't say much," Morrison announced to the others.

"Ah, a quiet one," said Entwistle, grinning.

Keith Moon shook his head. "Bloody birds of a feather." And began to beat a tattoo against his legs.

Morrison leaned forward, resting his elbows on the back of the Reverend's seat and my own. "I gotta hand it to you two, you're not freaking out like I expected. I—whoa, pull over."

We did, and Jerry Garcia climbed in.

"Come see Uncle John's band," I muttered under my breath.

"I always hated that fuckin' song," said Garcia.

"Really?" asked Cobain. "That's, like, one of my guilty-favorite tunes of all time."

Garcia shrugged. "What's it hurt to admit it now?"

Cobain thought about it for a moment, then nodded. "I see what you mean."

"Hey, *Nevermind* was a great record," said Garcia. "You were a great songwriter, my friend. *Sloppy* guitarist, but a great songwriter."

"Thanks," said Cobain. "I think."

"You're welcome," said Garcia. "Maybe."

I looked over at the Reverend. "If Ms. Holiday was right, Reverend, if you got some idea what's going on, I'd sure appreciate being let in on the secret."

It was Morrison who answered. "Hasn't it crossed your mind to wonder how it is a van that's designed to hold only eight people is holding almost twice that many right now?"

I looked in the rearview mirror and saw an empty van reflected back at me. "I guess it's because you're all ghosts, right?"

Morrison laughed, as did everyone else. "Shit, *no*, Sam! *Ghosts* are, like, the spirits of real people who're hanging around because they've got unfinished business."

"Like that girl up there," said Hendrix, pointing to a young woman crossing the street.

"Do we need to pick her up?" asked the Reverend.

Morrison shook his head. "No. She's got nothing to do with this."

I stared at her. "Who is she?"

"Roberta Martin," said Garcia, Hendrix, and Buchanan simultaneously.

I put the van in park and turned to face them. *"Who?"*

"The greatest guitar player who ever lived," said Morrison.

I shrugged. "I've never heard of her."

"No reason you should have," said Buchanan in his soft, soft voice. "She was killed by a drunk driver on her way to a gig in Nobelsville, Indiana, in 1982."

"Girl was so good it was *scary*," said Hendrix.

Garcia nodded. "You got that right."

"Never recorded a demo for anyone," said Buchanan. "She was only twenty-two when she died."

"*I* was only twenty-five," said Tommy Bolin.

"Yeah," replied Hendrix, "but it was your own fucking fault. By the way, I want my ring back."

"This one?" said Bolin, holding up his hand. "My girlfriend gave it to me."

"That was the same ring I was wearing when *I* died," said Hendrix. "How the fuck she wound up with it, I don't know."

Bolin removed the ring and tossed it to Hendrix. "It was kinda tight, anyway."

"Says you." Hendrix slipped it back on his finger, and the two men smiled at each other.

"*She's* a ghost," said Cobain, pointing toward Roberta Martin. "*We're* . . . shit, I guess you'd call us . . . what?"

"Ulcerations of the idealized," replied Entwistle.

"Good going," said Morrison. "We're more than a memory but less than something alive."

"I still don't understand."

"Who says that *we* do, hon?" asked Billie Holiday.

In the street, Roberta Martin stopped and turned toward the van. Everyone inside became quiet. She smiled at us, lifted her hand, waved, and then disappeared into the sleet.

"Girl had the *fire*," said Hendrix, his voice suddenly sad.

"She sure did," replied Buchanan.

Cobain nodded. "A fuckin' shame."

Jerry Garcia leaned forward, passing halfway through Janis Joplin, who shared his seat. "You know anything about physics, Sam?"

"A little, I guess."

"So you know how black holes are formed by stars that collapse inward on themselves, right?"

"Okay . . . ?"

"And how matter can be reformed into anything as it passes through . . . I mean, at least theoretically?"

I shrugged. "I guess, sure."

"Then think of us as a something that's come out of a black hole . . . only in this case, it's a black hole of idealization, formed by a collapsing psyche."

I opened my mouth to speak, then shook my head and looked at the Reverend.

"They're not ghosts," he said to me. "They're the idealized versions of themselves. They're not the *people* they were, they're the icons, what they were imagined to be by those fans who idealized and worshipped them."

I nodded. "The legends, not the human beings?"

"Right." He looked back at our passengers. "Right?"

"Close enough," said Morrison. "At some point, every one of us has been idolized by someone. Be idolized by enough people, and that idol-image becomes more real to them than you ever could be. Fuck, man, I had so many people calling me a rock god that I started believing it myself."

"I wouldn't know, mate," said Paul Kossoff.

I looked back at the guitarist. "But you were *good*. *Back Street Crawler* was a kick-ass album."

"Thanks, mate. But after I left Free . . ." He shrugged. "All I was to the world—to whatever part of it that still noticed me—was 'ex-Free guitarist . . .' And the only thing Free did that people still remember or care about was 'All Right Now.'"

"But at least *that's* remembered," I said.

Kossoff smiled. "Yeah, there's *that*."

"All it takes," said Buchanan, "is one person. *One* person idolizes you, and you're screwed. Like it or not, from that moment on . . . you kinda split in two. Some part of you is always aware of the idol half." He gave his head a little shake. "And it can mess with you."

"Amen," said Cobain.

Morrison tapped my shoulder. "You need to get moving again."

"Where are we going?"

"Back to the good Reverend's shelter."

"Why there?"

"Because," said Entwistle, "the source of the ulceration that brought us here should be there by now."

"You and your bloody loopy syntax," said Keith Moon. "You always talked just like you played. Too damned busy for its own good."

"Coming from you," said Entwistle, "I take that as a compliment."

"You would." Then Moon smiled. "Good to see you again, Ox."

"Likewise."

I looked at the Reverend. "I'm scared."

He said nothing in return, and I knew.

Despite what Morrison had said to us, the Reverend was scared, as well.

6

It didn't help that none of them said a word after that, just sat back there staring out at the night and looking more and more like the ghosts they claimed not to be.

They filed into the shelter silently, each finding a cot or a chair at various spots around the main floor, where they sat, watching all the doors and windows.

The dog—Lump—sat up as soon as we came inside, his ears jerking. Missy sat down to pet him when he started growling, and Beth looked at her daughter, then to me.

"Lump *never* growls," she said. "I don't know what's gotten into him all of a sudden."

"It's just a bad night," I said, as if that could explain everything. "Where's your son—sorry, I forgot his name."

"Kyle? He's downstairs taking a shower."

"How're you doing?"

"Hm? Oh, me . . . I'm okay." She patted her stomach. "The food really hit the spot."

"Well, if anybody wants seconds . . ."

"You're very nice."

"I try."

"Would it be all right if the kids watched *Rudolph* again? Kyle and Missy really like it, even though the Bumble kinda scares them."

"The Bumble?"

"The Abominable Snow Monster. Remember, Yukon Cornelius calls it the 'Bumble'?"

"That's right. Huh. Thing scared me half to death when I was a kid and saw it for the first time."

The Reverend called me over to the kitchen area, where he, Jackson, and Grant McCullers were warming up some stew and wrapping other food for the refrigerator. Grant was doing most of the wrapping, and doing it quickly. I only mention this because he's got a bad hand that looks more like a claw than it does a human hand. It's been that way for as long as I've known him. Arthritis. But he can play a mean harmonica, serve drinks more smoothly, and wrap food faster and with more dexterity than anyone I've ever seen.

"Hey, Sam, I hear you're something of a music expert," said Grant.

"Not an expert, but I know trivia. *Some* trivia."

"Did you ever hear of a band called Parallax?" asked Grant.

I looked at Jackson and the Reverend, both of whom were staring at me like the answer to this was something important.

"Sure. They only did three albums, but they were pretty good."

Grant finished wrapping a half pound of hamburger, tossed it onto the pile of to-be-frozen foods. "They were from Ohio, right?"

I nodded. "Two of them were from Zanesville, but the guitarist, Byron Knight, he was from here, from Cedar Hill."

Grant exchanged an I-told-you-so look with Jackson, who nodded his head and gestured for the Reverend and me to follow him into the back.

"It was real nice of you to bring over all this food," I said to Grant.

"The new freezer's a tad smaller than I'd planned, so I had to do something with this chow, ya know?"

I grinned at his white lie. "How's the Hangman coming along?"

"I look to reopen in about two weeks."

"You gonna replace the old jukebox?"

He stopped for a moment, thought about something, then shook his head. "You know, I don't think I will. It works just fine. In fact, I'm getting rid of that new one."

The Reverend came up behind me. "Are you two finished with this architectural discussion? I could use Sam's help."

"You can *always* use Sam's help," said Grant. "In fact, I wonder if you'd get anything done if you *didn't* have Sam's help."

"And yours, and Ted's, and God's. I am useless without any of you."

Grant laughed. "Just wanted to hear you say it."

"It's unbecoming of you, Grant. Fishing for a compliment."

"Been a bad couple of months. But you don't want to hear about my dreadful personality problems."

"Your lips to God's ear."

They looked at one another and smiled. The Reverend took hold of my elbow and we fell into step behind the sheriff.

"This guy was in pretty bad shape," said Jackson, "so Grant and I put him back in your office. Hope you don't mind too much."

"As long as he hasn't puked on everything."

Jackson grinned. "Not *that* kind of bad shape. The guy was shit-scared half out of his mind. Wanted to be put someplace where no one could see him."

"Did he get here before or after Bill Emerson?"

"After." Jackson grinned. "Can't say any of us were much help to Bill."

"Still no word about Joe, then?"

"Afraid not. I've got my deputies out looking for him, as well, now. Don't worry, We'll find him."

"God, I hope so."

We arrived at the door to the Reverend's office-slash-living quarters. Jackson gripped the doorknob, then looked at us. "I was kinda into Parallax, too, when I was younger. That's why I about fell over when I saw who this was." He opened the door and we stepped into the room.

Byron Knight—that's right, *the* Byron Knight—was lying on a cot beside the Reverend's desk. It had been almost thirty years since anyone had seen him. Most people who cared to remember him at all assumed he was dead, what with his dramatic disappearance back in the early eighties.

The years had not been good to him. His once muscular frame—featured on the covers of both *Rolling Stone* and *Melody Maker* in the same month—was now an emaciated ruin. The clothes he wore were torn, patched, and tattered. And the sickly gray pallor of his skin betrayed an illness I was all-too familiar with: cancer. I'd watched it slowly chew my mother to death after Dad abandoned us when I was twelve.

"The source of the ulceration," whispered the Reverend.

"The source of the what?" asked Jackson.

The Reverend, ignoring the sheriff's question, turned to me. "You stay here with him, Sam, all right? Don't let anyone except me or Ted or Grant through the door, understand?"

"Yessir."

"What the hell is going on?" asked Jackson. "I only ask because it seems to me that neither one of you were too surprised to see him here. Me, I see a rock star from thirty years ago who I thought was dead, I get curious."

The Reverend took hold of Jackson's arm and led him out of the room. "Lock the door behind us, Sam."

"Don't have to tell me twice."

They left, I locked the door, and I heard a voice from behind me say one word.

"Mudman . . ."

Wow.

Okay, it wasn't quite the same as hearing Morrison call himself the Lizard King . . . but it was close.

The Buckeye State has produced only four rock acts that ever amounted to anything more than passing curiosities: Devo (Akron), The James Gang (Cleveland), Guided By Voices (Dayton), and Parallax (Zanesville/Cedar Hill). Parallax came out of central Ohio in the mid-1970s, just as the progressive rock movement was hitting its zenith. Bands like Yes; Emerson, Lake & Palmer; Flash; King Crimson; and a trio of Canadian upstarts calling themselves Rush were engulfing the airwaves with long, complex "concept" pieces like "Close to the Edge," "Tarkus," and "2112." It was not uncommon (thanks to the earlier success of Iron Butterfly's seventeen-minute "In-A-Gadda-Da-Vida") to turn on your FM radio and hear only three songs played over the course of an hour. Ten-minute songs were almost *short* compared to a half-hour epic like "Karn Evil 9." It seemed that if you were going to be taken seriously in the prog rock movement (by anyone who wasn't Lester Bangs of

Creem magazine), you had to produce a "concept" piece that would initially befuddle listeners while giving the DJs time to take a leisurely piss break. A lot of it was pretentious crap, but some of it was kind of amazing. It didn't matter if you thought Rush's "The Fountain of Lamneth" was overblown silliness, because Yes's "The Revealing Science of God" might blow you away right after.

One of these concept pieces that you could hear played on FM radio back then was an eighteen-minute beauty by Parallax entitled "Kiss of the Mudman."

What made "Mudman" so unique that even Lester Bangs admitted a grumbling admiration for it (Bangs was infamous for loathing everything about the prog-rock movement) was its fusion of traditional blues with Hindi music. Critics were divided on whether or not it was a successful piece, but even those who disliked it had to admit that it was unlike anything produced during the short-lived prog era—and that it was performed by your basic rock trio, using only a bass, drums, and a single guitar, without any studio trickery or overdubs, served, according to *Rolling Stone*'s review, "as a testament to Parallax's serious-minded goals, if not their cumulative musicianship, which seems too agile at times to move 'Mudman' into the realm of potential classic. Still, Canada's Rush might soon have reason to be looking over their shoulders if Knight, Shaw, and Jacobs continue to move in this direction."

Kiss of the Mudman (both the album and the song) made Parallax instant (if fleeting) icons. Their two previous albums (both of which had done okay but not great) were reissued and sold like crazy, giving them two gold and one platinum album in the same year, 1978.

And then Alan Shaw, the bassist, died of a heroin overdose, and Tracy Jacobs, the drummer, was killed in an auto accident (it was later determined that he'd been drunk at the time). Byron Knight recorded a terrific solo album that just bombed, and then he dropped off the radar. Some college stations still dusted off "Mudman" from time to time when the DJs felt like making fun of it (or needed a leisurely piss break), and it, like the band who recorded it, was now nothing more than a curiosity piece.

Still, if you were a fan, (like I'd been) to hear the man who'd written and sang the song mumble the word *mudman* was, well . . . still kind of a thrill, and I couldn't help but remember the verse that had been all the rage for a few months back when I was a teenager:

> *You wonder where it all went wrong and why you feel*
> *   so dead*
> *Why it seems that every day you're hanging by a*
> *   thread*
> *Are you still who you were and not what you've*
> *   become?*
> *Is this the taste of failure that lingers on your*
> *   tongue?*
>
> *Your dreams are ending in a place*
> *Far from where they began*
> *Because what's on your lips*
> *Is the memory of the kiss*
> *Of the mudman . . .*

Okay, "Blowin' in the Wind" it wasn't, but as a soul-sick cry of loneliness and alienation, it works—and that's what "Mudman" was, an eighteen-minute musical suicide note, chronicling the last minutes of a dying rock star's life as he looks back on all the people he's hurt and left behind, knowing that none of it—the fame, the money, the women, and riches—was worth it, that all he'd ever wanted he'd pissed away, and now had to die alone, and deserved his fate.

I'd always wondered just who or what the Mudman was (as did all the fans of the piece), but Knight would never say.

"Sonofabitch," he slurred from the cot as he attempted to sit up. I went over and helped him, got him a glass of water, and watched as he pulled a bottle of pills from his pocket and popped two of them into his mouth. "For the pain," he said, taking a deep drink of the water. Setting down the glass, he wiped his mouth, rubbed his eyes, and looked at me. "Was I dreaming, or did you say something about an ulceration?"

I shook my head. "That was someone else, the Reverend, the man who runs this shelter."

"Ah." He blinked, coughed a few times, and rubbed the back of his neck. "I'm kinda sick, I'm afraid."

"Cancer." It was not a question.

He looked at me. "Seen it before, have you?"

"Yes."

"Don't worry, I'm not gonna flip out on you. I just needed to get a little shut-eye in a warm place."

"You're Byron Knight."

He paled at the mention of his name. "I *was* Byron Knight. Now I'm just a sick transient who's come back to his hometown to die. Think the Reverend would have any objection to my doing it here?"

"We've had people pass away before. The Reverend never forces anyone to leave if they don't want to."

"That's good, because I don't want to. Don't have anywhere to go, anyway." He ran his fingers through his hair, then stuck out his hand. "You are?"

"Sam," I said, shaking his hand.

"What the fuck happened to that ear of yours?"

I touched it, as I always do whenever someone asks me about it. "Frostbite."

"You hear out of it? No, huh?"

"Nope."

"So I guess it was a dumb question."

"Not really."

He sniffed, then looked around the room. "Your Reverend, he wouldn't have any booze stashed around here by chance, would he?"

I knew the Reverend kept a bottle of brandy in his desk. I got it out and poured Knight a short one.

"Is that a good idea?" I asked as I handed the glass to him. "I mean, on top of the pain pills?"

He laughed, but there was no humor in it. "Sam, I think I'm way past worrying about the effects this'll have on my health." He lifted the glass in a toast. "To *your* health, then." He downed it in one gulp. "Oh, that's nice." He held out the glass. "One more? I promise that'll be it."

I poured him another, this one a little higher than the last. This time he sipped at it.

"I wish you'd stop looking at me like that."

"I'm sorry," I said. "It's just that . . . I was a big fan."

"That's nice." He sounded as if he really meant it. "It's nice to know that someone remembers."

"You guys were good."

"No, we *could have* been good. Fuck—we could've

been *great*, but it just got too easy to hear everyone else *tell* us how great we were. 'Better the illusion exalts us than ten thousand truths.' Alexander Pushkin said that. Don't ask me who he was, I couldn't tell you. I read that line in a book of quotes somewhere. Always stayed with me." He dug around in his pocket and produced a hand-rolled cigarette. "Yes, Sam, this is grass, and I'm gonna light up. I can do it in here or we can step outside; it's up to you."

I nodded at the joint. "That for the pain, too?"

"*Everything's* for the pain these days, Sam."

"There's a sheriff out in the shelter."

"So? Here or a jail cell, at least I'll be inside when I buy the farm." He struck a match and inhaled on the joint. The room was instantly filled with the too-sweet aroma.

"Want a hit?" he said, offering the joint.

"No. Go ahead and bogart it, my friend."

He laughed. "I'll bet the first time you heard that song, it was in *Easy Rider*. Am I right? Tell me I'm right."

"You're right."

"Thought so." He took a couple of more hits, then licked his fingers and doused the business end. "No need to use it all at once."

The smoke lingered. A lot.

No, wait—*lingered* isn't quite the right word. What this smoke did was *remain*. It didn't drift off, didn't start to break apart and dissipate; it just hung in the air, a semisolid cloud that didn't appear to be in a hurry to go anywhere.

"That must be some strong stuff," I said.

"It does the trick, if used in combination with the right ingredients."

"Like brandy and pain pills?"

"Give that man a cigar."

"Can I get you anything else?"

He pointed to something beside the door. "You can bring me my ax, if you don't mind."

Turning, I saw the beat-up guitar case leaning against the wall. I picked up the case, noted that the handle was about to come off (the duct tape used to reattach it was just about shot), and carried it over to Knight. He opened the case and removed the guitar, a gorgeous, new-looking Takamine twelve-string with a dreadnought-sized cutaway white-bound body, solid spruce top and rosewood back and sides, a mahogany neck with white-bound rosewood fretboard, a rosewood bridge, and a black pick guard.

It was one of the most beautiful instruments I'd ever seen.

"Yeah," said Knight, seeing the expression on my face, "she's a beauty. I've had this baby for most of my life. Half the time—shit, *most* of the time—I took better care of her than I did of myself." He gave it a light strum, and the room filled with that rich, clear sound that only a perfectly tuned guitar can produce.

"So, Sam . . . any requests?"

"You should play what you want."

"Hmm." He began playing a series of warm-up riffs, nothing spectacular, then slowly eased into a standard blues riff, then the same with variations, something he described as the blues minor pentatonic scale, consisting of the root, the minor third, the fourth, the fifth and the minor seventh.

"Something to hear, if you know how to listen," he said. "You know, it never occurred to me before how frighteningly easy it is to reshape a single note or scale into its own ghost. For example, E-major, C, G, to D will all fit in one scale—the Aeolian minor, or natural minor of a G-major scale. Now, if you add an A-major chord, all you have to do is change the C natural of your scale to a C-sharp for the time you're on the A-major. Music is phrases and feeling, so learning the scales doesn't get you 'Limehouse Blues' any more than buying tubes of oil paints gets you a *Starry Night*, but you have to respect the craft enough to realize, no matter how good you are, you'll never master it. Music will always have the final word."

And he continued to play.

"Mr. Knight?"

"You can stay here and keep me company, Sam, *unless* you're gonna call me 'Mr. Knight.' The name is Byron."

"What happened after your solo album? I mean, I don't want to pry, but you just disappeared. Everyone thought you were dead."

He stopped playing, flexed his fingers, and adjusted the tuning on the E string. "Seen any other dead rock stars tonight, Sam?"

My mouth went dry. "Yessir."

"I'm guessing there's more than a few legends milling around out there in the shelter, am I right?"

"Yes."

"Anyone in that crowd seem . . . I dunno . . . a little out of place?"

"Billie Holiday."

He looked up at me. "No shit? Wow. She actually showed up this time."

"Why her?"

"Because I loved that voice, Sam. Never has there been a sadder voice in music. Never."

I finally pulled a chair away from the Reverend's desk and sat across from Knight. "They told us that they weren't ghosts, that they were—"

"Let me guess. They called themselves 'ulcerations'?"

"How did you know?"

"Because I'm the source."

I stared at him.

"I'm guessing that doesn't really tell you anything, does it?"

"Not really."

He downed the rest of the brandy, looked at the empty glass, and said, "I'll tell you one hell of a story, Sam. You'll be the only person I've ever told it to, but it's gonna cost you one more glass of the good Reverend's hooch."

I poured him one more glass. He sipped at it, then played a little as he spoke.

True to his word, he told me one hell of a story.

7

"It was right after our second album, *Redundant Refugee*, came out. We were doing well enough, opening for bigger bands, being called back for a few encores every night. Things were moving along. We'd recorded maybe half the songs for the *Mudman* album but I still had no idea what we were going to do for the concept piece. We wanted something long, a whole side of record, and we were beating our heads against a wall. We decided to take two weeks off from the project and each other.

"I was involved with a model at the time—you might remember her, Veronique? Very hot at the time. She talked me into going to India with her. She was taking her first stab at acting, a cameo in a big-budget film.

"I hated almost every minute I was there. The humidity was oppressive as hell and it seemed that, regardless of how far away from the cities you were, the sewer stink always found you. There were areas near the hotel where we were staying where the garbage and shit—and I'm talking real, honest-to-God human waste—reached to my knees. But, man, there were places in that country that were so beautiful—the old Hindu temples and shrines, for instance—but I never could decide whether that odd, damaged beauty was a result of my being stoned most of the time or not. But the thing is, there was this one afternoon when I was stone-cold sober that I remember clearer than anything.

"I wandered away from the movie set and walked to a nearby village. I passed a Hindu temple and saw peacocks flying, men squatting in fields as the sun was setting behind them, a woman making dung patties as she watched an oxen pulling a plow toward the squatting men, all of them turning into shadows against the setting sun; unreal, ya know . . . *holy* things. Young boys with sweat- and ash-streaked faces rode past on bicycles with cans of milk rattling in their baskets. I could hear the echo of a lone, powerful, ghostly voice singing the Moslem call to prayer. I closed my eyes and simply followed the echo, breathing in the dust from the road as a pony cart filled with people came by, feeling the warmth of the evening breeze caress my face, and when the singing stopped I opened my eyes and found myself before the iron gates of the cemetery of Bodhgaya.

"I remember how still everything was. It was as if that ragged, lilting voice had guided me into another, secret world." He fired up the joint once more, took a hit, slowly releasing the smoke. It drifted into the cloud and remained.

"I started walking around the graves until I came to this big-ass statue of Kshetrapala, the Guardian of the Dead."

For a few moments I thought maybe I was getting a contact high from the smoke, because the room began yawing in front of me, expanding to make room for the smoke from Knight's joint that hung churning in the air.

"You should have seen him," whispered Knight. "A demon with blue skin, a yellow face, bristling orange hair, three bulging red eyes, and a four-fanged grin. He was draped in corpse skin and a tiger-skin loincloth and was riding a huge black bear. He carried an ax in one hand and a skullcap of blood in the other."

I blinked, rubbed my eyes, then blinked again.

I wasn't imagining things.

While Knight had been describing his encounter with Kshetrapala, the smoke from his joint had churned itself into the shape of the demon.

Another hit, another dragon's-breath of smoke, and more figures took form around the Guardian of the Dead, acting out Knight's story as he continued.

"There was a group of people standing around the Guardian's base, all of them looking down at something. None of them were making a sound. I made my way up to them and worked toward the front for a better look."

I watched as the Knight smoke-player moved

through the other shapes to stand at the base of the statue.

"An old beggar woman in shit-stained rags was kneeling in front of Kshetrapala holding a baby above her head like she was making some kinda offering. Flowers had been carefully placed around the base of the statue, as well as bowls of burning incense, small cakes wrapped in colorful paper, framed photographs, dolls made from dried reeds and string, pieces of candy, a violin with a broken neck . . . it was fucking unbelievable. I don't remember what kind of sound I made, only that I did make a noise and it drew the old woman's attention. Without lowering her arms, she turned her head and looked directly into my eyes." He shook his head and—it seemed to me—shuddered.

"Man, I'm telling you, Sam, I have never before or since seen such pure *madness* in a someone's eyes. For a moment, as she stared at me, I could feel her despair and insanity seeping into my pores. She was emaciated from starvation and had been severely burned at some time—the left half of her face was fused to her shoulder by greasy wattles of pinkish-gray scar tissue. She was trying to form words, but all that emerged were these . . . guttural animal sounds.

"The baby she was holding, it was dead. Not only that, but it had been dead for quite some time because it was partially decomposed. It looked like a small mummy."

I could clearly see the baby take shape from a few stray strands of smoke.

"The old beggar woman lowered her arms, laid the baby's corpse on the ground, and began keening—

that's the only word for it. She *sang* her grief. I looked at the others and saw these placid expressions on their faces . . . they seemed almost distracted." He looked at me for a moment, then directed his gaze to the shadowy smoke-play unfolding in the air between us.

The figure of the beggar woman thrust one of its hands under its shawl and pulled out something that could only have been a knife; a very long knife.

"She began hacking away at her own chest, ripping out sections of muscle and bone until this bloody cavity was there," said Knight, his eyes glazing over. "I backed away but I couldn't stop looking. I mean, I'd read all the stories of Yukio Mishima's committing public hara-kiri as a way of merging life with art but I never tried to picture something like that in my mind—and now, right here in front of me, this poor, crazy woman was disemboweling herself in an apparent act of worship, and the 'congregation' looked like a bunch of disinterested Broadway producers forced to watch a cattle-call audition."

The woman collapsed, took the dead infant, and shoved it into the cavity, then lay there sputtering smoke-blood from her mouth.

"I was transfixed . . . but unmoved, ya know? The image of that dead child floating in the gore of the beggar woman's chest fascinated me on an artistic level, so I stood there and watched her dying, searing the image into my brain. And then I heard the music."

Instruments appeared in the hands of the smoke-crowd: drums, a flute, something that could only have been a sitar.

"I have no idea where the instruments came from. To this day I swear that the others were empty-handed when I got there but now, suddenly, all of them had instruments and were playing them with astonishing skill—ghatams, tablas, mridangams, a recorder, and sitar—and the sound was so rich, so spiraling and glad! I could feel it wrap itself around me and bid 'Sing!' I couldn't find my voice—believe me, if I could have, I would've sung my heart out—so one of the women in the group began to sing for me: 'I am struck by a greater and greater wonder, and I rejoice again and again!' She was singing in Hindu—*Hindu,* a language I don't know, yet I understood every word in her song. 'Oh, see him in the burdened, In hearts o'erturned with grief, The lips that mutter mercy, The tears that never cease,' and the others responded in voices a hundred times fuller than any human's voice should be: 'I am, I am, I am the light; I live, I live, I live in light,' and now I'm shaking not only from the damned *weirdness* of it all but because the music, this pulsing, swirling, pure crystal rain sound is inside me—I know how that must seem to you, but I swear I felt it assume physical dimensions deep in my gut. It shook me.

"I went down on one knee because I thought I was going to be sick but the sound kept growing without and within me, and I was aware not only of the music and the people playing it and the dying woman in front of me, but of every living thing surrounding us; every weed, every insect, every animal in distant fields, the birds flying overhead . . . it was . . . I'm not quite sure how to—oh, hang on.

"I once met a schizophrenic who described what it felt like when he wasn't on his medication. He said it was as if all of his nerves had been plugged into every electrical appliance in the house and someone had set those appliances to run full-blast. That's what it was like for me that day in the graveyard. For one moment all life everywhere was functioning at its peak and I was plugged into everything—but only as long as this music deemed me worthy of possession."

I began shaking my head. Slowly, at first, then with more determination, in order to rid my ears—*both* my ears—of a buzzing pressure that was growing inside my skull.

Knight continued: "I managed to pull my head up and look at the beggar woman. She had reached over and taken the violin with the broken neck and was holding it against the baby—both the dead infant and the instrument were slick with her blood—and she made the smallest movement with her head, a quick, sharp, sideways jerk that I knew meant 'Come closer.' I leaned over until my ear was nearly touching her lips and I heard her whisper three words: *'Shakti. Kichar admi.'* It wasn't until later, when I'd gotten back to the set and asked one of the Indian crew members about it, that I found out what *Shakti* means: Creative intelligence, beauty, and power. The cosmic energies as perceived in Hindu mysticism, given to mankind by Brahma, Vishnu, and Shiva so it might know some small part of what it feels like to be a god.

"Then she pushed me away with surprising strength. I fell backwards onto my ass and felt the music wrenched from my chest. I was suddenly separate from all of them, from the earth, my own flesh, the glow of the setting sun; the surrounding life had withdrawn from me, unplugged itself. I was being asked to leave, so I did. With their glorious music still spinning in the air behind me, I moved toward the road and did not look back until I was well past the gates."

The smoke-players began to reverently shift their positions. I rubbed my temples and turned my head to the side; not only was I hearing the song Knight had described, but underneath it was the cumulative babble of a million whispering voices speaking in as many different languages.

"As soon as I stepped from the cemetery I heard a new sound join the music, a lone, sustained note that floated above everything, a mournful cry that sang of ill-founded dreams and sorrowful partings and dusty myths from ages long gone by, then progressively rose in pitch to soften this extraordinary melancholy with promises of joy and wonder—'I am light's fullest dimension, I am light's richest intention, I am, I am, I am the light!'—and I turned for one more look, one last drinking in of this gloriously odd, golden moment, and I saw the child standing in the midst of the musicians; such a beautiful child, the violin tucked firmly under his chin. He looked at me and smiled a smile unlike any that had been smiled before, full of riddles and mischief and answers and glee, and in that smile I knew his name: *Shakti*. He was giving me a final chord, a last bit of the music to remember for the rest of my life, and in that last moment he opened me up to the majestic cacophony to such a degree that I heard . . . Jesus Christ, I heard *everything*.

"I ran. It was the only thing I could think to do to break this hold on me. I turned and ran back toward the film set. And even though it seemed that every person I passed on the road wore the beggar woman's face or was clutching a dead infant to their chest or was in some way sick or damaged, I felt . . . elated. I know that must sound crazier than a soup sandwich, but I knew all of these people, with their lips that muttered mercy and their tears that never ceased, were walking toward the cemetery where the pain and sadness would be lifted from their eyes, and that I was being watched over by a child of wonder who would always be waiting at the entrance to my secret world.

"And all of them said the same thing to me as they passed by. *'Kichar admi.'*"

"Did you ever find out what that meant?"

He nodded, then strummed the guitar once again. "'Mudman.'"

"Holy shit."

"Yeah." He began playing the opening to "Kiss of the Mudman," that almost-traditional twelve-bar blues riff where you can tell something is just a bit *off* but can't put your finger on it.

"What is the Mudman supposed to be?" I asked him.

"I always figured it was just another name for Kshetrapala, but later, when I woke up in the middle of the night after me and Veronique had practically went through the floor with our fucking, I thought . . . man, I thought, what better way to describe what it feels like after you wake up from a night of excess. The taste of booze in your mouth, maybe a little puke-burp rolling around in the back of your throat, your body aching, your head splitting, your face feeling like a glazed donut from going down on wet pussy . . . excess. You wake feeling like you got kissed by the Mudman."

He stopped playing. "I was still hearing that song they had been singing, so I picked up my guitar and started fooling around with it, and I realized that what they'd been singing was . . . I don't know if

this'll make sense . . . but they'd been singing something like an *inverted* traditional blues riff."

He played it again, and this time I *heard* it, the off
thing, a single note in the middle of the riff that
didn't seem to fit.

"The progression seemed so logical," said Knight.
"Leave the G string alone—tuned to G, of course—
so the high and low E strings go down a half step to
E flat. The B string goes down a half step to B flat,
the A and D go up a half step, to B flat and E flat.
The result was an open E flat major chord, which
made easy work of the central riff. For the intro, I
started on the twelfth fret, pressing the first and
third strings down, dropped down to the seventh
and eighth fret on those same strings for the next
chord, and continued down the neck . . . as the progression moved to the fourth string, more and more
notes were left out and it became a disguised version
of a typical blues riff. The idea was to have a rush of
notes to sort of clear the palette, not open the back
door to hell . . . but that's a road paved with good intentions, isn't it?"

"What do you mean, open the back door to hell?"

"The Mudman, dude. Whatever name you wanna
give him, he's *real.* He is Shakti's shadow. He feeds on
creative energy, and when that energy runs out, he
feeds on the person who used to carry it. And this series of notes"—he played the opening again, only
much slower—"is his invitation to enter this world.
Not at this tempo; it's got to be a little faster."

"How do you know this?"

He grinned. "Because I called him up by accident
one night. I'd just finished the first leg of my solo

tour, and I was bored out of my skull at the hotel at three in the morning, so I started fiddling with the riff, and I increased its tempo and . . . there he was." He set aside his guitar and opened his shirt. The middle of his chest was a mass of scar tissue.

"Fucker tried to take a piece out of me, Sam. That's why the police found all the blood and that section of my flesh in the hotel room. The Mudman demanded a sacrifice from me, and I wasn't ready to make it." He buttoned up his shirt and picked up his guitar once again.

"I've been running away from him ever since. But I'm too sick now. I can't run any more."

I scratched at my dead ear. "So why are . . . why are the others out there looking for you?"

"Because they've been kissed by him. He devoured all their creative energies, then chewed up what was left. That's how he works, Sam. He finds someone who's really creative, and he feeds on their energy, all the while giving them too many temptations, access to too many excesses, because that way, their energies will be spent faster. He gorges himself on their energy, then eats them for dessert. What you've got out there, those are the ulcerations that remain, the aftertastes, the memories of the legends."

"The icons, not the people."

He nodded. "You might buy the farm, but your legend never does . . . and as long as the legend remains, even if it's just in the mind of one person, then you're tied to him and his desires. It sucks. If you're born with any kind of creative talent, you're on his hit list from the beginning. They're all here because I dug their music. I'm one of the ulcerations that keeps them alive."

"So why not . . . why not just not play the notes?"

"You think it's just as simple as that? Dude, it doesn't have to be me who plays them. The notes, they're out there. They're everywhere. A bird, the sound of the wind, a car backfiring . . . the notes are all over the place. And every so often, enough of them come together in the same place, at the same, and in the right tempo, that the doorway opens and he comes shambling in. And there's not a goddamn thing you can do to stop it."

There was a knock on the door and I rose to see who it was.

"It's me," said the Reverend.

I let him in. He took one look at Knight, sniffed the air, and said, "Hawaiian seedless?"

"A man of the cloth who knows his weed," replied Knight. "Will wonders never cease?"

"Not any time soon, from the looks of things."

Knight stared at him. "Please don't tell me Elvis just showed up."

"I think he'd feel a little out of place with this crowd."

"Is Billie Holiday really here?"

"She is."

Knight shook his head. "Damn. I finally rate Billie. Wow."

The Reverend closed the door. "Is it always the same bunch?"

"Some of them change. Depends on who I've been thinking about or listening to before the Mudman finds me."

The Reverend did not ask who or what the Mudman was. One look at him, and I knew that he knew. Don't ask me how, but the Reverend . . . knows things. Most of the time it's pretty cool, but sometimes . . . sometimes it's just creepy.

"What are we supposed to do?" he asked Knight.

"Damned if I know, but if I had to guess, I don't think it's up to *you* to do anything. Whatever's gonna happen . . . it's my call." He rose from the cot, finished his brandy, and patted down his hair. "And what I'm gonna do, if it's all right with you, is play in front of an audience one more time."

The Reverend considered this for moment. "I think that would be wonderful."

And Byron Knight smiled the last genuine smile of his life.

8

Everyone gathered around the center of the room as Knight situated himself on a stool.

Even Morrison and the others looked on him with a sad kind of respect.

"Any requests?" asked Knight.

It was Grant McCullers who spoke up. "I've always been partial to Bach's 'Sheep May Safely Graze.' It's kind of a Christmas tune, don't you think?"

"I do."

And Knight began to play it, smoothly, hauntingly. It was majestic and sad and melancholy and glorious, and yet there was something hesitant about the way Knight played the song; the notes brushed you once, softly, like a cattail or a ghost, then fell shyly toward the ground in some inner contemplation too sad to be touched by a tender thought or the delicate brush of another's care.

It was perhaps the most beautiful thing I'd ever heard.

And then someone screamed from the basement.

Timmy was the first to respond, snapping his head in the direction of the scream and muttering, "Terrible, just terrible," as he ran across the room and down the stairs. Linus hopped up on his cart and made a beeline across the floor, then pushed himself off and took the stairs with his hands as Beth, Lump, and the still-damp Kyle followed after him.

That's when I realized that it had been the little girl, Missy, who'd screamed.

I reached the top of the stairs just as Timmy came around the corner, carrying Missy in his arms, her small, shuddering body wrapped in a towel.

He was pale and shaking. "Terrible, *just terrible.*"

He sounded horrified.

A few moments later Lump gave out with a snarl and a bark, then came charging up the stairs, Beth and Kyle right behind him.

"I saw the *Bumble,*" cried Missy. "He w-w-was . . . he was in the wall!"

Beth took Missy from Timmy's arms and began stroking the back of her daughter's head. "Shhh, hon, there-there, c'mon, it's all right . . . c'mon, you just got a fright, that's all. The Bumble scares you and you just imagined it."

She might have just imagined it, but Lump had seen or sensed something that was making him crazy; his legs were locked in place, his lips curled back, eyes unblinking as he stared at the bottom of the steps and growled.

"Where's Linus?" asked the Reverend, coming up beside me.

"He's still down there."

Ted Jackson joined us. He'd unstrapped the top of his holster and was touching the butt of his gun, ready to pull it. "Jesus Christ in a Chrysler, I about jumped out of my shorts."

"Probably nothing," said the Reverend. "The little girl got spooked, that's all."

I could tell from the tone of his voice that he didn't believe it any more than I did.

Knight was standing now, holding his guitar like a child, his eyes closed, his face almost peaceful.

Morrison and the others were gone.

And from somewhere in the basement, something moved.

Something big.

"What the hell?" said Jackson, gripping his gun but not pulling it from the holster.

Timmy came up to the Reverend and grabbed his arm, saying, "Terrible, just terrible," over and over, getting louder and more excited.

"Timmy," said the Reverend, gripping both of Timmy's arms, "I need you to calm down. C'mon. There you go, deep breaths, all right. Good. Now . . . did you see something down there?"

Timmy nodded.

"Are you sure you actually saw something that was there, or was it—"

Timmy pointed at his eyes and shook his head. No, it wasn't one of his visual hallucinations, he knew the difference, thank you very much. *"Terrible . . . terrible . . . just terrible."*

Beth was rocking Missy back and forth, whispering

comfort in her ear, kissing her cheek, while Kyle sat on the floor beside them, holding his little sister's hand.

Whatever was in the basement moved again, and this time with enough force to shake the foundation of the building.

A few second later, Linus came barreling out on his hands, covered in sweat and shaking, his face even paler than Timmy's had been.

"You're gonna think I'm crazy," he said as he took the stairs two at a time, "but I just saw goddamned Godzilla down there!" He hopped onto his cart and sped over to Missy, Beth, and Kyle.

Lump still stood at the top of the stairs, ready to attack.

"Okay, that's it," said Jackson, removing his weapon and clicking off the safety. "I'm going down there."

"Not alone, you're not," said the Reverend.

Grant McCullers joined us. He was holding a wooden rolling pin. "Hey, it's the most dangerous thing I could find in that kitchen."

"Hang on," said the Reverend, running back to his office.

He was gone maybe thirty seconds, just long enough for the whole building to shake once more. The chandelier began to swing.

Everyone was gathering in the farthest corner of the room, watching that chandelier.

Then the lights flickered once, twice, and went out.

The emergency generator kicked in a few seconds later, and the Reverend was standing next to me, handing out weapons.

"Goddammit," said Jackson. "Do you have permits for these things?"

"Bet your ass I do."

He handed Grant a pump-action shotgun, then stuck a .22 in my hands.

The Reverend had opted for a 9mm.

"Look at us," said Grant. "The poor man's Wild Bunch."

The Reverend almost smiled at that. "Let's go."

And we started down the stairs.

9

When I was eleven years old, my mother was diagnosed with cancer. She went fast, lasting just over one year, but it was an agonizing year. My dad, who never was worth much of anything, put her to bed and left her there, leaving it up to me to make sure she got her medicine on time, to change her sheets, and to clean her up when she didn't make it to the bathroom on time.

Toward the end, I became so angry with him, with his cowardice and drunkenness, that I actually made the mistake of hitting him one night.

He beat the shit out of me, then threw me out the back door into the yard. It had snowed a lot that week, and there was about a foot of snow and ice on the ground.

I remember landing on my side, half my face buried in the snow.

I remember that I couldn't move because it hurt so much.

And I remember thinking how *cold* my ear was getting.

I regained consciousness about five hours later. A neighbor had come home and seen me lying in the yard. They took me to the hospital, where I stayed for almost two weeks. I had pneumonia and frostbite. They had to remove my ear, which was okay because I was deaf on that side, anyway.

Somewhere in there Dad took off and just left Mom alone. The whole time I was in the hospital, I was so scared because she had no one there to take care of her (one of our neighbors was keeping an eye on her, but I didn't know that).

By the time I was released, Mom was all but dead. She lasted just two days after I got home.

There was no money to cover the hospital bills, so the house was sold, and I was put into the care of the county.

I remember that as I sat there in the courthouse, waiting for someone from children's services to come and collect me, that I had never felt so alone and afraid in my life. I hated myself for not being there for Mom, and I hated Dad for being such a worthless coward, and I hated looking like a freak with one ear, and I hated everything.

But mostly, I hated feeling *that afraid*.

And I promised myself that I would never, ever, *ever* feel that afraid again, no matter what.

A promise that I had kept to myself until the moment the Reverend, Grant, Sheriff Jackson, and I hit the bottom of those stairs and turned in the hallway.

And I came face to face with the Mudman.

10

The east wall had almost completely collapsed, spewing out wood beams, bricks, and mud.

So much mud.

And it was moving.

"Holy Mother of God," whispered Grant.

A demon with three bulging red eyes and a four-fanged grin rose up from the muck before us. It was draped in corpse skin and riding a huge black bear. It carried an ax in one hand and a skullcap of blood in the other . . . and from every side of its form, faces peered out, faces made of black mud, their dark lips working to form words.

I saw them all—Hendrix, Morrison, Garcia, Ms. Holiday, Cobain, all of them.

And I felt the buzz in the center of my head as their words began to come clear.

I am, I am, I AM the darkness . . . I AM, I AM, I AM darkness's empty belly, the pit at the end of your days. . . .

It rose up to its fullest height, cracking the ceiling with its back, and lumbered forward, blood spilling from the skullcap, snot and foam dripping from the bear's snout and mouth, smashing holes into the wall with every swing of its ax.

Its eyes glowed brighter with every step.

The Reverend was the first to fire. The bullet slammed into the muck with a loud *splat* that did no damage at all. No sooner was the hole made than it oozed closed, healing.

And with every step, the thing grew larger, the singer's words louder.

I AM, I AM, I AM Kichar Admi, I AM, I AM, I AM the source of all the songs you sing. . . .

Grant McCullers pumped four rounds into it but it would not stop coming.

I AM, I AM, I AM the song the darkness sings, in the pit of my starving belly. . . .

We continued backing up, all of us firing into its center, none of the bullets having any effect.

The mud dripped and oozed, clumping into the face of a beggar woman, the body of a dead child.

The singers continued, *I AM, I AM, I AM what you made me, what you wanted me to be, I AM, I AM, I AM only my song and nothing more. . . .*

The lights flickered again, and the building shuddered.

I ran out of bullets, as did everyone else.

And then I felt a hand on my shoulder.

I turned and saw Byron Knight beside me. His face was a mask of peace and acceptance.

I had to watch his lips, because I could no longer hear anything; the roar of the gunfire was still screaming through my head.

"I've had this appointment for a long time," he said. "Just . . . let me go."

Cradling his guitar, he pushed past us and walked forward.

The Mudman stopped moving.

The singers fell silent.

And the bear rose up on its hind legs.

The ax swung down swiftly and surely, deeply burying itself in Knight's chest. The demon threw back its head and howled with laughter, then pulled Knight from the floor, his legs dangling as blood from his wound pumped down in heavy rivulets, splattering across the floor.

The demon opened its mouth, its jaws dislodging, dropping down, growing wider, until its face was nothing more than a slick, dark maw, big enough to swallow a man whole.

Which is what it did.

Then it spat out Knight's guitar, which hit the floor and shattered into half a dozen pieces, the snapping strings a final death groan that echoed against the walls.

The demon turned around and walked toward the collapsed wall, then crouched down and began to move into the mounds of dirt, sludge, and muck, becoming less and less solid until it became what it had been; just mud.

I closed my eyes and began to cry. The Reverend came over and put his arms around me.

It didn't help much.

11

We don't talk about that night. Oh, every once in a while, when the four of us get together to play cards, Grant McCullers will call us the Wild Bunch and everyone will get this look on their faces, but that's as close as we come to discussing it.

One night Ted Jackson told us a story about something he'd seen after a recent labor riot that made me cringe, and Grant told us what had really happened at the Hangman.

We listened, and we all believed, but we don't talk about it.

Like the Reverend says, this is Cedar Hill. Weird shit happens here.

Grant gave Beth and her kids five hundred dollars and put them on the bus to Indiana himself. Lump even got a seat, but he had to ride in a carrier, which didn't please him too much. Beth and the kids promised to write and call Grant as much as they could, but if they've ever been in touch with him, he hasn't said.

The basement was finally repaired after the Reverend got really pushy with a couple of local contractors. So far, it's holding up fine.

Linus is touring with another carnival, once again as Thalidomide Man. He sends us postcards all the time.

I'd almost managed to learn how to live with what I saw, until one afternoon a couple of weeks ago when I was waiting at a crosswalk for the light to change.

A bird chirped.

A car backfired.

A child laughed somewhere.

The wind whistled.

And those four notes, in succession, in the right tempo, began *that tune,* and I remembered Knight's words: *"The notes, they're out there. They're everywhere. A bird, the sound of the wind, a car backfiring . . . the notes are all over the place. And every so often, enough of them come together in the same place, at the same, and in the right tempo, that the doorway opens and he comes shambling in. And there's not a goddamn thing you can do to stop it."*

I can't listen to music anymore. Oh, I hear it, but I've trained myself to think of it as background noise, nothing to pay attention to.

It has to be this way, because I have been made aware of the sequence of notes that, if heard, recognized, and acknowledged, will bring something terrible into the world.

Of all the things I have lost in this life, it is music that I miss the most.

Ethel, God love her, has noticed that I don't seem

as "chipper" as I used to be. I smile, shrug, and tell her not to worry, that I'm fine, still seeing the doctor, still taking my medication.

"You need to stay cheerful, Sam," she says. "It's a sad world, and you got to fight it or else it'll eat you alive."

She has no idea.

She tells me that I ought to be like the seven dwarves when I work, that I should whistle a happy tune.

A happy tune.

But I can't remember any.

RICHARD LAYMON

THE MIDNIGHT TOUR

For years morbid tourists have flocked to the Beast House, eager to see the infamous site of so many unspeakable atrocities, to hear tales of the beast said to prowl the hallways. They can listen to the audio tour on their headphones as they stroll from room to room, looking at the realistic recreations of the blood-drenched corpses....

But the audio tour only gives the sanitized version of the horrors of the Beast House. If you want the full story, you have to take the Midnight Tour, a very special event strictly limited to thirteen brave visitors. It begins at the stroke of midnight. You may not live to see it end.

ISBN 10: 0-8439-5753-0
ISBN 13: 978-0-8439-5753-2 $7.99 US/$9.99 CAN